A String Of Perils

A STRING OF PERILS

Linda S. Clayton

iUniverse, Inc.
New York Lincoln Shanghai

A String Of Perils

All Rights Reserved © 2004 by Linda S. Clayton

No part of this book may be reproduced or transmitted in any form or by any means, graphic, electronic, or mechanical, including photocopying, recording, taping, or by any information storage retrieval system, without the written permission of the publisher.

iUniverse, Inc.

For information address:
iUniverse, Inc.
2021 Pine Lake Road, Suite 100
Lincoln, NE 68512
www.iuniverse.com

This is a work of fiction. Names, characters and places are used fictitiously, and any resemblance to persons living or dead is unintentional.

ISBN: 0-595-32460-6 (pbk)
ISBN: 0-595-66586-1 (cloth)

Printed in the United States of America

For Paul, Alicia, Carolyn, Tim and Dan—my lifesavers.

Acknowledgements

Several folks helped me with ideas for the cover of this book. A great big thank you to Festi and Hans Weitekamper, Terry Keane and Chuck McNear for allowing me to scramble over their boats taking pictures and asking questions. And they never once said they thought I was crazy. Thanks to Allan Miller for permitting me to photograph the terrific view of the marsh from his deck.

A special thanks to Festi Weitekamper for her outstanding help with the French language.

Many thanks to Suzanne Mousseau, who knows everything about boats and the waterways around Hilton Head.

This book was a family affair. Bear hugs for Becca Clayton, who helped me with ballet terms. I wouldn't know a *tour jeter* from a *Tour de France*.
And for Carolyn Clayton-Luce and Sam Clayton-Luce who once again used their considerable computer and artistic skills to save the day.
And for Dan Clayton, who taught me how to fly an airplane without leaving the ground—which was probably a very good thing.
And for the best editor in the world, Elizabeth Clayton, whose eagle eye caught every inconsistency and error. I couldn't have done it without her. You are all an amazing bunch.

I am also extremely grateful to Judy DeMint, Let's just say the book wouldn't be the same without her contribution.

Over the past months several people offered encouragement and support, which I truly appreciated. I'd like to give big hugs to Susan and Bob Blank, Mary Biggs, Sue and Don James, Patty and Tom Woods, Althea and Eric Shepherd, Debbie and Steve Hancotte, my tennis buddies and Rendy Parrish. Thanks, guys.

PROLOGUE

▼

Winter, 2003

It was late on a Friday afternoon in February. A chill hung over the deserted city streets. One by one the men, dressed in warm overcoats, entered the Stadpark. Nodding imperceptibly to each other, they strolled leisurely to Leystraat. At intervals they entered the building and presented their identification cards to the guards. Once inside, they disabled the surveillance camera and inserted a tape of their own. Others used their keys to open the locks. They worked quickly, emptying the contents of the vaults into large sacks. When they could carry no more, they exited the building silently. At a prearranged hour, they met again to divide the loot. The theft went undiscovered until Monday morning when employees returned to work.

＊　　　＊　　　＊　　　＊

Summer, 2004

The Cessna 182 banked to the left over Calibogue Sound and pointed its wing at the Harbour Town lighthouse. The famed Hilton Head yacht basin looked like a tiny horseshoe dotted with white, toy boats. Sandwiched between blue sky and sparkling water, I sat mesmerized with fear, clutching the sides of the seat until my knuckles turned white. I had to have been crazy to leave the safety of the ground with Otis Murbaugh.

I looked out the window as we flew along the shoreline. Twenty more minutes and we'd be back at the airport. I couldn't wait.

Suddenly, instead of continuing on course, the plane turned out to sea, and the nose rose until all I saw was blue sky. I could feel us losing air speed as the plane began to shudder. Terrified, I grabbed Otis by the arm and screamed, "What's wrong? What's going on?" As if in answer, a loud horn began to squawk. "We're going to die," I yelled. I had a horrible mental picture of us falling into the Atlantic Ocean. *Not with Otis Murbaugh*, I prayed. *Please God, not with Otis Murbaugh*. Actually, not with anyone. I still had things to do, people to see.

As quickly as we'd climbed, we suddenly plunged towards the water with a speed that took my breath away. I closed my eyes and braced myself for a horrifying splat. After what seemed like an eternity, I felt the plane straighten out. When I dared to look, Otis was laughing.

"Well, Ms Bloom, what did you think of that?"

"I think you're a lunatic," I sputtered. "You're lucky you don't have the contents of my stomach spilled all over your nice plane." I peeled my white knuckles off the edge of the seat. "Could you please put this aircraft down now?" Fearing he would take me literally and land in the ocean, I hastily added, "At the airport. The airport would be fine."

"Ah, Maggie, I just wanted to show you my new toy. You have to admit, she's a honey."

"Listen, Otis, it's no wonder you can't get anyone to fly with you. That was terrifying. People don't like to be scared."

Otis looked disappointed. "Thought you'd like a bit of fun. Didn't realize you were such a girl."

I stifled the urge to defend myself. It would only goad Otis into attempting some other outrageous aeronautical feat, only this time we might not be lucky enough to escape.

Linda S. Clayton 3

"I'll never do this again, but your plane is very nice," I said politely. I could afford to be cordial. The airport was in sight and unless Otis completely botched the landing, I was going to live to see another day.

CHAPTER 1

▼

I found Otis lying on his back in the woods next to the bicycle path. He was squashed between some palmetto fronds and thick weeds, with one arm draped around the stump of an old oak tree. His body was covered with pine straw and leaves so that only his foot was visible. He was also dead. I knew this because his eyes didn't blink as sunlight flashed through the trees onto his face. And his mouth was open, as if he'd been in mid-sentence when the life went out of him.

If I hadn't had my eyes glued to the ground, I'd have stumbled over his leg and fallen flat on my face. Fortunately, I was watching for snakes and therefore remained upright. The warm Hilton Head sunshine attracted more than tourists to the well-manicured bike paths. Resident reptiles loved them, too. I can tell you, it is disconcerting to have one fall on your head or slither in front of you when you're concentrating on cardiac performance. Jogging requires constant vigilance.

I had daintily jumped over the appendage before my brain processed what my eyes had seen. Wally and Willow, my English cocker spaniels, were not as slow reacting. By the time I turned around and ran back, both dogs had set up quite a howl. Willow maintained a discreet three-foot distance, but Wally, who would stick his nose into a pot of paste if there were the slightest chance of finding something edible, ventured closer, sniffing audibly.

I looked around for an abandoned bicycle, thinking a rider had perhaps fallen and injured himself. Seeing none, I parted the bushes.

I was so undone at the sight of him, I jumped around like a mad woman, waving my arms and screaming "Mama Mia, Tower of Pisa, I am weaka in the kneesa." at the top of my lungs. I am not Italian and I am not crazy, but lately, in times of crisis or excitement, the most inane, totally inappropriate words have been bursting out of my mouth. It's probably a hormonal thing, but at the moment I am incapable of controlling it.

Blood covered one side of his face and matted his dark hair. His green T-shirt was smeared with the substance, as if he'd tried to mop up the gaping wound on his head.

No one could mistake that oily black hair or the pudgy face. Poor Otis Murbaugh. I suddenly wished I'd been more charitable the last time I'd seen him. He was an obnoxious boor, but he didn't deserve this.

I bent down and using two fingers, gingerly searched for a pulse. There was none.

I straightened up and pulled my cell phone out of my pocket. 911 responded immediately. Since the nearest emergency vehicle was only a few blocks away, I figured help would be here soon.

Willow, apparently as repulsed by the body as I was, sat obediently at my feet, but Wally crept closer—no doubt intending to investigate Otis as thoroughly as he does my laundry hamper. He also had an unseemly habit of lifting his leg against any foreign object on the ground. I didn't like Otis, but there was a certain amount of decorum associated with death, which should not include urine stains on the corpse. I yanked my puppy away, chagrined to see he already had something in his mouth that he had obviously stolen from Otis's body.

I pried Wally's teeth apart and extracted his find. It was a business card. Centered on a background of blue sky, the dusky pink wall of a house and a green palm tree were the words:

Peter S. Bloom
Import/Export
Riyad El Nabil
Marrakech, Morocco

Excuse me? I looked again. Yep, that's what it said. Peter S. Bloom, Import/Export, Marrakech, Morocco. This couldn't be. There had to be some mistake. Unless there were two men with exactly the same name, Peter S. Bloom was my ex-husband, and as far as I knew, he was a lawyer in Boston, MA—not an importer in Marrakech.

The sound of a siren jerked me away from more scrutiny of the strange writing. As the emergency rescue vehicle drove down the path to where I waited, I quickly pocketed the card. I know, I know—removing evidence is against the law—but I reasoned I could always turn it over to the sheriff at a later time. I'd talk to the paramedics first and then, in the privacy of my home, figure out what Peter was up to and why Otis Murbaugh would be clutching my ex-husband's business card in his dead hand.

Sheriff Griffey was not happy to see me. In fact, he almost snarled. The words shot like sharp darts out of a corner of his mouth. "You again. I reckoned I'd seen the last of you." We'd met each other last year when I'd participated in a little incident involving a yacht and a shoot-out on Broad Creek. "How'd you happen to find the body?"

As he talked, he moved into the thick growth of live oak trees, tangled vines and bushes bordering the path. You wouldn't get me in there if you promised me dinner at the French Laundry in Napa Valley as a reward. Sea Pines—snazzy as it was—still housed enough snakes to make treading on pine straw in dark places extremely unwise.

"I was jogging," I called after him. "The dogs and I were running. You remember my dogs," I added, trying to be polite.

"Do you know why the deceased was here?" He didn't ask me if I knew Otis because everyone did.

8   A String Of Perils

"Sure don't. The deceased and I did not socialize. Did he fall and hit his head or something?"

My question met with silence. Soon heavy footsteps tramped through the underbrush and Sheriff Griffey reappeared at my side.

"Get the yellow tape up, boys. This here is a crime scene."

"Are you saying he didn't fall?" I asked.

"I'm saying someone gave him a whack on the head and then for good measure shot him in the back. Would you call that an accident?"

I gulped. "No sir. Are you saying he was murdered?"

Sheriff Griffey gave his holster a hitch and wiped his sunglasses on his shirt. "What I'm saying is that someone wanted to make very sure he was dead. This here is what you would call 'overkill.'" He laughed at his attempt at humor. "The fact is; there are two bullet holes in his back. He's tore up pretty good."

I felt my breakfast jump towards my throat.

"Hope you're not involved in this, Ms Bloom. Last time you got away with a rap on the knuckles. This time we won't be as easy on you."

"I didn't have anything to do with this," I said indignantly. "I told you I found him when I was jogging."

The sheriff eyed me unenthusiastically. "Don't go anywhere."

This order was ambiguous. Did he mean don't leave the scene of the crime or the country? "If you don't need me anymore, I'll just take the dogs home," I told him.

He nodded absentmindedly as he consulted with his deputies. I interpreted that to mean scamper on home. As I was preparing to scamper speedily, he said, "I'll be in touch. We'll need to talk again."

My fingers closed around the card in my pocket. I knew I was withholding information, but there was no way I could give it to him now. What would I say? *Oh, by the way, my dog found this in Otis's hand and it just happens to have a name on it that strongly resembles my ex-husband's, and I was going to give it to you just as soon as I did a little investigating and made sure the Peter Bloom I knew was busy being a lawyer and not involved in a murder.* I had a feeling Sheriff Griffey would not find that amusing. I walked away, hoping he wouldn't wonder why I had my left hand jammed in my pocket, while two energetic dogs lunged from leashes held in the right.

CHAPTER 2

▼

The phone was ringing as I opened the front door. Wally and Willow raced to the kitchen—Willow for a drink of water, Wally to see if the dish towel was within reach so he could tear it to shreds. I grabbed the receiver just as the answering machine was about to pick up.

"Have you heard the news," Lucy Rotblumen yelled excitedly. "It's about time someone rubbed him out."

"Lucy! You shouldn't say such things. And surely you don't mean Otis Murbaugh. You couldn't possible know about that."

"Well, I do, darling. You know how quickly news travels on this island. Sarah Evans just happened to be driving down Greenwood Drive when she spotted Chet Branson standing on the grass watching the paramedics. Of course she pulled over and asked him what was going on and voila! She called me on her cell phone. Such a wonderful invention."

"I was there," I informed her. "In fact, I'm the one who found him. I'm surprised your informant left out that piece of information."

"Just a minute, Maggie." She covered the phone with her hand, but I could still hear her words. "We'll have cocktails in the sunroom now. A bit of that goose paté would be nice. And crackers."

"I could whip up some tuna fish spread," I offered. "I'm afraid I'm fresh out of goose innards."

"Sorry, Maggie. I was giving instructions to Emerald. Thank heavens Julius has given up his silly diet. I've never seen so much kelp. He's back to enjoying his drink before dinner. So civilized, don't you think?"

I had to laugh. Lucy sure had come a long way. She and I had grown up together in Pooler, Georgia. In the third grade she was a head taller than all her classmates. In high school the boys' basketball coach fantasized about her—not for her body, which resembled a sturdy tree—but for her amazing ability to reach the net on the basket while standing on her toes.

Later, men eyed her differently when she earned her living as an exotic dancer at the Purple Pelican, a strip joint on the way to Savannah. One night Fate brought the diminutive Julius Rotblumen into the club. His Ferrari was being repaired, he had a few hours to kill—the rest is history. He choked on a pretzel, Lucy, who was busy wrapping her leg around a pole and moaning in ecstasy, jumped off the stage in her G-string and pasties and performed the Heimlich maneuver. To hear Lucy tell it, she knew from the second his little head bounced against her impressive chest as she squeezed his middle she was destined to be Mrs. Julius Rotblumen, wife of one of the wealthiest men in the United States.

They had a gorgeous oceanfront home in Sea Pines, a chalet in Beaver Creek, a villa in Gstaad, an apartment in New York and a yacht big enough to sail across the Atlantic to Europe.

Most of the time Lucy dressed as if she were going to work in a circus—bright colors, feathers, sequins, glitter—the more the better. And because of her extreme wealth no one ever criticized her. She could walk through Sea Pines in a gold caftan, scarlet turban covering her flame colored hair and tennis shoes, and certain folks, eager to be invited to a soiree at the Rotblumens, would gush over her divine clothes. In spite of all the perks she enjoyed, she was still the same Lucy I'd known all my life. And she was my best friend.

"You weren't going to drink alcohol for six weeks," I reminded her. "Wasn't it something about body purification and water being the healthiest beverage?"

"There's no reason to be fanatical about these things. A cocktail now and then helps lower cholesterol. Would you like to come over and have one with us?"

"No, thanks. That's nice of you, but there's something I have to do." I debated whether to mention the business card I'd taken from the scene of the crime, but since I always ended up telling her everything, I plunged right in.

"Hmm."

I could hear her tapping her teeth.

"What does 'Hmm' mean?"

"It means, here we go again. You know what Ben's going to say."

"I don't know what you mean," I said defensively, but I could feel my face grow hot. Ben Jakowski would, I knew, have a fit. He had this silly idea I attracted trouble, and he definitely did not like anything about my ex-husband.

Ben was a freelance journalist. He was also the most gorgeous man I knew. He had a thick head of sandy hair, a strong athletic body that made my knees wobble, and the most beautiful blue eyes I'd ever gazed into. More and more, my daydreams about him had long-term ramifications; for instance I could picture us sharing a container of Metamucil and filling out Medicare forms together. I hadn't, however, shared any of this with him yet. It was complicated. I was sure I loved him, and I thought he loved me, but if I let my guard down, he might turn into a first class schmuck like my ex-husband and break my heart.

"I'll agree that Ben is going to be a little bit upset, but it's not as if I'm involved in something dangerous. I simply have to find out if the Peter S. Bloom on the card is my Peter. It's kind of important since Otis seems to have been murdered."

"First of all, he is no longer your Peter S. Bloom. And secondly, that name is not particularly unique. There could be others, you know."

"I'm well aware of that. I'm just going to do a bit of snooping, Lucy. Make a few calls. That's all."

"I hope so. Try to stay out of trouble. What am I saying? That's like telling Wally to behave himself."

"Hey," I yelled, "leave my dog out of this." But she had already hung up.

I wandered into the sunroom and looked out the window at the marsh. At this time of day a soft orange glow spread over the Spartina grass. A blue heron swooped over a loblolly pine and landed gracefully on the sand. I watched as he pecked the wet ground with his beak, searching for a tasty meal.

I thought about Peter. Our marriage had ended in disaster after I discovered he'd been having an affair with a silicone-enhanced bimbo almost young enough to be his daughter. I still distinctly remembered the day I found out. We were having dinner at a trendy restaurant in Boston. Somewhere between the *insalata mista* and the *tiramisu* he said, "Do you ever notice we seem to travel down parallel roads with very few intersections?"

Being totally clueless and naïve enough to think he was talking about some kind of career path, I stretched my foot under the table until I could tickle his crotch with my toe and said, "I think we intersect a lot. When we get home, we can intersect some more."

When he jerked away as if I'd tapped him with a hot poker, I knew we weren't going to be intersecting. Not then, not ever again. The bimbo, of course, left him as soon as she realized he wasn't going to move to Santa Monica and roller blade on the beach with her.

Last year, just when I finally managed to stop fantasizing about amputating some of his vital parts, Peter sailed his new boat into Harbour Town, intent on reconciliation. I almost fell for his glib talk until I realized he didn't really want me. He wanted someone to stroke his ego after his girlfriend dumped him.

14   A String Of Perils

To Ben's credit, he said very little about Peter during that time. But I know I hurt him. So, telling him I was going to do a little investigating on Peter's behalf was not going to go over very well.

Let's get one thing straight, though. I have no romantic interest in my ex-husband. Frankly, and this is the absolute truth, I sort of hoped he would fall off a steep cliff or get strategically gored by a bull in Pamplona. At the very least, I wished he would have a hard time attracting willing females to his hot tub. He should learn what it's like to roam around an empty house eating Chunky Monkey ice cream and potato chips until dawn. It won't happen, but a girl can dream. I owed Peter, the skunk, absolutely nothing, but for old time's sake, I couldn't let the sheriff know about the calling card in Otis's hand before I had a chance to talk to my ex-husband.

It was too late to call his office. Lawyers in the firm of Hale, Simmons and Bloom didn't work after five o'clock. I'd have to call him at home. With a stab of nostalgia, I dialed the familiar number. Peter had moved back into our Georgian colonial as soon as I cleared out. After three rings a silky female voice purred into the phone, "Bloom residence. Whom may I say is calling?"

So much for roaming around the house eating junk food. I cleared my throat nervously. I was willing to bet my non-existent alimony the sultry salutation belonged to another of Peter's minimal age Barbie dolls. The man was incapable of spending a minute without female company.

"Ah, this is Maggie Bloom, former wife of Peter Bloom. May I speak to him please?" I sounded like Mary Poppins.

The voice never missed a beat. "I'm sorry, Ms Bloom. Mr. Bloom is not available. Would you care to leave a message?"

"Not really. I need to speak to him. It's very important, so it would be greatly appreciated and extremely helpful if you could tell me where he is."

"I'm sorry, but he left instructions not to bother him."

I was beginning to regret my decision to warn Peter. And I was also getting annoyed.

"This isn't a social call. There is an urgent problem I have to discuss with him."

"Perhaps you could confide in me and I'll relay the message."

"Look, cupcake, apparently you don't understand. Your boyfriend is going to wind up in jail if I don't speak to him soon. Now be a good girl and tell me how to get in touch with him."

I thought I detected a slight tremor in her voice. "Say, what's this all about."

That was more like it. "I'm sorry," I said smugly, "I'm not at liberty to say."

"I can tell you he left town and won't be back for a week."

"You're doing fine," I said encouragingly. "Now tell me where he went."

"That's just it," the voice wailed. "He made the reservations himself and took his passport. I know it's gone because I, ah, happened to be looking for something in his desk."

This bit of information sent a chill through my body. Passport meant he went out of the country and making his own reservations indicated he wanted to keep his destination a secret. Surely he wasn't in Morocco. But on the bright side, if he had left the United States, he couldn't have had anything to do with Otis Murbaugh's death.

"Would you happen to know if he had business in North Africa?"

"Is that somewhere near Switzerland?"

I sighed. My ex didn't pick his babes for what they had between the ears. It was what they had between the neck and the knees that counted. They could be as slow witted as a turtle, but if they had bodies that defied human anatomical proportions, Peter pronounced them perfect. The last one thought the Alps were in Sweden.

"Switzerland is on a different continent, dear," I said not unkindly.

"Huh?"

"If you hear from him, could you please tell him to call Maggie? He knows the number."

"He does?"

Peter's pet rock had obviously over-taxed her brain. I hung up before she started spouting gibberish.

CHAPTER 3

▼

Even sleuths have to wear underwear. I was in Saks shopping for Jockey cotton briefs when Janna Maletesta's cheerful voice called to me from a display of lacy bras.

"Maggie, how lovely to see you. It's been ages."

As always happened when I saw Janna, I wished I paid more attention to my clothes, hair, make-up, posture, teeth, nails, vocabulary, reading material and general outlook on life. Even I had to admit she was some dish. Barely five feet four inches, she had a body that other less fortunate women paid big bucks to duplicate. And that process would have involved a lot of liposuction and silicone implants. Janna was nearly perfect. Her honey blonde, casually coifed hair skimmed her shoulders. Her deeply tanned legs and arms looked sensational in crisp white shorts and a coral top. On her feet she wore spiffy Manola Blahnik sandals that I knew for a fact cost $100 a toe.

I, on the other hand, looked like I'd been dressed by my dogs. "It's nice to see you, too, Janna," I said, trying to hide a muddy paw print on my jogging shorts. Jake, Janna's husband, kissed me on both cheeks before casually draping an arm over his wife's shoulder. He also looked sensational in a white pole shirt, a gold chain around his neck and navy shorts. Jake was an investment banker and part time Sea Pines residence. The Maletestas lived in an oceanfront home near Lucy and

- 17 -

Julius. We didn't travel in the same social circles, but Janna owned a dozen hand-painted Maggie Bloom plates and stemware, which made us speaking acquaintances.

"Terrible thing about Otis, isn't it?" Jake said. "Couldn't believe it when Miles Fishburn called me today. That land deal thing riled a lot of people. Guess one of them decided to get even."

Otis's trouble started when he bought a piece of land on the May River in Bluffton. He laid claim to not only the land but also a stretch of water beyond it—water the local folks always fished for shrimp and oysters. When people complained, Otis waved an official looking paper in their faces and threatened them with lawsuits if their boats penetrated his space. It's fair to say a great many residents were extremely angry.

"Otis wasn't an easy person to like," I said. "I can't believe someone would kill him, though."

Janna smiled, revealing perfect white teeth. "I understand he has no heirs. Such a shame. A beautiful, new home and no one to enjoy it."

"All that money, too. Lately he'd been throwing it around as if he'd been printing it in his basement," Jake added. "Maybe the deal with your ex-husband turned out to be lucrative."

I'd been looking for a way to escape, so I hadn't been giving the conversation my full attention. My head snapped around so fast, I feared whiplash.

"Huh?"

"I know Otis was pleased to have the esteemed Peter Bloom as a business partner."

"Huh?"

Janna laughed—a tinkling sound that set my teeth on edge. "You act like you don't know. Didn't Peter tell you?"

I recovered enough to say, "Peter and I never discussed his affairs—at least not the ones that involved actual business transactions. I'm sure you're mistaken, though. As far as I know, Peter didn't know Otis."

Linda S. Clayton　19

"Of course he did," Jake insisted. "Otis told me he'd met Peter several times for dinner."

Relieved, I said, "I know that's not right. Peter was on the island for one night and he was with me. He absolutely did not meet Otis." Here I felt I was on solid ground. Peter came to Hilton Head to win me back. I rejected him, and he hightailed it out of here as fast as he could.

Jake shook his head. "I don't think Otis meant here on Hilton Head. At least that's not the impression I got. They could have met anywhere—or do you keep track of all your ex-husband's movements?"

I felt my face flame. "Of course not. I thought you were referring to last year when Peter came for a visit. I have absolutely no contact with him so I obviously can't say definitively he didn't meet Otis. I'm just saying it's highly unlikely." I consulted my watch. "Would you look at the time. Must go. It's been great seeing you again."

Janna kissed the air near my face. "Take care. I love your little dishes."

"We'll call you if we hear anything more about Otis and Peter," Jake yelled as I rounded the corner of cosmetics and headed for the door. I fervently hoped no busybody heard him. One thing was certain. I had to do some sleuthing. Everyone seemed to know more about my ex-husband than I did.

When I returned home there was a message from the sheriff on my machine. "Ms Bloom," he said in his South Carolina twang, "I need to speak to you again. There are a few things I'd like to clear up. I'll call tomorrow and we'll set up an appointment."

Great. He probably found out about the calling card and was going to haul me off to jail. That was the trouble with living on this small island. Everyone knew everything. It was practically impossible to keep a secret.

CHAPTER 4

▼

At eleven thirty at night a full moon blazed over the marsh, making flashlights unnecessary. I tried to ignore sounds of movement in the tall Spartina grass. An unseen animal howled briefly and splashed in the water. Terrified, I threw my arms around Ben's neck, hoping the critter wouldn't smell my fear and hunt me down.

Ben Jakowski held me tightly. "I hope you realize you owe me big time, although I'm having a hard time figuring out why I listen to you. All of your wild schemes end up in disaster."

"Because you want to protect me and keep me out of danger." Recovered, I released Ben and pretended I wasn't nervous. "And please stop muttering. Someone might hear you."

"You're crazy. You do know that, don't you? You have an alarming disregard for personal safety or other people's private property. Why you aren't locked up in a maximum security prison with a girl named Tanya as your roommate is a mystery to me."

He sounded upset and I didn't really blame him. After the phone call from the sheriff, I telephoned Ben and enlisted his help. Now we were plodding through marsh grass and muck. Cold slime oozed out of my tennis shoes, and mosquitoes attacked relentlessly. The Murbaugh manse was situated on a prime piece of real estate facing Broad Creek and the Intracoastal Waterway. And best of all, it was conveniently

- 20 -

located a scant half mile as the crow flies from my house. A crow, however, was able to wing its way across the marsh. Unfortunately, we had to crawl

I stopped next to Ben and whispered in his ear. "You're doing this because you'll be suitably rewarded when we're finished. That is, if no one calls the police because you're being so loud."

As always happened when I caught a whiff of Ben's after-shave, I suddenly felt dizzy. I wondered if I made him dizzy, too. He didn't look weak-kneed. Still, I strongly suspected I was the reason he moved to the Lowcountry. You can't tell me a New York Times correspondent pitches it all in and moves to the South just because he has a hankering for fun in the sun.

"That had better not be an empty promise," he whispered back. "I can turn around any time. I have no problem with letting you get arrested by yourself."

I put my hand over his mouth. We had reached the back of Otis's house, and I didn't want any unnecessary commotion.

Otis's home was a tribute to atrocious taste and too much money. There were turrets and towers and a widow's walk that spanned two wings of the house. We crept past a swimming pool rimmed with blooming gardenia plants and climbing jasmine. My plan was simple. We would enter—break-in is such a nasty word—look through all of Otis's stuff, confirm that not only were my Peter and the Moroccan Peter two different people, but my Peter and the odious Otis also didn't know each other. Then Ben and I would return to the comfort and pleasures of my home. I couldn't see how anything could go wrong. My ex-husband didn't deserve this kind of personalized attention, but I didn't intend to let him become involved in this mess if he were innocent.

Maybe I was overreacting. The sheriff didn't know about the business card and even if he did, it didn't prove Peter was guilty of anything. But it would cast suspicion. And cause questioning. Let's face it—the bottom line was I had to know why my ex-husband's name was on a card with a Moroccan address and why Otis had it in his hand. I didn't care what Peter did in Boston, but this was my turf and it was my business to get some answers. The likeliest explanation for the missing passport was that Peter was frolicking on the coast of France with some starry eyed bimbo, but I had to find out for sure.

The house was dark—which was no surprise since Otis was obviously in no shape to occupy it. We circled the property hunting for a way to enter, but the Murbaugh domicile was locked up tighter than a drum. There was, however, a window on the second floor that appeared to be slightly open.

"See that? I pointed upward. "All we need is a ladder. Could you see if you can find one in the garage?"

"I think not. Let's go. Sea Pines security patrols these streets regularly. There is no way I'm going into the garage to hunt for a ladder. Let me repeat. Let's go."

"Thanks, sweetie." I patted his arm. "Hurry back. We don't want to hang around here too long."

While I waited for Ben to stop staring at me, I fiddled with my hair, tucking it under my baseball cap. It was taking an awfully long time for him to get moving. In fact, it was taking so long I looked down at my legs, wondering if I'd forgotten to put on some crucial piece of clothing—like my pants. No. I wasn't looking my best, but sleuthing required comfortable attire. I'd learned from experience that you didn't barge through brush and bushes without protective covering. I wore jeans, a long sleeve shirt and tennis shoes. I had a tote bag with supplies slung around my shoulder. Ben, who had never been on an investigation before, slapped at mosquitoes feasting on his bare legs.

"I'll look for a ladder," he finally said through his teeth, "and I'll hold it for you because otherwise you'll probably break your neck, but once you enter that house, I'm going home. You are, as I believe I stated earlier, certifiably crazy."

"Fair enough. Now please get that ladder. We're wasting time."

As soon as he disappeared in the direction of the garage, I pulled a baseball from the bag I carried, wrapped it in a towel and whacked out a glass pane in the kitchen door. I reached through the broken glass, unlocked the door and stepped into the house. Ben came flying around the corner just as I was placing the baseball a distance from the door on the floor.

"What was that noise? Are you okay?"

Satisfied with my work, I stood up and rubbed my hands.

"The sheriff will never know the house was broken into. He'll think some boys hurled a baseball through the window."

"This was your plan all the time, wasn't it? You never intended to use a ladder."

"Would you have agreed to this? Don't worry. I take full responsibility. You can truthfully say you knew nothing about it."

"You've forgotten one thing. There is no house around here. A kid would have to have an arm like A-Rod to heave a ball this far." When I looked at him blankly, he said, "You know, Alex Rodriguez, the best player in baseball? A Yankee? Oh, never mind. All I'm saying is, a kid couldn't do this."

"Let's not deal in minor technicalities," I said briskly. "Are you going home now or are you coming with me?"

"Give me the flashlight. You hunt for whatever it is you want and I'll light your way."

Otis's house smelled like bacon and sweat. Several dirty dishes sat in a sink big enough to bathe in. There was a container of Viagra, a bottle of prescription sleeping pills and a half empty glass of water on the granite counter. I scooped a pile of unopened mail into my bag. At a quick glance it seemed to be mostly junk mail, but I'd have a closer look at home.

"I'm going to watch your back while you do your snooping," Ben told me. "If I whistle, come running fast. And hurry up. I'm not staying here forever."

I brushed past him on my way to the living room, which I gave only a cursory inspection. Otis's taste ran to red brocade furniture and lamps with tasseled fringes. Had I been able to turn the lights on, I'd have bet money I'd see paintings of sunsets on velvet. I skirted a bearskin rug in front of the fireplace. The mouth of the poor animal was open in what was supposed to resemble a ferocious growl. I played the beam of my flashlight on a framed photo of Otis and a woman. Both reclined on the bearskin rug and both wore big grins and not much else. Ugh! The funny thing was, the woman was quite attractive. I shook my head. You'd have to be drugged and blind to go out with Otis Murbaugh. But there was no accounting for taste.

There was an office—a small room with built-in bookshelves, a desk, a computer and a painting of a woman with white hair and wire rim glasses. His grandmother? His secret fantasy? The books appeared to be for decoration only. Their spines were stiff when I opened them. The drawers were disappointingly empty. If Otis was involved in some nefarious business, he didn't keep receipts in his desk.

I eyed his computer. What harm would a quick glance do? I knew it was risking discovery to turn it on, but if it yielded important information, it would be worth it. As the computer hummed to life, I tried to think. Otis had the business card with Peter's name in his hand when he died. That meant he had either used it or intended to use it. As far as I could remember, there was no telephone number on the card. Did that mean he needed the address? To send something?

I turned my attention to the computer monitor. There were only three icons on the desktop: Flight Simulator—and please God, don't let that be how Otis learned to fly—Turbo Tax and Address Book. I clicked on Turbo Tax, hoping it would reveal Otis's assets. It was empty. His address book, on the other had, was approximately the size of the Hilton Head telephone directory.

I scrolled through the Bs. Bailey, Bedford, Biggs, Black, Blank, Bloom, Bloom. My name and address were there as well as Peter's Sudbury address and phone number.

I nearly jumped out of my shoes when Ben tapped me on the shoulder. "Find anything?"

"Look at this. Damn! I had no idea he knew Peter. How in the world do you suppose they met? Otis wasn't Peter's type."

"Could have been last year when Peter brought his boat down. Doesn't Otis own a boat?"

"He has some kind of sailboat, but I don't think he keeps it at Harbour Town. As far as I know he rented it out most of the time. Otis wasn't much of a sportsman."

As I talked I inspected more of the address book. I was fairly certain he didn't know all these people. Poor Otis. He had deluded himself into thinking these folks were his buddies.

"He even has an address for Bitsy Foster's husband in London. This is really pitiful. Bitsy and her husband have been divorced for years."

"So the man collected names—which makes Peter's name in his address book unremarkable."

"But it doesn't prove it isn't my Peter S. Bloom on the card."

Ben slammed his hand down on the desk. "*Your* Peter S. Bloom? Is that how you think of him? Why do I have the feeling you're still in love with the guy."

"I meant my Peter as opposed to somebody else's Peter. Don't be so silly, Ben. I told you I feel nothing for him except concern." I tried to read the expression on his face, but he turned away, avoiding me. I put my arms around his waist and pressed my cheek against his back. "Please believe me. I know in my heart that my ex-husband doesn't have anything to do with Otis Murbaugh or Marrakech, Morocco, but if Sheriff Griffey gets wind of this and starts sniffing around before I can prove Peter isn't involved, it could be very bad. Peter's not here to explain things or defend himself. I have to do it for him. After all, we were married for fourteen years. I guess that mandates some kind of loyalty—even if I can't stand the man."

Ben took me in his arms and held me tight. His lips skimmed the top of my head. "Keep looking. I don't like, it but I guess I understand. I hope that if I ever get into trouble, you'll do the same for me."

"With pleasure," I said happily as I took the stairs two at a time. Ben was one in a million.

I was using a coat hanger to poke through Otis's underwear drawer when I heard the noise. At first I thought marsh rats had invaded his attic. This was fairly common for folks who owned homes on the water or marshes. I knew from first hand experience that they could chew through the roof and set up housekeeping with very little noise. Before you knew it you had a family of several hundred munching on your insulation and running through your walls.

This sound was more like a rustling. Since many nocturnal critters crossed the roofs in Sea Pines, I ignored it. But what I heard next made me slap my hand over my chest so no one would hear the frantic thumping of my heart. Unless I was very mistaken, rats did not tiptoe stealthily down the hall.

There was someone else in the house.

I held my breath and listened. The footsteps stopped. I looked around the room for something I could use as a weapon. Otis's bedroom had a circular bed covered in some kind of fuzzy material. There were several large pillows arranged on the floor in a corner. A dozen or so colorful Mardi Gras masks decorated one wall. And that was it, except for another bearskin rug—a smaller version of the one downstairs—in front of the fireplace.

I crept to the door and stuck out my head. A shadowy figure moved down the hall and entered a bedroom. This puzzled me because whoever it was must know Ben and I were in the house. We hadn't expected guests, so we hadn't been exactly quiet. That meant, I decided, that the person wasn't worried because he/she was armed and could shoot holes in us if the need arose.

Panicked, I backed into the room and hid behind the door. I had to get downstairs and warn Ben before someone whacked me over the head and the lights went out. I grabbed a silver mask with a long, pointed proboscis, horns and bright pink feathery hair, slammed it over my face—and almost passed out. Someone had actually worn the thing. It smelled of sweat, perfume and stale cigarette smoke. Nevertheless, it was all I had. I figured a good scare might be as effective as a pointed pistol. Well, maybe not, but our clandestine marauder wouldn't expect to see a half crazed lunatic in a Mardi Gras mask prancing around the hall. The shock might give me time to grab Ben and get away.

I didn't waste time worrying about the logic of my plan. I took a deep breath, dashed out the door and raced down the stairs as if my pants were on fire.

Ben was in the living room looking out the window. He turned around in time to see me hurl myself at his mid-section. Understandably concerned about his immediate physical well being, he stiff-armed me in the chest, sending me flying backwards over the brocade couch. I landed with a thud on the floor.

"It's me, Ben," I gasped. "We have to get out of here."

Ben stood over me with his fists clenched. "Who's me?"

"Maggie, you idiot. Who did you think it was?"

He reached down and pulled the mask off my face. "Why are you...? Never mind. I don't think I want to know."

"Ben," I said urgently. "We have to go right now." I pointed to the ceiling. "There is somebody up there. I saw him with my own eyes."

We both froze as we heard soft footsteps above us. I took Ben's hand. "He's using the back stairs. In a few seconds he'll be in the kitchen, What are we going to do?"

Ben had already taken my hand and was pulling me through the hall to the front door. "Ladies first," he said as he opened the door. We flew across the lawn and into the marsh. Neither of us said a word until we were safely in my house, drinking coffee and pretending we were both fine.

CHAPTER 5

▼

All I wanted to do was stay in bed. Preferably with a pillow over my head and the curtains pulled tightly across the windows. But Wally and Willow had other plans. They sat on my stomach and examined me carefully, looking for signs of life. Wally took a few tentative swipes at my face with his tongue. Since ignoring them wasn't going to work, I got up, pulled on shorts and a T-shirt and padded to the kitchen.

Today, in spite of the fact that I still had lingering shakes from last night's adventure, I had to take my newest creations to Susan Lowerby at Fashion Court, an upscale boutique in Harbour Town. Since the divorce from Peter, I earned my living painting things. I'd begun modestly with flowerpots and wastebaskets. Much to my astonishment, these hand-painted handicrafts actually sold well. Now I supplied several snazzy boutiques with decorated stemware and pitchers. I named my business *In Bloom*, developed a web site and sold my things online as well as other locations in the southeast.

Now I selected several glasses and pitchers with the ever-popular magnolia motif, carefully packed them in a box and loaded it into my car.

At this hour of the morning Harbour Town was quiet. Tourists were still snoozing, and the shops were still closed. A crew of four scrubbed the decks of a yacht docked in the harbor. A few early birds sat in the rocking chairs, sipping coffee and watching the activity.

The door to Fashion Court was open. Cotton Duncan stood at the back of the shop arranging Vera Bradley bags on the shelves. When she saw me she bounded over and took the box out of my hands.

"I talked to Ma last night," she said as she set the stemware on the counter.

Ordinarily this statement would be quite harmless, but when it was uttered by Cotton Duncan, you had to worry. Cotton's mother, Wisteria, died five months ago. Since then, Cotton had been having regular and public conversations with her deceased parent. According to Cotton, Wisteria, or at least her voice, appeared every night and dispensed gossip, special tips for folks in trouble and greetings from the recently departed. Cotton published these tidbits in a monthly newsletter she called *Gems From The Other Side*.

I had to admit that even though I publicly denied ever having laid my peepers on the publication, I did, from time to time in the privacy of my bedroom, glance through it. I didn't want some surprise from the Great Beyond sneaking up on me when I wasn't looking.

"So how is your mother?" It was a polite and necessary inquiry. If I didn't ask, she'd tell me anyway.

"She seems to be fine. Looks a little wrinkled. I suspect it's a bit windy Over There."

Cotton shoved a clump of curly copper colored hair out of her face. "She says the gossip is pretty good and soon she'll have some great news for us. Candy says like maybe she'll give us the winning lottery number. She can do that, you know."

Candy was Cotton's twin. The story of their birth was still a popular tale. On warm evenings when folks on Hilton Head were sitting on their porches inhaling the soft breezes floating off the ocean, the conversation very often turned to Wisteria and the conception of her offspring. In fact, the story had been told so often and with so many embellishments that it was hard to determine where truth left off and fiction began.

Legend says that at the age of forty, Wisteria experienced a sudden urge to see the world. She left the family home and traveled all the way to North Carolina. Somewhere along the Outer Banks she met a sailor whose ship had docked for a brief port call. Here the story grows a bit cloudy because Wisteria never specified the country of origin of the ship or the nationality of the sailor.

In any event, when Wisteria began to gain weight, she attributed it to copious helpings of grits and red-eyed gravy and vowed to eventually go on a diet. She was visiting the State Fair in Raleigh when her water broke and labor began. With the help of a passing taxi driver she delivered her first daughter on the pavement next to a cotton candy machine. During her brief labor Wisteria kept her eyes glued on the pink confection swirling in the plastic dome. When the baby was placed in her arms, she happily named her Candy.

Thinking this amazing event had reached a conclusion, Wisteria struggled to get to her feet, only to be felled by more contractions. Eleven minutes later a second daughter was born. At a loss for a name and anxious to be on her way, she glimpsed the cotton candy sign and made a decision. The second baby would be Cotton.

And even though in the eyes of the medical establishment these babies were indisputably twins, in Wisteria's eyes she had an older and a younger daughter. Those eleven minutes must have seemed like years to the bewildered new mother. Forever more Candy was known as "the oldest" and Cotton referred to as "the baby".

Back home on the island, Wisteria announced that the girls' father was at sea and wouldn't be back for a long time. Gradually folks just forgot there was supposed to be another parental unit.

Somehow, in the explosion, partitioning and fertilization of the egg that produced the twins, Cotton's half missed out on an adequate portion of gray matter and common sense. She was pleasant, loveable, docile and eager to please, but she was never going to finish the Sunday New York Times crossword puzzle.

Candy lived in Memphis and called her sister once a week. Cotton lived in her mother's house on the north end of the island and worked part time in Harbour Town.

"Anyway," Cotton told me, "I'll be putting the gossip in *Gems From The Other Side*. Isn't that exciting?"

"Right up there with a root canal. What's that you're unpacking?"

Cotton held a string of beads in her hand. "Aren't these pretty? I found them in this little wooden box by the back door this morning. Guess Ms Lowerby forgot to pick them up last night."

The beads were large and milky white. Each was decorated with flowers and leaves painted in delicate pastel colors. "The artist did a super job on these," I said admiringly. "The style is primitive but effective. I wonder where they came from."

Cotton examined the box in her hand. "There's no address label and there's no packing slip. It doesn't even say it was intended for this shop but since it was outside our door, I figured Ms Lowerby would want it unpacked."

"How many necklaces are in the box?"

"Twenty. I thought I'd put one or two in the window and see if they appealed to the tourists."

"Better wait until Ms Lowerby comes," I advised. "Just in case a customer wants to buy one. You don't know how they would be priced." I examined the necklace again. I didn't think Susan would have any problem selling them. They were extremely attractive—and would look splendid with a dress I recently bought. "Say, do you think I could have one? They really are pretty and very unique. I'll write a note to Susan and tell her to subtract the price from the items I brought today."

"That's fine. Ms Lowerby will be happy to see I made a sale," she said, handing me paper and pen. She carefully wrapped the necklace in tissue and put it in a pretty blue bag. "Want to know what Ma said?"

"Some other time," I started to the door. "I've got a ton of things to do this morning."

Cotton followed me out of the shop. "Janet Ormund is getting divorced."

"Janet Ormund is always getting divorced." Janet was a long time local who lived in Spanish Wells and had been married five or six times.

"Ed Harris ran his boat aground in South Beach. Ma said he'd been drinking Tequila."

"He switched from vodka?"

"Your ex-husband is in a mess of trouble. Pretty soon the sheriff is going to be looking for him."

"What!"

"That's what Ma said. She said, 'Tell Maggie her sweetie did a real bad thing.'"

"He is not my sweetie," I gasped, "and I'm sure I have no idea what you're talking about."

"Umm, that's not what Ma says. You never pay attention to me, Maggie. I could save you a lot of trouble if you'd just listen."

She had my full attention. I faced her squarely. "Okay. Tell me exactly what your mother said. I assure you, I am listening."

"Certain vibrations tell her his aura and yours are very cloudy. And they are mingled, which means you two are involved in something together. It'll only be a matter of time until she has all the facts."

Good grief. This girl had more bats in her noggin than a church bell tower. But this was the kind of reckless chatter that would upset Ben and make the sheriff very curious. I had to make sure she kept her ghostly gossip to herself.

"You know, Cotton, how much I love hearing the nightly tidbits from your mother. It really is amazing how much she manages to learn from the, ah, newly departed. She dispenses information like a doctor does medicine. That's why you should think of yourself as a sort of specialized caregiver. When your mother's news applies to only one specific person, you mustn't tell it to anyone else."

"I mustn't?"

"Of course not." I tried to look serious. "Patient confidentiality and that sort of thing."

"I have patients?"

"I think you could say you do."

Cotton looked dazed but happy. "I never thought of it that way, but I think you're right. I must protect my people."

"I'm so glad you understand. I truly appreciate you telling me about Peter's aura and you can be assured we'll work on cleaning it up."

"You don't actually clean it, Maggie. What you have to do is go through a purification ceremony. I could arrange it for you if you like."

"I'll have to talk to Peter. In the meantime, can I trust you to keep this information strictly private?"

She almost saluted. "I advise you to do the same. And call on me for any advice you may need. After all, I am the professional here."

Heaven help us. But I made sure I had my back turned before I rolled my eyes.

The sheriff drove up my driveway as I was watering the geraniums on the front porch. He climbed out of his patrol car and strolled purposefully towards me. "Wonder if you could give me some information," he said, pulling out a notebook and a pen.

"I don't have anything to tell you. I didn't see anyone around Otis and I didn't hear anything."

"Not what I want to know." He flipped through some pages. "I'm interested in people who had business dealings with the deceased."

"That wouldn't be me," I said. "I certainly wouldn't have been that dumb." He raised his eyebrows. "I mean, his business reputation wasn't very savory, was it. Everyone knew that."

"How about friends of yours who might have worked with Murbaugh?"

This was sliding very close to asking about Peter. I was convinced the sheriff was toying with me. "I don't know of anyone," I said stiffly. "If you don't mind my saying so, that is an odd thing to ask."

He slapped his notebook closed. "If you have any information, make sure you tell me. It's against the law to withhold evidence." He marched to his car, leaving me clutching my watering can with one hand and my rapidly beating heart with the other.

Carole Parker, Peter's secretary at Hale, Simmons and Bloom, told me Peter was out of the country. "Don't know where he went, honey. I'm out of the loop because he made the reservations himself this time. He said he'd be back in a week. I could ask one of the partners, if you like."

"No, that's okay. I'm just wondering if he did this often. Make the reservations himself, I mean."

"Sometimes. Actually he's been doing it a lot lately. I figured he wanted to keep something secret." Her cheerful voice trailed off. "I'm sorry, Maggie. I forgot you were married to him."

I'd known Carole since she became Peter's secretary ten years ago. During the divorce she'd maintained a friendly relationship with me, in spite of the fact her boss could have canned her for consorting with the enemy.

"What you're trying to say is that he is traveling with one of his girl-friends."

"Well, yes. I have a feeling he is."

I thought about the voice on the phone. Surely Peter didn't have a bimbo for home and a different bimbo for travel. That would be excessive, even for Peter. My bet was he was traveling alone. Dirty deeds are best carried out without witnesses.

"One last question, Carole, and I promise I won't bother you again. Do you know the name of his present girlfriend?"

Carole hesitated. "I probably shouldn't be saying this, but what the heck. There is some gossip around the office but I'm not sure how accurate it is. Her name is Petal Rose and she's a hostess at a ritzy restaurant here in town. Rumor has it she will soon be Mrs. Peter Bloom."

What! I felt like I'd been hit in the stomach. Married? How did we get to married? It was just last year he'd come to Hilton Head trying to win me back. I certainly didn't love Peter and I didn't want to be married to him, but I also didn't want him to get hitched. I'd envisioned a long, empty life for him, full of remorse at losing me. To help me remember what a louse he'd been, I conjured up an image of the time I'd found Peter and the bimbo cavorting in our hot tub. After that, no amount of scrubbing could get it clean. I eventually used it to bathe the dogs.

"What's she like?" I managed to croak.

"Your typical trophy wife. Very young, very blond, great body that is probably all due to Mother Nature. She's one of those incredible women blessed with super skin, super hair and a super figure. You know the type."

Actually, I didn't. Janna came close, but I knew some absolutely divine person named Romano colored her hair, and I suspected she'd had a few nips and tucks. On the other hand, my face had freckles, my knees had creases, my chestnut hair color was due to three different shades of Clairol and I required glasses to read the telephone book. Suddenly I felt very old.

"Thanks, Carole. I don't think he took her on his trip. A female voice answered the phone at his house."

"Well then," she laughed. "It's settled. He went alone. Probably had to take a vacation from all that youthful energy."

"Hah, hah," I laughed. "Men can be so ridiculous, can't they?" Secretly, I hoped he'd overdose on Viagra.

CHAPTER 6

▼

"Just because Peter's secretary said he was out of the country doesn't mean he is. He could be anywhere," I said. "He could even be the person who conked Otis over the head. I tell you, Lucy, I'm feeling like I really don't know my ex-husband. And the sheriff is making me nervous."

"If I were you, I'd forget about this whole thing. You are the only one who has connected Peter to Otis. I think you're becoming a tiny bit tedious about all this."

Lucy's breath came in gasps as she spoke, and sweat created rivers in the make-up spackled on her face. "How far have we run, anyway?"

"About fifty feet. Do you want to quit?"

We had walked from Lucy's oceanfront home to the bike path on South Beach Drive. After a complicated series of stretches and maneuvers aimed at making our bodies—according to Lucy—'more receptive to exercise', we finally started to jog.

"I don't think we should overdo it, do you? I mean, we don't want to damage our muscles." Lucy glanced at her shocking pink satin jogging shorts and mint green tank top. She had pulled her flaming red hair into a ponytail and stuck the end through a hole in a pink sequined baseball cap. "I notice a bit of moisture on my shorts."

"That's called perspiration. Honestly, Lucy, didn't you sweat when you worked as a dancer?"

"Of course I did, but in those days a glistening body was almost a requirement for the job. After I met Julius and left my work at the club, I gave up glistening." She looked at her watch. "I think we should have an appropriate libation and then do lunch." She patted her stomach. "I've worked up quite an appetite."

A hot sun warmed our faces as we took seats outside at the Salty Dog Café in South Beach. Several tourists stood at the railing of the marina, watching fishing boats return with the morning catch.

"I believe I'll have a shrimp salad," Lucy told our server. "And a Bloody Mary to begin with."

I ordered a cheeseburger and fries. Real women ate real food. I'll bet Petal Rose feasted on cotton balls.

"So," Lucy began as she settled back in her chair. "I know you're not going to let this go with Peter. Sometimes you're as tenacious as a tick."

"How can I let it go? I was married to Peter. I don't want my family tree to read, *Peter S. Bloom, husband of Maggie Bloom—Incarcerated For Murder*. It's absurd to think he'd commit a crime, and I intend to prove he didn't. I wish I could determine is if the woman I talked to on the phone was Petal. Seems to me the person Peter intended to marry would know where he was, and I'd swear this girl didn't. She sounded extremely upset by the end of the conversation."

"Do you realize you're obsessing about this? Let me remind you—and I'm saying this as plainly as I can—there is no known connection between Peter and Otis. You are the only one who knows about the calling card."

"But I am not the only one who knows about a business deal between them—although I still don't believe it. Jake Maletesta insists they were partners. Even Cotton hinted at something. And how do you know Otis didn't have a dozen more cards in his pocket?" I asked. "The police could be sitting on that information while they hunt for more clues. They probably already suspect Peter of murder. They're waiting until they can prove it."

Lucy stirred her Bloody Mary with a stalk of celery. "That could be true, but why do you care so much? You're going to make Ben awfully mad if you keep picking at this."

I took a bite of my sandwich and chewed vigorously, enjoying the taste of fat and melted cheese. A girl could subsist just so long on fish and veggies. I mean, a body needs to ingest a certain amount of animal products. As soon as my mouth was empty, I said, "Ben understands my concern. He knows as well as I do that Peter couldn't be involved in anything illegal."

"How would you know that? You have no idea about Peter's business dealings."

"He doesn't have business dealings. He's a divorce lawyer. Trust me. Peter litigates. He doesn't know anything about the real world."

"Actually Ben doesn't understand anything about your fascination with your ex-husband either, but since he's fairly fond of you, he's willing to keep his mouth shut."

Lucy's lips weren't moving, so I deduced someone else was speaking. Ben brushed my lips with his and sat down.

"Am I interrupting you girls? I just ran six miles so I could do with a rest."

"Exactly what I said to Maggie," Lucy murmured. "We, too, have been running." Lucy rubbed her thigh. "I think I've got a slight pull in my deltoid."

"Then you'd better rub somewhere else. You've got your hand on your hamstring."

"It doesn't matter what it's called," Lucy said crossly. "The point is, I've injured myself. I'll require a few days rest before I can jog again."

Ben tried valiantly to hide a grin. "Wise decision, Lucy." He ordered an ice tea and a salad. I nonchalantly covered the remains of my cheeseburger and fries with my napkin "I have some news about Otis, if you're interested."

Linda S. Clayton 39

Lucy drained her Bloody Mary and looked longingly towards the bar. "One more couldn't hurt, I think. Especially if we're going to be discussing things."

"I was talking to Jack Woodward, who knows the sheriff fairly well. It seems they did find something else at the scene of the murder—something they haven't mentioned to the press," Ben said.

"I knew it," I wailed. "What did I tell you, Lucy? Peter's cards were probably stuck in every pocket."

"No, I didn't hear anything about cards. They found a rather unique money clip. It was in the shape of the dollar sign and was made of brightly colored beads. Sort of like the kind of thing you find out West."

My heart stopped. I know it did because I suddenly couldn't breathe. Ben looked at me in alarm. "Maggie, what's wrong? You're the color of paste. Do you have something stuck in your throat?"

Lucy jumped to her feet, prepared to grab me around the middle and squeeze. I pushed her away.

"This money clip—did it have strands of leather at the top?"

Ben looked at me curiously. "Yes, I believe it did. How would you know that?"

"Because I bought it for Peter when we visited the Grand Canyon. I had no idea he was still using it." Back in the days when my ex-husband and I still enjoyed being with each other, we drove to Arizona for a vacation. We rode donkeys down the narrow canyon trail and spent the night at Phantom Ranch, where I'd found the key chain.

"There could be others," Lucy said without much conviction.

"No, there couldn't. Do you believe me now? Peter is mixed up in the murder. And I'll bet something terrible has happened to him. Why would he leave his money clip at the scene of the crime? It doesn't make sense."

"It does if he clonked Otis over the head. Maybe there was a struggle and it fell out of his pocket."

"Ben!" I jumped to my feet, knocking my chair over. "How can you say that?"

A mother, father, two children and a grandmother at the next table stopped eating and stared at us. In fact, the grandmother turned in her seat so she'd have a better view.

"Sit down, Maggie," Lucy said gently. "We'll have three Bloody Marys," she said to our server, who hustled over to see what was wrong. "Now then, let's try to sort this out. If the money clip does belong to Peter, it implicates him. What we have to do is figure out in what way."

"How can we investigate anything? No one answers the phone at Peter's house. His office doesn't know where he is. And by the way, I've already thought of trying to call his girlfriend at her home. There is no listing for Petal Rose in Boston. How much do you want to bet that's not her real name."

"It certainly seems like we've reached a dead end." Lucy smiled as she sipped her drink.

"Why are you smiling? I don't think this is funny." The grandmother leaned closer, dropping all pretense of ignoring us. "And keep your voice down. People are listening."

"I think that rather than getting your knickers in a knot, you should listen to my suggestion."

I took a huge gulp of my Bloody Mary and instantly regretted it. The spicy seasoning burned my throat. Ben offered me his ice tea, which I immediately drained. "I didn't realize you had a suggestion. Let's hear it."

"Yes," Ben echoed. "Let's hear it. Anything to get this resolved."

Lucy looked like she had swallowed a yellow tweetie bird. "What I was thinking is this; we simply go to Marrakech and find out what's going on."

I stared at my friend. The vodka had melted her brain. "Sure, we can do that, Lucy. I'll just use petty cash to pay for the plane fare and hotel room and off we go. What's the matter with you? If you're going to offer a suggestion, make it a sensible one."

Lucy nibbled on the stalk of celery. "Are you finished? If you would let me explain…"

"Please do. I'm all ears." I winked at Ben to show him what I thought of this nonsense.

"Julius is going salmon fishing in Alaska. Therefore, I will have to amuse myself for a few days. I'd enjoy a jaunt to Marrakech, and since I don't want to go by myself, I'll take you. You too, Ben. It's that simple."

I know my mouth opened, but no words came out. I was too stunned.

"Now that we have it settled, I thought Tuesday would be a good day to leave." She reached into the fanny pack she wore around her waist. "Here is your ticket, Maggie. Delta to Paris, Royal Air Maroc from Paris to Tangier and Marrakech. I assume you have a valid passport. No visa is necessary. Ben, I didn't know I'd see you this morning so your ticket is still at my house. We'll get it later. Why are you looking at me that way?"

"Because you're crazy, that's why. I just can't pick up and go. What about my dogs?"

"You can leave them at my house. Emerald will be happy to watch them. Well, not happy perhaps, but well paid."

I turned to Ben. "Tell her she's nuts. This has to be the craziest idea I've ever heard."

Ben ignored me. "I'll pay you for the ticket, Lucy, but I am definitely coming. There's no way I'm letting you two run loose in a foreign country. Besides, you need me. I spent a few months in Morocco doing a piece for the Times, so I know Marrakech."

This was ridiculous. "You're supposed to be talking her out of this. I'm not going to Morocco and that's final."

Three days later I fastened my seatbelt as the Paris bound Delta 767 screamed down the runway at Atlanta's Hartsfield International Airport. Final destination—Marrakech, Morocco.

CHAPTER 7

▼

The Royal Air Maroc 727 descended slowly from the cobalt blue sky through white cumulous clouds. A stiff wind from the Mediterranean swept across the runway in Tangier, bending the palm trees and rocking our aircraft. Its wheels thumped hard on the tarmac as the plane landed. After an hour on the ground, we took off again, this time bound for Marrakech.

My deodorant failed me at 35,000 feet somewhere over the south of France. By the time we reached the ultra fancy Mamounia hotel in Marrakech, I was so ripe I couldn't stand myself.

Lucy sailed up the marble steps of the hotel looking as if she'd just stepped out of the shower. In fact, she was wearing a different outfit than the one I'd seen her leave the house in twenty hours earlier.

"I changed in the bathroom on the plane, sweetie. Rule number one: always carry spare clothes in your travel case. Also—she wrinkled her nose delicately—deodorant, toothbrush. perfume, make-up and a complete change of underwear." She smoothed the jacket of her orange and purple pants suit. "I do hate not feeling fresh. This way we can check in and explore the city. I'm assuming we can eat and relax before we begin our sleuthing."

I wanted a bath and bed. Lucy, who donned an eye mask the second the plane was airborne, slept her way across the Atlantic and was obviously fit for evening activities. Ben and I, on the other hand, had consumed many glasses of a very exceptional French Chablis. We stayed awake, chatting and drinking until the first light of morning broke over the coast of England. After that, there was no point trying to sleep.

Consequently, I boarded the Royal Air Maroc flight to Marrakech with an excruciating headache and an overwhelming urge to put my head on a pillow. It was not to be. Several passengers on the aircraft, who had remained sedate during the takeoff and climbing maneuvers, became annoyingly animated as soon as the pilot turned off the seat belt sign. They opened their duty free bottles of whisky and passed them around the cabin to ever increasing sounds of merriment.

By the time we piled into a taxi at the Marrakech airport, I longed for death—any death as long as it came swiftly. I hoped Ben felt the same way.

"I'm with you, Lucy," he said. Just give me time for a quick shower. I'd like to take you to a restaurant in the old town."

I shot him a dirty look.

Even in my odoriferous, sleep deprived state, I couldn't fail to be impressed with the splendid lobby of Hotel La Mamounia. It was as if we had stepped into some ancient palace. There was marble everywhere and graceful arches and wooden beams, intricate mosaics and an exquisite ceiling crafted of inlaid mahogany. I'd never seen anything so magnificent in my life. I leaned against a marble pillar while Lucy and Ben checked us in.

"You and I are sharing a suite," she told me. "Ben has a connecting room. That way we'll all be nice and cozy."

I was astonished at the spectacular accommodations Lucy had arranged for us. Heavy silk drapes hung on either side of double French doors, which opened to a balcony overlooking the garden and swimming pool. Above each bed was a beautiful tiled mosaic framed by yards of twisted gold silk. I stepped onto the balcony and inhaled the heady fragrance of jasmine, roses and orange blossoms. In the distance the famous Koutoubia minaret rose against a backdrop of the High Atlas mountains. I felt like a character in a Moorish fairy tale.

I also felt an urgent need for a bath. Forty minutes later I had soaked in the modern Jacuzzi, washed my hair with lavender soap, wrapped myself in a thick terry robe—and passed out. Lucy and Ben settled for salads from room service and also called it a day.

Just as a slim ray of dawn appeared in the night sky, the muezzin called the faithful to prayer. I knew this because I consulted my guide-book, and I heard this because I was experiencing a severe case of insomnia and dehydration. I was learning the hard way that it is unwise to consume large quantities of alcoholic beverages at 35, 000 feet. My mouth felt like a sand box and tasted nasty.

Careful not to wake Lucy, I climbed out of bed and quickly donned a lime green cotton dress and sandals. Around my neck I wore the only piece of jewelry I'd brought with me—the necklace I bought from Cotton at Fashion Court. I grabbed a map of Marrakech from the writing desk and went out onto the balcony. Down below, a man dressed in a white garment that covered his entire body swept the swimming pool deck. A lovely warm breeze carried the aroma of blooming flowers across the balcony.

"Beautiful, isn't it?" Ben stood beside me wearing a thick, blue terry cloth towel around his waist. He ran his fingers through his freshly washed hair. "I'm starving. Want some breakfast?"

I touched his tan, muscular arm. "That would be nice," I murmured.

I felt his arm tense. "Food it is, unless you're interested in something else?"

"What do you have in mind," I asked, my heart thumping.

He glanced into my bedroom. "Think Lucy will sleep for a while?"

"Probably. Why?"

For heaven sakes, why couldn't we be like Wally and Willow. Then I could swish my tail in his face and he could jump my bones. The human courting process was far too complicated.

"Well, I was thinking…"

"Good grief, Ben, let's go. We're wasting time out here." I grabbed his hand and pulled him across the balcony to his room. I knew I should have shown more maidenly restraint but subtlety is not my style. And I didn't think he was offended by my boldness. He trotted quite eagerly beside me.

An hour later we ordered everything that sounded remotely like breakfast food from the menu in the dining room.

"What I want to do is find out what's going on with Peter. Once we have that out of the way, we can explore Marrakech," I said as I took a bite of a delicious warm croissant. "Do you think it's too early to hunt for the address?"

"Let's have a look at your map. It'll save time if we know where we're going."

I moved my plate to one side and spread the map on the table. "I glanced at this last night. Only the major roads seem to be marked. Most of these side streets have no names. How are we supposed to find Riyad El Nabil?"

"We'll ask. I remember that most of the major roads have French names—for instance, most of them start with *Rue*. Many of the areas near the souks, on the other hand, start with Riyad and include either a man or a woman's name. As I recall, Riyad means courtyard and Nabil is a Moroccan male name, so Riyad el Nabil would roughly translate to *Nabil's Courtyard*. I'll bet the place we are looking for is small, and we find it near the souks."

I looked at him admiringly. "You are, indeed, a helpful person to have on this jaunt." Remembering the hour we spent in his bedroom, I felt my face flush. "I'm not talking about that," I said when he began to laugh. "I mean how you figured out Nabil is a man's name. I didn't know that."

"Glad to be of help. I want to get this solved as much as you do. Maybe more."

We stopped talking as a family of four sat down at the table next to us. The father led the way to the table, followed by two well-behaved children and the mother. The woman wore a *jellaba,* a long gray garment that covered her hair and her body. Across her face she wore a veil.

"I feel like I'm in another world," I said to Ben.

"You are. Every time I come to Morocco I think I'm stepping back in time. It's fascinating."

"This was probably a dumb thing to do. Coming here, I mean. Now that I'm actually in Marrakech I realize the probability of finding out anything about Peter is zero. I think Lucy just wanted a boondoggle."

"Not necessarily. It's worth a try. We weren't getting anywhere at home." He took my hand across the table and stared into my eyes. "I want you back, Maggie. I don't want Peter coming between us, And I'll do anything I can to get this resolved."

"You are a great guy. You know that, don't you?"

"A guy never gets tired of hearing it."

I took one last sip of *café au lait* and wiped my lips on the linen napkin. "Don't let it go to your head," I said as I stood up. "There's always room for improvement."

What was the matter with me? I ruined a perfectly good moment by shooting off my big mouth. And for this I had to blame Peter. His mid-life crisis had sapped my self-confidence so badly, I was afraid to completely trust any other man. Ben was the one for me, but before I let him know that, I would require a blood oath and one of his kidneys. A girl had to protect herself from heartache.

The scene at the Jemaa el Fna was unlike anything I'd ever seen. The huge square in the old city of Marrakech—a short walk from the

Mamounia—resembled a spectacular circus with lots of different acts performing at once. I watched in awe as acrobats dressed in shiny green shirts and black and gold pants, formed a human pyramid.

A snake charmer with a leathery face and missing front teeth wrapped a live cobra around his neck. He grinned happily as I jumped away in fright.

"Look over there," Ben said, pointing to a throng of people clustered around a seated man. "That's a story teller. He comes here every day and spins new tales for the folks. Too bad we can't understand him because I've heard the stories are remarkable."

I was too busy absorbing the activity around me to care about the storyteller. A water seller, dressed in the traditional red Rifi costume and wearing a wide brimmed straw hat with dangling tassels, offered me a drink from a brass cup. When I declined—I mean, there were probably amoebae growing in that stuff, and heaven only knows how many strange lips had touched the rim—he pointed to my camera and held out his hand.

"He wants you to take a picture and then give him a *dirham*," Ben told me. I obliged, thinking the snapshot would be a nice souvenir of the trip.

"The souks are at the far end of the square." I pressed closer to Ben. "Let's try to have a look."

A young boy using a crutch to support his body, which was crippled with some horrible deformity, hobbled towards us. "A *dirham*, lady. I can be your guide."

"No, thank you," I replied and walked faster. The boy, however, was not to be deterred.

"Lady, I will take you where you want to go. Here, you like? Eat this. Is very good." He offered me a squishy ball that looked like pasty molasses. "It is *majoun*. Very tasty. You eat all."

"Do you want to try this, Ben? It seems to be some kind of local delicacy."

"No, and you don't either." He shook his finger sternly at the boy. "That is the Moroccan equivalent of an Alice B. Toklas brownie. It's made from the crushed seeds of the marijuana plant and you definitely don't want to eat it."

Temporarily discouraged, the boy kept his distance as Ben and I tried to make our way through the crowds of people. Our progress was slow.

"Lady, I will take you where you want to go. Not safe for a lady to walk here alone." The boy materialized suddenly at my side.

"I'm not alone." I turned to point to Ben, who had stopped to watch a dentist extract a patient's tooth in his open-air office. The boy dismissed Ben with a wave of his crutch. "He not from here. I help you, lady. Very cheap. Five *dirhan* for whole day."

"I told you I don't need a guide." I tried to reach Ben but, against my will, the crowd of people swept me forward. I clutched my tote bag to my chest and tried not to fall.

Miraculously, the crippled boy experienced a healing in the midst of the throng. He straightened up, tucked his crutch under his arm and broke into a jog. "I help you, lady. You stay with me. Your friend is gone." As he reached for my elbow, I aimed a kick at his shins and trotted away. This time the mob of people worked to my advantage. I let it carry me along until I reached the entrance to the souks.

Without thinking—which is a deplorable habit that often gets me into trouble—I entered the dizzying complex of open shops and twisting alleys. Enterprising merchants sold copper pots, rugs, shoes, spices, leatherwork and jewelry. I stopped by a dyers stall, fascinated by the skeins of dripping red, blue and yellow wool that hung from clotheslines.

Hands reached out to me and plucked at my clothes, trying to entice me into the stalls. I suddenly needed oxygen, but there was none. The hot air was thick with cigarette smoke and unfamiliar smells. I tried to retrace my steps but it was like trying to run up the down stairs of an escalator—it wouldn't work. The crowd was too thick. I was propelled through the souk by strange bodies that pressed against me. I could feel warm breath on the back of my neck. Genuinely afraid I was about to faint, I lurched to the right and grabbed hold of the first thing I could put my hands on—a wooden pole with directional signs. Gasping, I held on for dear life as people gave me curious looks and pushed past me. When I felt I could breathe again, I looked at the sign. My hand covered *Riyad el* but under my thumb I could plainly see the word, *Nabil.*

The sign pointed directly into a stall. A small boy with huge, solemn black eyes sat on a dirty carpet fashioning a piece of brown leather into the shape of a sandal. In a back room, three men sat in a circle drinking peppermint tea. As I timidly poked my head in the door, one of them scowled, stood up and approached me. "We are not open. Please come back. Very nice shoes tomorrow."

I pulled the business card with Peter's name out of my wallet. "I'm not interested in shoes. I'm looking for Riyad el Nabil. Could you tell me how to get there?"

The man smoothed his thick black mustache as he considered my request. "This is Riyad el Nabil," he informed me. "What are you looking for?"

"An import/export company. I'm not sure of the name." Looking around, I felt certain there had to be some mistake. This dirty little stall surely wasn't a business office. "Perhaps there is another Riyad el Nabil," I asked hopefully.

The man glanced at my hand. "May I see the card?"

I clutched it to my chest. "I am looking for information about Peter S. Bloom."

"Bloom." He rolled the word over his tongue. "There is no one here by that name."

"Just as I suspected. Thank you for your time. I won't bother you anymore," I babbled as I backed out of the room. Losing interest, the men returned to their tea.

The little boy tugged at my skirt. "Lady, you go there." He pointed to an alley next to the stall.

"Is that Riyad el Nabil?" I asked.

He held out a dirty hand. "You go there, lady. *Dirhan?*"

I took the desired money out of my wallet and held it in my hand. "Not so fast. Do you speak English?"

He looked at the men in the back room and then at me. "You go there, lady. Riyad el Nabil. You find."

I resisted the urge to say *where is your mother.* Obviously, she wasn't here making sure her child wasn't being exploited. I gave the *dirham* to the boy and cautiously moved down the alley.

The alley ended at the ochre colored wall of Marrakech. Directly ahead of me was a gate with a bell. Since there was no way to get around the wall, I would have to go through it. I stiffened my spine and pushed the bell.

A swarthy man wearing the traditional white garment opened the gate and looked me over. "Yes, lady, you need help?"

My eyes took in a courtyard with a fountain. On the far wall, above an archway was a sign. *Riyad el Nabil.*

"Is this a hotel?" Ben was right. Riyad did mean courtyard. But it was also some kind of guesthouse or lodging.

The man started to close the gate.

"Wait," I said, suddenly struck by inspiration. "I'm looking for Peter Bloom. He told me to meet him here."

The gate opened slightly. "Peter Bloom is not here."

"That's fine," I said firmly. "I will wait."

"You cannot wait, lady. He not come back."

"I don't believe you." I ventured into the courtyard and looked around. It was cool and quiet. I detected the faint odor of mint tea and cigarette smoke.

"Tell me," I said, "when did you last see Peter Bloom? And what does he look like? Could you describe him for me?" It occurred to me I wasn't very adept at the interrogation part of my investigation, but in all fairness, I haven't had a lot of practice.

The man stared at me curiously. "You ask too many questions. Wait here. Do not leave."

He shouldn't have said that. There was something slightly sinister in the way he spoke. As soon as he left the courtyard, I hightailed it out of there. I tore through the gate and pounded down the alley to the souks.

When two men appeared on either side of me, so close they were actually touching my body, I had no idea what was happening. I also had no intention of becoming involved in some kind of Moroccan sexual fantasy. I gave them each a jab with my elbows and tried to break away. Imagine my surprise when strong hands grasped my arms and, lifting my feet off the ground, hustled me between them back into the Riyad el Nabil. I tried to scream but fear temporarily paralyzed my vocal chords.

My feet were still flailing when we raced through the courtyard into a room furnished in shades of deep purple and pink. The men plopped me unceremoniously onto a purple satin chair and stepped back as the man I spoke with earlier in the souk came into the room.

"I am sorry about this," he said as he nodded at the two goons, "but I would like to have a little chat with you. Would you care for some tea?"

About like I'd care for some ground glass. "I think not," I said.

His English, which had been broken during our last conversation suddenly became quite fluent. "What do you know about Peter Bloom?"

I managed to find my voice. "I am Mrs. Peter S. Bloom and I don't think my husband would appreciate you treating me this way." I peered out the door, praying that Ben wouldn't pick this precise moment to find *Riyad el Nabil* and rescue me. Even though I was terrified, I wasn't sure how I'd explain my last statement.

The man looked me up and down as if he were assessing a side of beef. I tried not to fidget but it was disconcerting to have him stare at me that way.

"You are not Peter Bloom's wife," he said coldly. "Who are you?"

"Well, technically, I'm not his wife," I told him. "But I was married to him for fourteen years, so I'll bet I know him a little better than you do."

"That doesn't explain what you're doing here."

Suddenly I had a brilliant idea. This man wasn't about to answer my questions. What I had to do was pretend I was one of them. A fellow conspirator.

"Peter sent me to check up on the operation."

He looked amused. "Which operation would that be?"

"You know—the import/export thing."

"Which one? Import? Export?"

"Import," I replied briskly. When he began to smile, I said, "Oh, you're talking about the export part of the business."

"Lady, you're a phony. I have no idea who you are, but Peter Bloom's wife is quite a looker."

His English had become pure American. I placed it somewhere in the Midwest.

Stung by his implication that I was not a looker, I felt my bravado disappear. However, part of me felt relieved. This couldn't be my Peter Bloom because I knew my ex-husband wasn't married. At least I was pretty sure he wasn't.

"Could you at least tell me if this is the Peter S. Bloom who lives in Sudbury, MA, practices law in Boston and is allergic to shellfish?"

He took my elbow and escorted me to the door. "I don't know how you got that business card, but there is nothing here that concerns you. The best thing for you to do is take a nice sightseeing tour and then leave Marrakech. It could be dangerous if you stay here."

"What happened to the Moroccan accent," I yelled as I was thrust into the alley. "I'll bet you're from Peoria."

"Des Moines," he answered. "Good old Des Moines, Iowa, U S of A."

CHAPTER 8

▼

I spotted Ben sitting at a table by the pool. Waving frantically, I skidded across the tile deck and hurled myself into a chair next to him. "You'll never believe what happened? I was abducted. And where were you, by the way? I turned around in the Jemaa el Fna and you were gone." I wiped my forehead with his linen napkin. "It was terrifying."

Quickly, I recounted the events of the morning.

Ben regarded me solemnly. "Did you notify the police?"

"Well, no. I don't know how to say 'two men lifted me off my feet and forced me into a stall in the souk' in Arabic. Or French."

He carefully folded his newspaper and put it on the table. "This is what I've been talking about. You are simply not capable of strolling through a store, a souk or even a street, for that matter, without attracting some sort of trouble. What do you do? Insult people? Snatch their wallets so they have to chase you? Annoy them so badly they want to whack you over the head? I've never been able to figure it out."

"I do nothing of the sort," I said indignantly. "And I think you're taking a rather cavalier approach to a very serious incident. I could have been hurt."

Ben sighed and using his thumb and forefinger rubbed the bridge of his nose. "You weren't, though, were you? Once again Maggie Bloom escapes from a dangerous situation. You thrive on this stuff."

- 55 -

I hunted for a snappy retort. Finding none I said, "Now that I'm feeling much calmer, I'm going back there. Did I forget to mention I found Riyad el Nabil and you were somewhat correct. There is a courtyard but also some sort of hotel. I'd certainly appreciate it if you would come with me. You may not believe I was in any danger, but I know I was. I don't want to face those men by myself." I jumped up and straightened my spine until I was at least five feet five inches. "Of course, if you'd rather not, I'll go alone."

"Oh, for heavens sake, sit down and stop being so melodramatic. Right now I'm not going anywhere and neither are you. Lucy is visiting the hotel spa and instructed me to tell you she wouldn't be eating lunch. So, I've ordered us each a lobster and a salad and a very presentable Sancerre white wine and for at least a half an hour we are not going to talk about Peter or abductions or *Riyad el Nabil* or anything else remotely connected to your ex-husband. Okay?"

His voice was bland enough, but his eyes looked like blue steel. Normally I don't permit anyone to issue orders to me, but I decided to make an exception this time. There was no point in fighting with Ben in a foreign country where I kind of needed him for protection—and other things. I sat back down, vowing that once we were back home on Hilton Head, I'd make perfectly clear how I felt about masterful men trying to manage me. But I had to admit, my resolve to discover the truth about Peter was causing trouble between Ben and me.

The lunch was delicious. I tore into the succulent lobster with such gusto that bits of shell sprayed over the table. I'm ashamed to admit that instead of being aloof and angry with Ben because of his callous behavior, I let myself completely relax and enjoy the wonderful food, intoxicating aroma of flowers mingled with exotic spices and the warm sunshine.

Within a half an hour I was sated and satisfied. I leaned back in my chair, sipped the excellent wine and, for the first time, glanced at the other guests seated around the pool. Three elegant women—tall, slender, tanned an incredible bronze and wearing the equivalent of hair scrunchies for bathing suits—sat at a table talking animatedly in French. Several Arab women, accompanied by their husbands, waited quietly as the men chatted with each other—and eyed the French women.

One woman, dressed in a *jellaba* and veil, occupied a table by herself. She had neither drink nor food in front of her. Instead, she sat stiffly, surveying the people who walked across the pool deck.

I suddenly longed for a nap. A morning of sleuthing and kidnapping followed by a sensational lunch left me lethargic. I needed sleep. We could postpone the hunt for Peter for another hour or two. Ben was delighted to hear my plans. In fact, judging from the way he took my hand and nearly dragged me to the hotel entrance, I suspected he had something else in mind.

I had stepped into the cool lobby when a finger tapped me gently on the shoulder. Still a bit jumpy after the morning's activities, I whirled around with my fists clenched, ready to do battle. I nearly decked the *jellaba* clad woman who had been sitting by the pool. Startled, I backed away.

"Can I help you?" I couldn't imagine how, but I am a polite person.

Chocolate brown eyes, rimmed heavily in charcoal, smiled at me over the veil covering her nose and mouth. "*Eh bien, mon petit chou-fleur. Est ce que tu m'as oublié deja?*"

I shook my head. "I'm sorry. I don't speak French. Perhaps there is someone else you could ask."

"I must say, Maggie, your memory is not very good. In fact, it— how you say—stinks." A perfectly lacquered, blood red fingernail hooked the top of the veil and pulled it down, revealing smiling lips painted the same bright crimson.

"Islane Ketanni!" I screamed as I grabbed my old friend and hugged her as hard as I could. Ben, along with several guests, watched in alarm. When we separated, the hood of Islane's *jellaba* hung around her shoulders, freeing her shiny black hair.

58   A String Of Perils

"Can you believe this, Ben? It's Islane. I never thought I'd see her again," I yelled as he tried to speak.

Ben, of course, knew her, too. After the divorce from Peter, I'd been so—let's call it unstable—I'd run as far away from Boston and the bimbo as I could. When a good friend invited me to come to Bonn, Germany, I'd jumped at the chance. I rented a house, learned German and eventually was able to say Peter's name without gagging. I also met Ben, who was a correspondent with the Bonn bureau of the New York Times. Due to a nasty incident which was not my fault, I was accused of murder. Ben and Islane, who was married to the Moroccan ambassador, helped me clear my name. But I'll save that story for another time.

"It's wonderful to see you, Islane." I didn't think his voice sounded very sincere. He was probably thinking about the old days.

"You too, Ben," my old friend said with a twinkle in her eye. "You are looking very well."

"How is Hassan?" I asked as we walked through the lobby.

Her pretty face clouded. "Hassan died two years ago. Right after we left Germany. He had cancer. There was nothing the doctors could do."

"I'm so sorry. I wish I'd known." My heart went out to my fun loving, normally cheerful friend. Hassan had been several years older than Islane. When she was only fourteen years old, he visited her village in the High Atlas mountains looking for a bride. All the eligible young girls lined up for inspection. He chose Islane. They married, she moved to Casablanca and became a diplomat's wife. In spite of staggering odds against them, they had a successful, happy marriage.

"Tell me," I said, trying to make the conversation more upbeat, "what are you doing here? Do you live in Marrakech? And why are you wearing a *jellaba?* I smiled, remembering the time she lent me one as a disguise in Bonn.

"I will tell you everything, but not here. You must come to my house this evening. It is in the Palmeraie. I will send a car for you."

"That won't be necessary. I'm sure we can find it." I gave her another hug. "It's wonderful to see you again."

"You too. And I insist. The car will pick you up at six o'clock." She drew the veil across her face, tucked her hair into the *jellaba* and with a wave of her hand, disappeared through the main entrance of the Mamounia.

"This isn't good," Ben said as soon as she was gone.

"What isn't good?"

"You and Islane together again. You may have forgotten those days in Germany, but I haven't. There's only one other person in the world who can attract trouble as fast as you can and she's walking away as we speak."

"For heaven's sake, Ben, we are simply going to chat. You can be so paranoid."

"Remember those words, buttercup. I promise they'll come back to bite you. But at least this time I'm prepared. Your *modus operandi* is familiar to me. Now, what about that 'nap'?"

I pulled away from him. "If you're so familiar with my *modus operandi*, you will know that I can't 'nap' when I'm annoyed. And I am very annoyed right now. So...I am going back to the souks and do more digging. Are you coming?"

"Do I have a choice?"

"Not if you ever intend to 'nap' with me again."

Ben fell into step beside me. "Lead the way. Perhaps I should have a weapon in case your abductors show up."

"Not necessary. I'm mad enough to take on any bully by myself."

"This is supposed to be reassuring?" I heard him mutter. "I should have my head examined."

Since it really was a bit foolhardy to go back into the souks, I sort of agreed with him.

CHAPTER 9

▼

I couldn't find *Riyad el Nabil.* The alleys in the souk twisted and turned in dizzying directions. I had no idea which way to go.

"I know what I saw, Ben. There was a sign pointing to one of the shops and there was a little kid sewing shoes. Then you go through this alley and there is the wall of Marrakech…"

"I actually believe you. The story is so bizarre, I don't think you could make it up. Let me take a crack at finding it."

"Be my guest." As if he could do any better than I could.

Ben approached a man selling handcrafted jewelry and to my utter astonishment, carried on a lengthy conversation—which involved much pointing of fingers and nodding of heads—in Arabic.

"How long have you known how to speak the language?" I stammered. "I am speechless."

"I took a total immersion course a few years ago, then spent about four months in Fez doing research for the New York Times. I'm afraid I'm a bit rusty. Haven't had much occasion to use it lately. And I'm certainly not fluent."

"You're amazing—and a very useful man to have around," I said as I raced to match his long strides.

"Got that right, babe. Now try to keep up."

Ben led us to the stall I'd visited earlier in the day. I recognized the torn, dirty brown curtain hanging over the entrance. Much to my disappointment, the little room was empty. A partially completed sandal lay in the corner on top of a pile of leather scraps. There were three empty tea glasses on a table in the back room. No tools or order books or papers of any kind.

"What kind of a business is this?" I asked as I rummaged through the smelly leather scraps. "You'd think there would be invoices or something."

"Offhand, I'd say not much of one. Let's go. This doesn't feel right."

"Here's the alley," I said excitedly, pulling Ben along. "See? The wall is straight ahead."

"Let me do the talking," Ben warned. "Women don't command much respect here. And please try to control any urge to yell crazy nonsense. That could get us in deep trouble."

This time, the gatekeeper opened the door as soon as he saw us and ushered us in. Then he backed out the gate and closed it with a bang. A tall woman wearing black pants, a green silk, long sleeved blouse and heels high enough to give her a nosebleed sat on a bench in the courtyard. Her sleek blond hair was twisted into an elaborate French braid.

"Can I do something for you?" she asked in heavily accented English. "I understand you are looking for someone.'

Ben, who up until now had been disapproving of the whole sleuthing business, suddenly became very animated. Honestly, there's nothing like an attractive woman to make men act like idiots. He looked like he was about to drool.

"We're searching for information about a Peter S. Bloom. Show her that business card, Maggie."

Reluctantly, I pulled it out and gave it to her.

"I may have heard of him. Why do you hunt this Peter?"

"You've heard of him?" I couldn't believe my ears. "Have you met him?"

An amused smile tugged at the corner of her mouth. "Perhaps. He is a very sexy man, *n'est pas?*"

"Peter? I don't think so. Oh sure, when you first meet him he oozes charm, and of course his voice is kind of seductive, but he has an annoying habit of sleeping in his black socks, and he has to brush his hair fifty strokes every night. That's probably why it's falling out."

Ben put his hand over my mouth. "That's enough information. Actually more than we need. My name is Ben Jakowski," he said extending his hand to the woman. "This is Maggie Meadows."

I glanced at Ben. He used my maiden name, so he obviously didn't want the woman to know I was the former Mrs. Bloom.

"I am Fleur Durand. How do you know those things about Peter?"

Ben shot me a warning glance. "I'm from Massachusetts," I said. "An old friend had his business card and asked me to look him up." Then I just couldn't help myself. "He likes women, you know. I understand he doesn't have a faithful bone in his body. I hope you're not mixed up with the womanizing skunk. He probably has some kind of horrible sexual disease."

Ben rolled his eyes. Fleur was not impressed with my warning. "The man I met is married and very content with his wife. He would never—how you say—have an *affaire de coeur.*"

"I think we're off the subject here, ladies," Ben interrupted. "We'd appreciate any information anyone can give us about Peter S. Bloom's business enterprises in Morocco. Maggie is inquiring for a friend, but I may be interested in becoming a customer."

Fleur—can anyone really be named Fleur—turned her full attention to Ben. "What service are you interested in?"

"Are you able to help us?" Ben countered.

"Possibly. First you must tell me what you want."

Ben was stymied. Since we had no idea what business Peter S. Bloom was in, we had no idea what to request.

"Do you have a business card? I could call you."

Fleur laughed. "I think not. If you decide what it is you are looking for, come back here. Perhaps you will find me. *Au revoir, Madame, Monsieur.*"

As she disappeared into an interior room, I resisted the temptation to follow her. "I don't think this is the same Peter S. Bloom," I told Ben. "It sure doesn't sound like him. Fleur insisted he was married, and I know my ex is single. Don't forget I still have my sources inside Peter's office. If he had tied the knot, Carole would have told me. She knows everything."

"Then we can stop skulking around souks and enjoy ourselves. Ben put his arm around my shoulder. "There are a lot of sights we haven't visited yet."

"Hmm," I murmured as I gripped my tote bag. "There's just one little thing. Did you notice what was peeking out of the Hermes handbag she was carrying?"

"What? I didn't see anything."

"It was a corner of a brochure. All I could read was 'Limos to Log..'"

"I still don't see your point."

"I think it was a brochure advertising limousine service to Logan International Airport—which is located in Boston. Coincidence? I think not. This Fleur Durand knows more than she was willing to tell us."

I extended my tote bag to demonstrate the position of the brochure. When the bullet ripped through the fabric and tore the bag from my hand, I jumped as if someone had jabbed me with a cattle prod. "Holy smokes and leaping lizards. Someone shot me in the gizzard."

Ben pushed me to the ground. "Your gizzard is fine. Keep your head down. I really don't like this, Maggie."

"You think I do?" My lips quivered so badly I could hardly speak. I slithered away from Ben.

"What in the hell are you doing? Let's go."

"I have to get my wallet and my lipstick. They flew out of my bag."

"Are you crazy? Leave them."

"Ben, my wallet has my driver's license, and you know what a hassle it is to replace that. And I can't leave the lipstick. It's my favorite color." Like a commando, I inched my way across the marble floor, pulling with my elbows and scooting on my stomach. I tossed my stuff into the tote bag and crawled back to Ben. "I think it's safe to go now. No one tried to shoot me again."

He hauled me out the gate and down the alley. "You must have nine lives," I heard him mutter.

I sure hoped do. I was using them up faster than I could count.

CHAPTER 10

▼

My cell phone, which was supposed to function anywhere in the world for a slight roaming charge, refused to work in Morocco. So I was forced to use the phone in our hotel room. I knew the cost could be more than my monthly house payment, but I'd reimburse Lucy when we returned to Hilton Head.

There was still no answer at Peter's house. Silky Voice must have decided to save her own skin. A call to Carole confirmed no one in the office had heard from my ex-husband.

Cotton happily informed me that her mother's bunions no longer hurt and that she was busy helping newly departed folks adjust to life on the Other Side. "She's found her calling, Maggie. I'm just so happy for her."

I had given up trying to keep Cotton on some earthly, rational level. She was clearly having severe emotional problems since her mother's death and at some point would require medication and professional attention. But for now, as long as she remembered to put on clothes before she went outside, I supposed she wasn't harming anyone.

"That's wonderful about your mother," I told her. "I have to stop talking soon because this phone call is expensive, but have you heard anymore about the murder investigation?"

- 65 -

"Let's see, the sheriff is looking into a connection between your Peter and Otis. Max, who works over at Palmetto Bay Marina, told the police he saw Otis on Peter's boat."

She said it so matter-of-factly, I almost missed the meaning of her words. But there it was—the thing I'd feared the most had happened. The sheriff was checking up on Peter. I felt strangely calm, which surprised me.

"Otis can't have been on Peter's boat," I told Cotton. "Peter docked his boat in Harbour Town. As far as I know, he never anchored at Palmetto Bay."

"You don't know everything, Maggie. Peter could have gone there."

"But it makes no sense. Palmetto Bay is around the corner from Harbour Town. Why would he take his boat there?"

"Dunno. I'm only telling you what I heard. I have to tell you what else Ma said."

Sighing, I resigned myself to another fifteen minutes of expensive conversation.

"Ma said she talked to Otis. She's taken him under her wing—him being newly crossed over and all. She said he's making the adjustment to eternity pretty good."

"That's nice, Cotton. Could we speed this along a bit? You can tell me all about your mother when I get home."

"All right, Maggie. Goodness, you are such an impatient person. I'm talking as fast as I can."

Criticizing Cotton was like wounding a baby bird—not something you would ever do intentionally. I settled a heavy gold silk pillow behind my head and stretched out on the bed. I could always take out a loan to pay the phone bill.

"Anyway," she continued, "Ma said Otis told her about his murder. He said he was hit over the head and knocked unconscious when he left his boat in Harbour Town. Then he was put in the back of a silver pick-up truck and taken to the woods where you found him. Then he was shot."

"Cotton, listen to me carefully. Is this information the sheriff has released? I mean, how does anyone know about a silver pick-up truck unless someone saw Otis being transported. I know you said you heard it from your mother but are you sure this isn't gossip?"

Cotton refused to answer me directly. Instead she said, "Well, how about this? Otis said he was very upset with Peter and his friend."

I sat straight up in bed. "What is that supposed to mean?"

"That's what Ma asked him. She said did he mean Peter had killed him."

"And what did he say?" Up until now I'd believed Cotton's imagined conversations with her mother were harmless. They were simply fabrications invented in Cotton's tormented mind. But it was going too far if, in the name of Wisteria, she actually fingered Peter as the murderer. I wondered if I should contact her sister, Candy, and ask for help.

I heard Cotton laugh. "You know Ma. She likes to keep things exciting. She said Otis wasn't ready to make a declaration. I think Peter had something to do with Otis's death. Otherwise, why would Otis mention him?"

I stifled the urge to say Otis said no such thing and stop inventing such harmful stories. "You haven't mentioned this to anyone, have you? Remember what we said about patient confidentiality?"

"I've been thinking about that, Maggie. I don't think I can keep this a secret. Ma and Otis wouldn't like that."

"Cotton, it's against the law to make false statements about people. You could get into trouble."

"Not me," she answered blandly. "Ma said it, not me."

I clutched the receiver so tightly, my knuckles hurt. "Promise me you won't tell this to anyone. We'll discuss it when I get home in a few days."

"Tell you what I'll do. Tonight I'll talk to Ma and ask her what she thinks."

"Promise me, Cotton."

Unfortunately, the Moroccan phone system, which up until now had functioned flawlessly, picked that precise moment to fail. When I realized I was talking to myself, I hung up.

"I think something has happened to Peter. He still isn't answering his phone and no one at his office has heard from him."

Lucy, Ben and I sat in the back of a black Mercedes on our way to Islane's house in the Palmeraie, a plush suburb of Marrakech. Lucy fished a mirror out of her handbag and inspected her flaming orange hair, which for tonight's occasion was swept high on one side and fashioned into a thick braid on the other. The result was bizarre, but on Lucy, who was dressed in a purple and white silk pants suit and a purple silk blouse, it looked strangely appropriate. She used a fancy lace hankie to wipe a thumbprint off a significant diamond on her right hand.

"I'm more concerned about the person who took a shot at you. We've stumbled into something that has nothing to do with your ex-husband and we need to get out of here before we're all riddled with bullet holes. If you ask me, Peter is probably on a private boondoggle and doesn't want anyone, including his lady friend, to know where he went. May I gently suggest that protecting his reputation is not worth our lives. I think we should do some sightseeing, stay far away from the souks and for the time being, forget all about business cards and murder."

We fell silent as the car wound up a driveway and stopped in front of a spectacular house. I thought the driver had made a mistake and taken us to a ritzy hotel. At that time of day the sun turned the stucco walls a soft golden color. A round dome on the roof rose against a blue sky. Palm trees were everywhere. We walked up marble steps and paused to admire the awesome mosaics around the front door. Even Lucy was speechless. Islane greeted us enthusiastically and pulled us into the house.

My American friend had met her match. Islane wore a long caftan that shimmered like spun gold. Around her neck was a rope of gold thick enough to lasso a steer. Gold bangle bracelets clattered on her arms. Both of my friends sported scarlet lipstick, magenta eye shadow, heavy black mascara and an abundance of exotic scents. The ladies sniffed each other like female felines meeting for the first time. When they linked arms and marched into the living room, Ben and I heaved a sigh of relief.

"We'll go through to the pool," Islane said. "It is so beautiful in the early evening."

Indeed it was. Planters filled with fragrant blooming flowers framed a pool spacious enough to host Olympic events. We sat in comfortable wrought iron chairs and admired the lush gardens as Islane served us glasses of peppermint tea. I smiled at my friend. "This is an awfully big house. Do you live here by yourself?" It was an innocent question, so I was alarmed to see large tears roll down Islane's cheeks.

"I have been so stupid," she said. "You would think a woman of my age would have more sense. After Hassan died, I spent a year thinking I would never see another man. Hassan was so much older than I. And he had been sick for such a long time. I was so tired—emotionally and physically. Then one day when I was playing tennis I met Henri."

Sensing something juicy, Lucy put down the Fabergé egg she'd been admiring and moved closer to Islane so she could pat her hand.

Reassured, Islane smiled weakly and resumed her story. "Henri is Parisian. He is tall and—how you say—very easy on the eye. We liked the same things—tennis, nice restaurants, travel. I thought he liked me. We laughed and talked and I was not lonely anymore. Can you understand this, Maggie?"

You bet your bippy I could. When that snake, Peter S. Bloom, had his unfortunate mid-life crisis and took up with the silicone bimbo, I felt like I was the last person left on earth. Make that the last unattractive person.

"Of course I can," I said soothingly.

"Anyway, I have a little money"—she waved her hand at our opulent surroundings—"and in the beginning it was fun to buy things for Henri. Some clothes, a watch. Nothing important."

Lucy pulled the silk hankie out of her décolleté, dabbed at Islane's eyes and glared at Ben as if he were responsible for Islane's distress.

"Things went well for a while," she continued. "He took me to Mauritius for a holiday. I paid for the trip because he told me he had a temporary trouble with his trust fund."

Ben and I exchanged glance. We knew where this was going.

"One day the bank called and said I had no funds. *Mais ce n'est pas possible*, I told the man on the phone. I have a great deal of money." She shook her head so violently, her black hair whipped across her face. "*Mais non*. The bank was right. Henri had put my name on checks and taken everything. Then he disappeared."

Islane slumped in her chair, her energy spent. My heart went out to my old friend.

"When you saw me today," she said, "I was trying to find him. Friends told me he was staying at La Mamounia. He also has a new girlfriend. I intend to put him in prison."

"Bravo!" Lucy clapped her hands. "You go, girl. The pig belongs behind bars."

"So," I said, "you were slinking around the hotel wearing a *jellaba* because you were hunting for him and needed a disguise."

"*Exactement.*"

"You see, Ben," I said triumphantly, "I'm not the only one with an inquisitive nature. Islane, is there anything we can do to help?"

My friend smiled broadly. "I thought you would never ask."

CHAPTER 11

▼

"I heard he intends to go to Ouarzazate. What I am thinking is, you drive there with me and you can help me find him. He does not know you, so it will be easy. This place—Ouarzazate—has a hotel where people go to relax. He will be there." Islane's hands flew as she talked, her unhappy demeanor gone.

I held up my hand. "Slow down. First of all, we only have two days left before we go home. And where is this Ouarzazate? I've never heard of it."

"Actually, it would be an interesting trip," Ben offered. "Ouarzazate is on the edge of the Sahara desert. We would have to go over the High Atlas mountains. There would be some spectacular scenery." He rubbed his hands together. "I'd enjoy that."

"Then it is settled. You drive with me in my little Renault, Maggie. I think it would be too noticeable to drive the Mercedes." She looked at Ben and Lucy. "The car is not suitable for four people. You could perhaps follow in another."

"I don't know," I said doubtfully. "I'm trying to discover if my ex-husband is mixed up in something unsavory in Marrakech, and I'd like to keep investigating. I hate to go back to the States without some answers."

Lucy pointed her forefinger at me and pretended to pull the trigger. "Bang, bang. Aren't you forgetting something? Someone wants to shoot you. I, for one, would welcome the opportunity to leave Marrakech until it's time for us to go home."

"That goes for me, too," Ben said. "An excellent idea, Islane. I'll arrange for a car tomorrow."

Ben and I had a difference of opinion on the way back to the hotel. I stalked off to my room without even saying goodnight, which was a childish thing to do but felt quite good at the time. I had to find out the truth about Peter. He was wrecking my relationship with Ben.

If I had known exactly where we were going, I wouldn't have gone. But as they say, what you don't know won't swivel your shorts. Islane picked me up at the Mamounia at eight o'clock. "Would you please drive," she said as she slid into the passenger seat. *"J'ai une mal de tete."*

"Pardon?" It was too early in the morning to cope with foreign languages.

"I have a hurting head. It would be difficult to drive."

Ben wrapped on the window. "I want you to take this," he said as he handed me a walkie talkie. "I have one, too. If you run into trouble, all you have to do is call. I'll be right behind you."

I pocketed the walkie talkie and winked at him. "Don't let Lucy lead you on a shopping spree. She'd famous for creating diversions so she can visit stores."

Ben thumped the hood of the Renault. "Just be careful. I can cope with Lucy."

I hadn't driven a car with a stick shift for a long time. We jerked spastically down the Place de la Liberté to the amusement of the locals until I learned the gear wouldn't engage until the clutch was nearly all the way out. The traffic was horrendous, and signal lights didn't seem to mean anything. Cars whizzed through red and stopped on green. Three times I careened through the train station parking lot, unable to get back into the flow of traffic. Islane held her head and moaned.

Linda S. Clayton   73

By the time I successfully navigated the unfamiliar streets in Marrakech and headed out of the city, I began to relax. I was shifting like a pro and having fun. And Ben was right. The scenery was worth the trip. I opened the window as we drove past walnut groves and oak trees and oleander bushes. In front of us were the sunbathed peaks of the High Atlas.

As we approached the town of Taddert, my walkie talkie beeped. Ben's voice crackled in my ear. "Are you doing okay?"

I assured him I was.

"Lucy wants to stop at Taddert and look at rugs."

"I'm trying not to laugh or say I told you so. Don't worry about us. Call if you have trouble getting her out of there."

"I heard that," Lucy shouted. "You should stop, too. I understand the rugs are lovely. I need some for our sunroom."

She needed rugs for the sunroom like I needed a pound of fudge, but I knew there was no deterring her. I wanted to keep driving, find this Henri character, tell Islane she was better off without him and get back to solving the Peter mystery.

As we headed into the High Atlas mountains, the landscape turned more barren. The narrow, two-lane road wound through miles of brown sand with very little vegetation—and very few people. We passed a man on foot and a donkey laden with bundles of straw. They moved slowly, as if time had no meaning for them. In the distance a solitary shepherd watched his flock of sheep.

The road had no guardrail. I navigated the hairpin turns with my heart in my throat. I tried to avoid looking over the side, which dropped so steeply it gave me vertigo. Occasionally I saw the remains of unlucky cars that had hurtled over the side and splatted way down below. "You'd think they'd take those wrecks away," I said to Islane. "That can't be good for tourism."

She shrugged. "It is just so. We are used to it."

At the bend of a curve, a lone vendor tried to sell us trinkets made of silver and amethyst. He chased the car, banging on the window as I slowed to avoid hitting him.

What had been fun in the beginning was now becoming unpleasant. My arms ached from clutching the steering wheel and my eyes stung from eyestrain. I longed to pull over and stop. As we climbed higher and higher, the curves became sharper and the distance to the bottom—in case we should fall over—distressingly far.

"Can you look at the map," I asked Islane. "Are we almost there?"

"We must go over the Tizi n' Tichka Pass. Then we start down."

A dusty mini van hurtled down the mountain towards us, forcing me to swerve to the right. I knew we were close to the edge when Islane screamed and covered her eyes with her hands. I fought off the urge to cover my eyes, too. One of us had to see what was going on. For a few heart stopping seconds I didn't think we were going to make it. The car began to skid on the dirt and gravel as I attempted to brake. Throwing caution to the wind, I steered to the left side of the road, figuring a head on collision with an oncoming vehicle was preferable to sailing down a mountain. The result would be the same, but the rescue folks would be able to retrieve our bodies.

We were lucky. There was nothing coming from the opposite direction. I braked, eased to the right and continued up the mountain at a sedate pace. Islane managed a weak laugh. "That was close."

I had to agree. And this definitely was not fun. I couldn't wait to reach our destination.

I was concentrating so hard on the winding curves, I didn't see the car behind us until it nudged the bumper of the Renault. When I looked in the rearview mirror I couldn't believe my eyes. A black Mercedes with tinted windows was trying to push us off the road.

"Whazzat!"

Islane turned to look at me. "Did you say something?"

"Great jumping grasshoppers. Give the dog a bone. Let me out of here, Mama. I want to go home."

I pressed my foot down hard on the accelerator, but the Renault was no match for the Mercedes. The best it could manage was a slight increase in speed. I could have run on foot faster, and at the moment, that sounded like a perfectly reasonable option.

The vehicle behind me filled the rearview mirror. It banged our car with enough force to send us both lurching forward.

"Do something," Islane screamed. "Who is that behind us?"

I was too busy to reply. We couldn't outrun our tormentor and there was no place to turn off the road. The sound of breaking glass accompanied the next assault from the car. "The tail lights are broken," I yelled. Not that it mattered. I didn't plan to brake any time soon.

I tried to zigzag back and forth but the road was too narrow to allow any fancy maneuvering. Only a miracle would save us. Just as I was about to tell Islane to brace herself for an ugly crash or a horrifying plunge over the edge of the mountain, I spied an opening in the relentless rocks and stones. With one swift motion I jerked the steering wheel to the left. The Renault shot off the road, jarring our teeth and shaking our limbs.

Taken by surprise, the Mercedes flew past us. From down the road, I heard brakes squeal and car doors slam. I had my door open before we came to a complete stop.

"Quick. Get out. We'll have to start running. They're coming back." I grabbed Islane's hand, yanked her out of the car and dragged her over the dirt and stones.

A small boy watched us with interest. "Do you live around here?" I asked frantically. Huge dark eyes stared back at me. Without speaking, he stuck a finger in his nose and explored enthusiastically.

Islane pushed me aside. "Permit me to ask him. That way we know he will understand what we are saying."

Several seconds later the three of us raced towards a baked mud hut that blended so beautifully into the landscape, I wouldn't have known it was there.

The inside was cool and dark. Two women covered completely with jellabas sat on a carpet in the corner. They drew veils over their faces as we entered. "The boy says there is no other man here. Except the grandfather who is sick in the other room."

"We have to leave," I whispered. "We can't get these folks in trouble."

"I agree." After speaking a few words, Islane pulled some *dirhan* out of her handbag and carefully put them on the floor next to the ladies. An arm shot out, snatched the money and tucked it into the thick folds of her garment.

Once outside I considered our next step. Islane, however, showed no indecisiveness. She trotted at a brisk pace to the rear of the hut and pointed to a donkey that was contentedly lying in the shade. "Please climb up and we will go."

"Excuse me?"

"This animal…I have paid enough *dirhan* to own ten of them but it does not matter. I own this one. We will ride away and the men will not find us."

I believe I snorted. "Do you have any idea how fast you can go on a donkey? We might as well walk. What we need is some kind of speedy vehicle."

Islane slapped the donkey on the rump and yelled something unintelligible. The animal rose to his feet and pinned his ears back. "*Compte plutôt sur ton âne que sur le cheval de ton voisin.*"

"What?" I held my ears. "Don't do that, Islane. You're giving me a headache."

"I said, *Count on your donkey rather than on the horse of your neighbor.* It is an old French proverb. Now climb up. We'll ride together. You forget I was raised in these mountains. Trust me, I know how to make a donkey move."

My friend constantly amazed me. I did as I was told and within minutes we were moving at an amazingly rapid pace across the barren land. For approximately fifty feet. Two men moved stealthily towards us and the object one of them was carrying wasn't an umbrella. It was a large, ugly-looking machine gun. Islane turned the donkey around and led it behind a large pile of rocks. "We will hide here," she said in my ear. They did not see us."

"What about the people in the hut?"

"They will be safe. These men will not bother women."

I wanted to ask her how she came to that conclusion. They sure wanted to bother me. It was then I finally remembered the walkie talkie. I took it out of my pocket and beeped Ben. His cheerful voice turned to deep concern as I told him what had happened.

"Don't move. We're not that far behind you. Lucy couldn't find anything to buy so we didn't stay long."

"I don't know how to tell you where we are. You'll be able to see the car, but I can't stand out there and flag you down."

"I'll find you. I figure I'm about ten minutes away. Just sit tight— and stay hidden."

"It's a good thing I brought my gun," I heard Lucy say before I pocketed the walkie talkie.

The men entered the hut. From our vantage point, we could clearly hear the conversation. "They are not Moroccan," Islane whispered. They are speaking Arabic, but it is not their native tongue. I would say they are French." Her pretty mouth turned into a frown. "*Incroyable.* They are looking for you."

"But why? Who are they?" I was genuinely stunned.

"They say you have stolen something from them. In this country that is very bad."

"Will the ladies turn us in?" I gulped.

"I do not think so. They have much money now. They do not want me to take it back."

"I didn't steal anything, Islane."

"Of course not. These are very bad men. I wish Ben would come."

That made two of us. I was relieved to hear the conversation end and the men leave the hut. They spoke in soft tones, obviously considering their next move. One of them swept the area with his hand. They were going to do a search.

The cavalry arrived at precisely the right moment. Ben's Peugeot bounced across the stones and dirt and barreled towards us. The men took off at a run. Lucy rose through the sunroof of the car like an angry Valkyrie. Her wild, red hair flew behind her as she fired a revolver at the backs of the retreating men and yelled, "Stop, you sons of bitches." Islane, who had never seen Lucy in action, was speechless.

"You might have hit them," I scolded as soon as I was able to breathe again.

"Not a chance. There aren't real bullets in here. I just wanted to scare them."

I felt my knees go weak. "No bullets?"

She looked at me as if I'd gone mad. "Honestly, Maggie. You should know you're not allowed to carry a weapon on an airplane."

"But...a gun is a weapon whether you have bullets or not," I managed to stammer.

"What kind of logic is that? If you can't hurt someone with it, it isn't a weapon."

"But..."

"Give up, Maggie," Ben said gently. "You know what you mean, and I know what you mean, but you're not going to win."

He was right. And I'd had enough controversy for one day. Islane and I piled into the cramped backseat of the Peugeot and rode the rest of the way to Ouarzazate in silence.

CHAPTER 12

▼

"I am frazzled," Lucy announced. "This trip may have been a mistake."
Ben, Lucy and I sat together at the pool bar drinking vodka tonics.
Islane sat apart, clad in her disguise. "I am for relaxing here, hurrying
back to Marrakech and flying home. No more intrigue."

"I couldn't agree more," Ben stated. "I only hope the men who tried
to ram Islane's car haven't decided to also visit the Berbere Palace. That
could mean more trouble."

My sense of safety disappeared. The hotel, which was built in the
kasbah style, seemed solid and secure. Guest rooms surrounded a sparkling blue pool and large courtyard where a buffet table stood ready to
hold the evening meal. Adjacent to the pool was an elegant white tent,
its entrance protected by gold ropes.

"What in the world is that," I wondered.

"It's for someone important who wants absolute privacy and luxury," Ben informed me.

"The hotel rooms aren't good enough?"

"This person will appear and leave when no one is around, and he'll
be discreetly served the finest foods and drinks. No need to ever leave
the tent and no one will see him walking in the halls or eating in the
dining room. You have to be very rich to rate such treatment."

It seemed to me room service would accomplish the same thing, but what did I know.

Dinner was delicious. We dined under the stars on lamb, couscous and wonderful fresh vegetables. We had ripe tomatoes and plump red and yellow peppers, tender slender green beans and juicy, firm peaches. We dipped our fingers into the couscous, formed it into little balls and popped it into our mouths.

"Y'all shouldn't be eating uncooked vegetables," Lucy warned, as she took a bite of lamb. "You also had ice in your vodka tonics. It's best only to have bottled drinks."

"Nonsense. These veggies couldn't be cleaner." I finished a second tomato and speared a slice of pepper from the platter. "Besides, I have a cast iron stomach."

I probably shouldn't have said that, but hindsight is always perfect, isn't it.

Since we were at a larger table, Islane was able to eat with us. She glared at me from under her veil as I ate with gusto. "Can't you take that thing off?" I asked between bites.

"He might recognize me if I do. That is, if he is here."

"We still don't know what Henri looks like," I reminded her. "Do you have a picture?"

"*Non,* no picture. But I can tell you very well. Tomorrow. For today I am ready to sleep."

Half an hour later, drowsy from a day of adventure, roasted lamb, couscous and a honey dessert, we strolled across the pool deck to our rooms. Palm branches rustled in the soft breeze. A bright moon hung in the clear night sky. As we walked past the white tent, I noticed the entrance was slightly open and the lights were on. I caught a brief glimpse of an ornate rug, a copper samovar and a crystal vase filled with a bouquet of pink roses and lavender orchids. A tall, well-built man wearing a tuxedo stood with his back to us, talking to someone we couldn't see.

"Would you look at that," I said to Islane. "It certainly is luxurious. I wonder who the man is."

Islane suddenly sounded like she had swallowed a frog. She slapped one hand over her mouth and with the other, pointed to the tent.

"What's the matter? Are you sick or something?"

She shook her head frantically. "*Non, non. Il est la.*"

"Speak English. Tell me what's wrong."

"He is there. That man in the tent. That is Henri. I have found him." She pulled the veil from her face. "I am going in there and cut something off."

I was satisfied to note the urge to maim a cheating snake seemed to be universal. However, I held her back. "How do you know it's Henri? We can only see his back. And he's standing in the shadows. I can't see his face."

"Patooie," she spit. "Do you think I do not recognize his back? I know his back as well as his front. Please remove yourself."

"Islane, listen to me. If he took your money, we have to notify the police and have him arrested. If you run in there and confront him, he may get away before the law arrives."

I felt her hesitate. "This is true. But I am remaining here. You call the *gendarmes*."

As we babbled, the man turned to fill a champagne glass for his companion. It was my turn to gasp. Tonight the lady wore a slinky, long black skirt, a silver and black sequined top and six-inch high black, strappy sandals. Her hair was swept high on her head and secured with a diamond clip.

"That's Fleur Durand—the woman I met in the souk," I said excitedly. "She knows Peter. Why would she be here with your Henri?"

"He is not my Henri. Give me your gun, Lucy. I will shoot him."

Lucy obligingly produced a pistol from somewhere between the folds of her gold and white tunic.

"Will you please not do that," I said as I snatched the weapon and put it in my bag. "Ben, could you go call the police? I'll stay here and make sure these two don't kill anyone."

Ben trotted to the front desk, and I turned my attention back to the tent. I could see Fleur plainly as she raised her glass to her lips and smiled at Henri. He stepped forward and turned to kiss her on the cheek.

I had to admit, Henri was extremely good-looking. His face was tanned the color of bronze. He had a square, firm jaw, lustrous black hair and a rugged athletic build. I pictured him lounging by the pool in one of those skimpy thongs European men call bathing trunks and felt my knees wobble. It was certainly easy to see why Islane had fallen for him. I also had to admit he and Fleur Durand made a spectacular couple.

"I'd give anything to hear what they're saying, although people that attractive probably don't have a brain between them. Scintillating conversation wouldn't be necessary."

"I still want to shoot him," Islane said. "Give me your handbag, Maggie."

As we discussed the situation, an attractive girl walked across the pool deck to the tent. Barefoot, she wore a blue bra decorated with seed pearls and sequins. Attached to the elaborate belt around her bare waist was a skirt of pale blue layers of chiffon. In her hand she carried a small boom box. When she saw us, she drew a matching chiffon veil over her face.

"Ah, a belly dancer," Lucy said. "Our friend has arranged for entertainment."

Before she could enter the tent, I grabbed the girl's arm and pulled her gently aside. "Islane," I said quickly before she could scream, "ask her if she would like to earn some money."

Several *dirhan* exchanged hands and minutes later the girl left, wearing a tablecloth instead of her clothes. "Now what do we do?" Lucy looked at the chiffon in my hand. "If you're thinking what I think you're thinking, you can forget it."

"Come on, Lucy, this used to be your profession. You know how to do it."

"I have given up that life. Anyway, these things would never fit me. Look at this belt. It would barely fit my thigh."

She had a point. Since Lucy's retirement from the entertainment field, she had added a few pounds to her statuesque frame. She carried it well, but these skimpy duds wouldn't cover her tush. I turned to Islane.

"You want me to put these things on and dance for him? I cannot do that." She blushed the color of borscht. "He would recognize my body."

Two pairs of eyes swiveled to me.

"Well, I certainly can't. I haven't worked out for a while and there might be a little jiggle here and there. Nothing major, mind you, but I'd feel self conscious." I rolled the chiffon into a ball and tucked it under my arm. "It was a good idea, though."

"Just a minute. I think you'd better stop protesting and don the duds before we lose a great opportunity to find out what's going on." Lucy shook out the costume and held it up to me. "It will fit. Now come over here and let me work on you. When I'm finished, you'll be able to fool your own mother."

She wasn't kidding. From the depths of her handbag she drew out enough tubes, lipsticks and powders to make up the entire chorus line of a Las Vegas nightclub act. While she worked on my face, Islane wound a gold chain through my hair. "I keep it in my purse, in case I need more jewelry," she explained.

"I'll have to use safety pins to hold this belt together," Lucy announced. "It won't stretch across your middle."

I tried to suck in my stomach but it was no use. "This isn't going to work. I look like a sausage."

Lucy stepped back and eyed me critically. "You look like a belly dancer. They all have fat stomachs. Take a gander in the mirror. I have to say, I'm damn good."

My face and neck, arms and tummy were the color of pale copper. Bright red lipstick, thick charcoal, mascara and a variety of eye shadows completely changed my appearance.

Lucy gave me a swat on the butt. "Now get in there. Keep the veil over your mouth and pretend you're having fun. And don't let him see your panties. Do you realize you're wearing cotton Jockeys?"

My underwear was the least of my worries. I stumbled into the tent, praying the safety pin wouldn't let go in the middle of my gyrations. Henri and Fleur sat on a low, white couch. They looked up expectantly as I entered. Henri grimaced slightly but smiled cordially. I was terrified he'd yell, *She's no belly dancer. Look at her flabby triceps and bulging belly.* But he didn't. Lucy had done a great job.

I punched the button on the boom box, clamped the veil around my mouth and assumed what I hoped was a seductive pose. But I couldn't dance to the music. It might charm a cobra, but it wasn't doing anything for me, and I could tell Henri wasn't impressed either. The music had no beat. It would have been a piece of cake if I could have bumped to *The Stripper,* but I didn't know what to do with flute and stick melodies. Nevertheless, I did my best. I swiveled and swayed and pirouetted and pranced and most of all, listened.

For a few minutes Fleur and Henri politely watched. When it became apparent they weren't going to see anything remotely approaching a sensuous dance, they began to chat. And miracle of miracles, they were speaking English.

"There is something wrong on your side of the operation. You have a problem on the island. I think we should slow things down for a while. Maybe stop." Fleur's French accent was gone. She was pure New York.

"I assure you, everything is fine. I can take care of any trouble. Our setup is perfect." He caressed her cheek. "Don't get squirrelly on me now. I need you."

Squirrelly? A Parisian knows the word *squirrelly?*

"I don't like the ex-wife snooping around. How did she get that business card? And what's she doing here? I think she knows, and that means trouble. And she has a real talent for eluding us. My men haven't been able to get near her."

Henri laughed. "She's harmless. She and her friend have too much money and too much time on their hands. I wouldn't worry about them. They don't know anything."

Is that right. I bumped over to where they were sitting and shook my hips until I was dizzy. My rotating rump banged against the table and knocked a glass of champagne into Fleur's lap. Too bad. I was aiming for Henri. I was also shaking with excitement. These were the lunatics who were trying to kill me. I couldn't wait to contact the police and throw these people behind bars.

Fleur leapt to her feet and screamed at me in Arabic. When that had no effect—mostly because I couldn't understand a word she said—she switched to French. I thought my goose was cooked—until a female voice outside the tent yelled, "Fire!" in English, French and for good measure, Arabic. Those two stampeded out of the tent as if the afore-mentioned flames were lapping at their knickers.

We made a mistake. We should have finessed the floorshow, raced into the tent, yanked Henri and Fleur out of there by their over-coifed hair and hauled them both off to the police. Instead, we spent two hours in a dingy *gendarmerie* near the Boulevard Mohammed V explaining ourselves to the local police. Frankly, the law seemed bored with our story. A tall, slim man with a thick black mustache and garlic breath seemed to be the officer in charge. He picked his teeth as he listened to Islane's story. He leered at me. I could tell from the smirk on his face that he was going to side with the enemy. I didn't understand a word he said yet I knew from his body language and his attitude that he wasn't going to help us.

Islane confirmed my fears. "He said a man has a right to choose any woman he wants. The money Henri took from me was not important. I probably gave it to him willingly. He even told me not to bother such an important person. He said I had no business looking into the tent."

"Now see here, Bubba," Lucy said in English. "In America we don't treat women that way. It's a good thing I don't have my gun because I'd shoot your pathetic, pint sized…"

"Lucy!" I hauled her out of the police station before we had to extend our trip to include time in a Moroccan jail cell.

The tent, of course, was empty. In fact, everything was gone: the bouquet of flowers, the lavish rug, the serving table with champagne and glasses. Even the boom box. The front desk informed us they had no registered guests by the name of Fleur Durand or Henri Lafitte. What a surprise! Or as Islane would say, *Quelle surprise!*

CHAPTER 13

The next morning, determined to spend our *dirham* and get the heck out of Morocco, we checked out of the Berbere Palace and drove thirty miles to the kasbah of Aït Benhaddou, off the Marrakech road. Lucy ignored this famous fortress, which had been the setting for many movies, and concentrated on the stalls of souvenir junk.

Islane sulked. "I cannot believe you let Henri get away."

"Moi?" I said indignantly. "I did no such thing. I'm not the one who stood outside the tent and yelled *Fire* in three different languages."

She shook her head. "I should have gone into the tent and shot him. Or at least pulled him out and called the *gendarmes*. He would be in a jail cell by today. Or perhaps dead. Now I will never be able to get my money back."

"I don't think he'd be in jail," I told her. "Security would have hauled you off to the hoosegow."

"If you ladies could stop bickering for a minute, I want to show you something." Lucy held two carved figures in her hand. Each was about a foot tall and fashioned from stone. "These remind me of Picasso. They're humorous but compelling."

I snorted. "They're tourist bait. I'll bet these folks crank them out by the dozen, slap a fancy price tag on them and laugh all the way to their baked mud huts."

Lucy narrowed her eyes as she looked at me. "Really, Maggie, you're not an authority on all art, you know. It just so happens I have some expertise in this area. Last year Julius and I attended a very comprehensive lecture about South African art at the Whitney."

I waved my hand at the vast expanse of barren desert, kasbah walls and *jellaba* clad women. "We aren't in South Africa." Duh.

"We are certainly in Africa. I must have these," she said handing the figures to a smiling vendor. "I will also take three of those beaded necklaces. They'll make cute gifts."

I inspected the strands of colored beads. Each marble size, pearl-like bead had been partially dipped in pale tints of color. On top of this, the artist had painted palm branches and jasmine blossoms. "You don't have to buy these here," I told her. "You can find the same thing in Harbour Town." I showed her the one I wore around my neck.

"I think not. They are quite different. Look at the workmanship on this one." She showed me a string of green, pink and blue beads. "The painting is far superior to the one you're wearing. This is genuine African art. A hobby artist in Bluffton probably decorated yours. Adequate, but not comparable to these unique creations."

There was no point in arguing with her. Ben tapped his watch, indicating it was time to get going. In a few hours we would be on the plane, bound for home.

Islane went to the airport with us. "I am going to hunt for Henri if I have to travel across Morocco wearing my *jellaba*. But I have a sick feeling that he will leave this country. Especially if he and the whore Fleur Durand have—how you say—a dirty business."

"And I promise you I am going to find out what the connection is between Peter and these people. Ben will help me. He's good at digging up information." My friend looked skeptical. "Don't worry. These days it's very difficult to simply vanish." How could I say that? Peter was nowhere to be found—although I didn't believe his absence was voluntary. "We'll get Henri, and you'll get your money back."

"I hope so," she said as she gave me a hug. "You will call?"

"Absolutely."

The instant the door of the Royal Air Maroc 767 closed, I had to find the lavatory—where I remained for most of the flight to Paris. Lucy, who travels with a complete pharmacy in her carry-on, clucked sympathetically as she handed me several white pills. "Told you not to eat the vegetables. They were probably washed in the donkey's water bowl."

Ben smiled. "I have a cast iron stomach. Years of traveling in third world countries have made me immune to bugs."

"Isn't that special," I said as I clamped my hand over my mouth and raced for the bathroom. I sort of regretted I wasn't contagious.

Wally and Willow had a bit of an attitude when I picked them up at Lucy's. Wally, who in former days consumed plastic, metal, pieces of furniture and nearly all my underwear, refused to eat dried dog food. Willow sported a stiff pink bow around her neck and tried to bite me when I attempted to remove it. Both dogs ignored their baskets, preferring instead to sleep on the pillows on my bed.

I was glad to be home; glad to be back in my sunroom watching deer lope through the marsh and boats cruise down Broad Creek and glad to have my spoiled puppies once again destroying my house.

There were fourteen messages on my answering machine from Cotton. There was also one from Janna Maletesta. "Could you give me a call as soon as you can, Maggie? It's terribly urgent." I dialed her number, wondering what kind of a situation Janna would consider urgent. Perhaps she had broken one of my glasses—or a fingernail. That wasn't fair. Janna was okay. Just because she and I had different life styles didn't mean her problems weren't as valid as mine.

"Oh, Maggie, I'm so glad to hear from you. I would like to order two dozen more glasses."

I grabbed my order book and a pencil. "That would be fine. Tell me which pattern you want." For the next few minutes we discussed prices

90   A String Of Perils

and delivery dates. Business concluded, Janna said, "By the way, I don't know if this is any of my concern but I thought you should know." She hesitated.

"Know what, Janna? "You can't stop talking now."

"Well, I was contacted by the sheriff's office. The officer asked me questions about you—like how well did I know you and did I know any of your friends."

"What! Why would the sheriff be interested in me? I promise you, Janna, I haven't broken any law." As I spoke, I remembered the calling card. Surely Sheriff Griffey didn't know about that. My friends wouldn't rat on me.

"I have no idea what it's all about, Maggie. He was very mysterious. I just wanted you to know."

"And I thank you," I said warmly. "I'll call the sheriff myself and get this cleared up." Hoo boy, that was a lie. I might call him, but not in this lifetime.

I was sweating as I hung up the phone. When it rang again I jerked so violently, I bopped Wally in the head.

"How about dinner? I was thinking of something with couscous," Ben said.

"Very funny."

"Seriously. We have to eat. We could grab something quick at the Crazy Crab."

"I'll take a rain check. My stomach is not yet accepting solid food." And was also flipping violently, thanks to Janna's message.

"You sound strange. What's the matter?"

"Nothing. Well, maybe something. The sheriff questioned Janna Maletesta about me. I'm sure it has something to do with Peter."

"Maybe you should give the business card you found to the police and let them take over the investigation. I'm getting tired of seeing you torn up about your ex-husband."

"I'm not torn up," I protested. "I'm simply..."

"Talk to you tomorrow," he said curtly. Then he hung up.

CHAPTER 14

▼

Cotton was delighted to see me. "Ma said you were on your way home, and she's never wrong."

"I also told you when I was returning," I reminded her. "That might have given it away."

"No matter," she said gaily as she straightened rows of silver jewelry in the display case in the shop. "There's so much to tell you. The sheriff can't find Peter. He says he's called the house a hundred times—even sent the Sudbury police to investigate, but there is no one there. Also, them folks at Peter's law office don't know where he is, either. He didn't come back to work when he was supposed to."

Gulp. I had hoped Peter was on a romantic boondoggle, but in my heart I knew he was in trouble. It's an instinctive thing based on years of living together. I knew his patterns. He might fritter away a week in the Bahamas, but if he said he'd be back at work on a certain day, he'd be there. This certainly was not typical behavior.

"But the police don't have anything else, do they? I mean something that would connect Peter to the murder." They didn't know the beaded key chain belonged to Peter, and I was sure Ben and Lucy wouldn't divulge that information.

"Oh, my yes. I heard from Bud, who heard it from a sheriff's deputy that they had found papers in Otis's house showing that Peter and Otis

- 91 -

had some kind of business deal. Not bills or anything but something with Peter's phone number."

"You mean the phone number in Sudbury?"

"Nope. It was his cell phone. The lady in the law office said very few people had that number."

"How do you know all this?

She closed the glass door of the display case and straightened up to meet my eyes. "Folks tell me. And of course Ma knows everything. I get a lot of stuff from her." She bent down to retrieve hand towels from a drawer. Her muffled voice said, "By the way, Maggie, I haven't told anyone about Peter maybe being the murderer. Not yet, even though Ma said I shouldn't keep such important information to myself. I may have to say something soon, though. Spirits don't like secrets."

I wondered if she was trying to blackmail me. Should I offer her money to keep her mouth shut? I watched her arrange the towels on a rack. Let's face it, she was light on gray matter. Some unkind folks even suggested she was dumber than a sack of stones. I couldn't imagine her plotting an extortion scheme.

I glanced out the shop window at the folks strolling through Harbour Town. The season was nearly over, but many tourists still enjoyed the warm weather. A white yacht sounded its horn as it began to back out of a slip in the harbor. Now, I'm not an expert on boats. In fact, my nautical career consists of taking a rowboat out into Broad Creek, but I was sure I'd seen the departing yacht somewhere before. And up close and personal, too.

Wanting a closer look, I waved goodbye to Cotton and walked to the harbor. As the boat slowly turned its stern, I nearly swallowed my tongue. A year ago I'd flown out of those double doors leading to the salon and stomped away. It had a new name now, but unless I was badly mistaken, Peter's boat was about to head into the waters of Calibogue Sound.

I raced along the side of the dock, waving my hands and shouting *stop* at the top of my lungs. When this proved ineffective, I yanked my cell phone out of my pocket and called Ben. He lived in a Ketch Court villa and was able to see the harbor from his living room window. Thankfully, he was home.

"Ben," I yelled. "Look out your window. There's a boat leaving the harbor. I know you'll think I'm crazy, but I think it belongs to Peter."

I heard him sigh. "Why would I think you're crazy? It's already a proven fact."

"Could you please keep an eye on the yacht until I can rent a boat? You'll be able to see it for quite a while."

More sighs.

"Please, Ben," I pleaded as I thundered past the Quarterdeck Restaurant. "Is it turning towards the bridge?"

Finally, he spoke. "It has turned left, heading for the ocean—and it's moving pretty fast. You'll never catch it."

"I'm going to try." I raced to the long pier and hunted for something speedy enough to take up the chase. There weren't many choices. Most were still out, either on fishing charters or sightseeing trips. I shaded my eyes as a boat entered the harbor. Hallelujah! It was the Moondancer, and I knew the captain well.

Joey Archer can't have been very happy to see me. He and I had been involved in a bit of a shoot-up on Broad Creek a year ago. In fact, when he recognized me, he tried to turn the boat around. The maneuver didn't work. He was committed to docking at the long pier.

As he approached, he threw me a line. "Don't tie up," I yelled. "I need you to take me out."

"Tie it up, Maggie. I'm getting off the boat."

"Please, Joey." I danced around the pier with the rope in my hand. "Let me come onboard."

Ozzie, the captain of the boat in the neighboring berth, walked over as Joey and I jostled. He calmly took the line out of my hand, tied up, looked me up and down and returned to his boat. Joey jumped off the Moondancer and headed for the harbor. I threw my body in front of him to block his way.

"We are wasting time here, Joey. You have to take me out there."

"No, I don't." He feinted left and dodged around me. "You are a loony bird."

"I am not," I yelled as I ran after him. "This is a matter of life and death."

Joey began to trot. "Leave me alone, Maggie."

I trotted with him. Together we loped towards the shops. At Harbour Town Crafts he broke into a run. I picked up the speed and matched him stride for stride. Tourists turned and stared as we sailed past Bailey's and rounded the corner.

I felt someone fall into step beside me. "Curiosity has driven me to accompany you," Ben said as he ran easily next to me. "Why are we running?"

"We're chasing him," I gasped. "I need his boat."

At the sound of Ben's voice, Joey stopped running, which was good because my breath was coming in ragged rasps and my chest was on fire.

"Maybe you can convince her, man. She'd nuts. I'm not taking the Moondancer out until I've had lunch. And I have a charter this afternoon. Ain't no way I'm going to lose that."

Ben put his arm around Joey's shoulder and conferred with him in tones low enough to prevent me from hearing. While they chatted, I ducked into the General Store and bought three bottles of water and a Snickers bar. The candy was for me. After my run through the harbor, I needed instant fuel.

When I rejoined the men, Joey's attitude had changed. In fact, he was positively affable. "Y'all go ahead," he said. "I'm going to pick up a hot dog and then I'll catch up with you."

Ben hurried me to the long pier before Joey could change his mind. "What did you say to him," I asked.

"I gave him money. You can't expect to use his boat without paying for it."

"You're super," I wheezed as I climbed aboard the Moondancer. "Boy, this brings back memories. I never thought I'd ride on this boat again." Actually, I never wanted to. Our adventure last year on Broad Creek (which you can read about in *A Yacht To Die For*) made me so skittish around water, I hyperventilated when I took a bath.

Munching on a hot dog and carrying a bottle of Mello Yello, Joey untied the rope and tossed it on the deck. Once onboard he gunned the motor and steered the Moondancer out of the harbor.

"Peter's boat—if it was Peter's boat—turned left towards the ocean," Ben said. He pointed to the tip of Daufuskie Island. "I don't know whether it headed out to sea or rounded the corner to South Beach." He squinted his eyes at me. "I'd also like to know why you're so certain it's your ex-husband's boat."

"First of all, I recognize it. He told me those double mahogany doors leading to the salon were unique. And secondly, the name gives it away. I mean, when he came to Hilton Head, it was called *Magnolia*. That's when he thought he could win me back with a flashy yacht. The new name is *Legal Pad*, which I assume is Peter's charming way of advertising he's a swinging single lawyer with a seagoing bed."

"You're reading an awful lot into two words, aren't you? The boat could belong to a secretary in a law firm."

"You've got to be kidding," I scoffed. "Peter bragged about how much his yacht had cost. I think it might be beyond a legal secretary's wages."

We stood on the bow, water spraying our faces. "She's wide open," Joey called over the roar of the motor. "She can't go any faster."

We quickly left Hilton Head and Daufuskie behind. To our right was Tybee Island, off the coast of Savannah. We saw a fishing boat dragging for shrimp, a catamaran with two men onboard and an elegant yacht moving majestically towards France, but there was no sign of the *Legal Pad*.

"I don't have enough fuel to go much farther," Joey announced. "We'll have to stop at the South Beach marina."

This wasn't good news but even I recognized we wouldn't get far without gas. Logic also told me the possibility of finding Peter's boat was probably zero. He had too much of a head start. But logic and I have never been comfortable companions. Therefore, I jumped up and down on the deck, punched Ben on the arm and yelled, "We can't stop now. He'll get away. Give me an oar and I'll row."

Joey used his forefinger to point to his head and make a circular motion. Ben put his arm firmly around my waist. "How about a bit of lunch at the Salty Dog? Maybe food will restore your blood sugar level and consequently, your sanity."

"I do not intend to eat anything," I said hotly. "Please let me off and I'll rent another boat." This didn't sound like a good plan since we had only reached the mouth of the marina. And I also had no money. Like I said, logic and I didn't know each other very well.

Fortunately, both men paid no attention to me. Joey coasted slowly into the harbor towards the fuel dock. My eyes swept over the boats anchored at South Beach. Soon most of them would be gone. When the tide went out, so did all the water in the harbor, making navigation in and out impossible.

On the dock, tourists eager to buy local fresh shrimp gathered around the crew of a fishing boat. On the other side of the fuel pump, a boat heading out to sea caught my eye. It was moving too fast for harbor traffic. A woman dressed in shiny green Capri pants and a yellow tank top stood in the bow talking to a man. Once clear of the mouth of the harbor, the captain gunned the motor, creating a wake which rocked the wave runners. I guess my memory wasn't as acute as I'd hoped because it wasn't until I saw the name on the stern of the boat that I recognized it.

"Say, isn't that…"

"Yes, it's the *Legal Pad*," I shouted before Ben could finish his sentence. "I knew it as soon as I saw it. Joey, you've got to turn this boat around. Right now."

Joey, who was busy pumping fuel into the tank, rolled his eyes.

"I hope you understand he can't do that right now," Ben said calmly, as if he were talking to a temperamental child. "I am seriously beginning to worry about you, Maggie. And I'm fed up with this erratic behavior. You're becoming unbalanced."

"No time for that now. Help me find the radio. I have to call the Coast Guard. They'll stop that boat."

"What do you intend to tell them? That you suspect the yacht belongs to your ex-husband, who is somehow mixed up in a murder investigation? And you just happen to have some evidence you haven't shared with them. Is that what you want to say? They'll think you're crazy, and you know what? They would probably be right."

"Ben," I said excitedly, pumping his arm up and down. "Did you recognize the woman standing in the bow?

"I didn't see her. I wasn't paying attention until I saw the name on the stern."

"That's okay," I said magnanimously. "It took me a few minutes, too. But she had the same slim build and the same ponytail. Ben, I'd bet my dogs that woman was Fleur Durand—our friend from Marrakech."

CHAPTER 15

▼

I'll admit I am sometimes scatterbrained, but I almost always remember to lock my front door. Now it stood ajar. Ben and I cautiously mounted the front steps and peered into the living room. The first things we saw were the down cushions from my lovely, glazed chintz-covered couch. They were on the floor, torn to shreds. Thinking Wally had gone on a rampage, I threw open the door, stomped into the house and bellowed "Wally" at the top of my lungs. No dog came running to greet us joyfully, but I was too upset at the destruction in the front hall to wonder why.

Ben, however, was not quite as dense. He put a finger to his lips and whispered, "Don't say anything. Whoever did this could still be here."

Did what? I didn't understand what he was talking about. He picked up a Russian box from the coffee table. Its lid had been torn off and tossed onto the couch. Wally was a very naughty dog, but surely he couldn't do that. He also couldn't have smashed my Murano glass pelican with the fish in its beak onto the slate fireplace hearth. Or knocked the pictures on the wall askew.

"Someone has trashed your house," Ben said. "You stay here while I have a look around." He grabbed a heavy ceramic pot I'd bought in Adendorf, Germany and, brandishing it above his head, tiptoed down the hall to the bedroom. I concentrated on gulping gasps of air and remaining upright. The kitchen, dining room and sunroom were equally chaotic. Who would do this? And why? I didn't have anything valuable enough to steal. The only possessions I cared about were my dogs.

I let out a scream I'm sure folks could hear in Savannah. Ben came racing out of the bedroom. "What! Did you see someone?"

"It's what I don't see," I wailed. "My puppies are gone. They've been kidnapped."

"Good grief, Maggie. We've got bigger problems than your dogs. I'm sure they're around here somewhere. No one in his right mind would kidnap Wally. We have to call the police."

I wasn't listening to him. I picked up one of my terry slippers, which was minus part of the toe and hugged it to my chest. "Look. Wally was chewing this when he was snatched. He must have taken it from my bedroom while I was out."

"How would you know that? Have you seen the disorder in your closets? You could profit from some organizational tips."

I glared at him. "This would not be a good time to lecture me. I have to find my dogs." I started out the door, but I didn't hear footsteps behind me. "Are you coming?"

"I think we should call the police."

"I think we should hunt for Wally and Willow."

I won.

Within minutes we found Wally. Unaware of his freedom, he had wandered as far as the service yard where he'd tipped over a trashcan and now munched contentedly on green fuzzy cheese I'd found in the refrigerator. He wagged his tail enthusiastically as we approached. I bent down and hugged his silky body. This was one time I was glad he was dumb as a post. He wasn't smart enough to think about running away.

Willow, on the other hand, was not slow-witted. Assuming she hadn't been kidnapped, she was probably half way to Charleston by now. I never understood her urge to roam. At my house she had three

100   A String Of Perils

square meals, a soft bed—mine—and two walks a day plus swimming privileges in the Atlantic Ocean, and she still bolted every chance she got.

Hoping for the best but fearing the worst, I started out on foot, calling her name in a cheerful voice designed to fool her into thinking I wasn't mad. I walked through pine straw and azalea bushes at the edge of the marsh. At the construction site of a new home, I stopped and shielded my eyes. A cement truck finished pouring concrete for the footers and slowly backed across the mud to allow another to take its place.

On the far side of the site, surrounded by cinder blocks and heavy equipment, I spied my puppy. I whistled and waved a piece of ham—a sure lure. She ran a few steps, then stopped and lifted her paw. When she tried to resume running, she limped badly. "Ben, I found her," I called. He and I raced across the debris, tiptoed over the wet cement and scooped up my dog. When I touched her right front paw, she yelped. I cradled her in my arms as I carried her out of the construction site and up my driveway. It was only when I put her down on the floor that I noticed the piece of fabric in her mouth. It was green and shiny—exactly like the pants I had seen on Fleur Durand.

A trip to the vet fixed Willow up in no time. Diagnosing a severe sprain, Dr. Nixon applied a doggie splint and told her to stay off her feet for a few days. Willow seemed to understand. She curled up on the couch in Ben's villa and allowed me to cover her with a light blanket.

We were at Ben's because there was no way I was going to stay in my house—not until we figured out what it was that I had and someone wanted. I'd convinced him not to call the police. How could we mention the break-in without explaining the business card, the trip to Morocco and Fleur Durand.

"We're in too deep now," I told Ben. "In fact, we've probably broken a few laws by not calling the sheriff sooner. Let's wait until we have this solved."

Ben laughed. At least that's how I chose to interpret the strangled sound coming from his throat. He did, however, call a cleaning company to tidy up the mess in my house—not that I ever intended to live there again. He blamed the absolute chaos on "extremely disorderly tenants."

I left Ben to his gurgling while I walked around the harbor to talk to Susan Lowerby. The people who had ransacked my house—and now I was convinced it was Fleur Durand and her associates—had smashed my supply of painted platters intended for the shelves of Fashion Court. Susan had enough other lovely merchandise for sale, so I knew she wouldn't be upset, but she had saved space for me and I was sorry to lose it.

The bell over the door tinkled as I walked into the shop. Susan popped up from behind the jewelry counter. "Hi, Maggie. Give me a second and I'll be right with you. I just want to put out this display of necklaces and bracelets." I inspected the glittering pieces of Swarovski jewelry. "These are beautiful. Which reminds me, how did the beaded necklaces sell?"

Susan looked at me blankly. "Which necklaces do you mean? These are the only new ones we've received."

"You know. The ones Cotton was unwrapping when I came into the shop a while ago. I saw some similar pieces in Morocco. They were very unique. I figured they would sell well."

Susan shook her head. "She never showed them to me. Funny you would mention Cotton. She didn't come to work last week and I haven't been able to find her. She doesn't answer her phone and hasn't picked up her paycheck." She lowered her voice. "Between you and me, I only gave Cotton a job because she seemed so inconsolable after her mother's death. She sure wasn't the best sales person I've ever had. In fact, I really wanted to let her go."

"I think she appreciated having this job," I told her. "To some extent it distracted her from thinking about her mother. It worries me that you haven't heard from her because I don't think she's very stable."

"I don't either," Susan said, a concerned look on her face. "What do you think we should do? Should we notify the sheriff?"

Why did everyone want to call the sheriff? There had to be other solutions. I suggested one. "I'll run out to her house and talk to her. If she's in a funk, maybe I can get her to see a doctor."

"I'd be very grateful, Susan said. She moved behind the counter and opened a drawer. "Here's her paycheck. I'm sure she must need it. She always cashed it promptly."

"I'll give it to her," I promised as I headed to the door. If I could find her. And if she wasn't sitting in some tree communing with her departed mother. I'd had my quota of stress. I didn't need any encounters with the Other Side.

I waited until evening to drive to Cotton's house on the north end of the island. Ben had a meeting and announced he would return around ten o'clock. He hadn't sounded particularly cordial on the phone, which made me worry that we had overstayed our welcome.

Wally and Willow settled themselves on the pillows on my bed and immediately fell asleep. I threw my bag over my shoulder, scribbled a note for Ben, jumped in my car and headed down Lighthouse Road. Twenty minutes later I turned off Hwy 278 onto the road leading to Cotton's. I drove slowly, afraid I wouldn't recognize the house in the dark. When my headlights picked out the name *Duncan* on a dilapidated mailbox, I heaved a relieved sigh.

The branches of massive, old oak trees formed a canopy over a driveway that was so narrow, clumps of Spanish moss grazed my windshield. As I approached the house, I was happy to see a dim light burning in the front window. There was no way I'd have entered a dark house. Gingerly, I climbed the wooden front steps.

"Thank you for coming."

Linda S. Clayton   103

I nearly flew out of my socks. My heart jumped northward and landed with a thump in my throat. When a soft hand tapped me on the shoulder, I screamed like a banshee and flapped my arms as if I were warding off a swarm of bees. "Whoo, baby, my knees are wrinkled. Get out of the way before I tinkle," I roared. "I'm out of here."

"What's the matter with you? Like, are you sick or something?"

It was Cotton, lurking in the shadows of the porch.

"Why are you lurking in the shadows of the porch," I managed to squeak once my heart stopped its wild bouncing. "You almost gave me a heart attack."

"I am waiting out here."

I brushed aside this unnecessary comment. "Can we go into the house? I need to talk to you for a minute. And I've brought your paycheck from Ms Lowerby."

She grabbed my arm and held on as if she were in the last stages of childbirth. "I don't want to go in there."

"Well, dear, I'm not wild about staying out here." There were strange rustling noises, which were probably slippery slimy snakes slithering through the overgrown azaleas surrounding the front porch.

"Watch when you go near the door," Cotton said. "There's a big banana spider in a web on the left side. Almost big enough to eat a mouse. Ma told me to leave it alone; it was somebody's soul who had passed to the Other Side."

Eeeek! I put my hands over my head and charged. Cotton could follow me or stand out there all night. When it was time to go home, I planned to leave via a window. Fortunately, she followed me. As soon as she was in the house, I slammed the door. "Could we turn on more lights?" I said as I moved around the room searching for lamps. "It's way too dark in here."

"Ma doesn't care much for electricity. She says it scares the spirits."

I stumbled over a brown horsehair hassock and banged into a table holding bottles filled with weird looking objects. The glass jars rocked precariously, and I lunged to keep them from falling. There weren't many lamps to turn on. Cotton reached into the mouth of a blue ceramic fish and pushed a button. A thin beam of light picked out a cobweb on the ceiling. Slowly the beam began to revolve and then blink like a strobe light.

"That's one of Ma's favorites. She says departed souls prefer it to normal light. They focus better. There aren't anymore lamps," she said apologetically.

"That's okay. I can't stay very long." I sat down on the edge of the couch, ready to bolt if Mama started to chat with me. "What's wrong, Cotton?" I asked. "It's kind of obvious you're not very happy."

"Ma is mad at me," she said. "I can't figure out what happened. We were having a nice conversation and then all of a sudden her voice got all funny and she told me I had been doing bad things."

Oh dear. This was not good. "Look, sweetie," I began. "I know you think you're having chats with your mother, and that's very understandable. She has only been gone a few months."

"She's not gone," Cotton interrupted. "She is right here."

"Where?" I looked around the room, afraid I'd find Wisteria sitting in a chair.

"Silly. You can't see her. I told you I talk to her."

"Yes, I know that. And I'm sure you are communicating with her. In your heart. What you're doing is thinking about her and sensing her answers. Isn't that right?" I nodded my head encouragingly. Cotton shook hers vigorously.

"Nope. Ma talks real loud to me. Usually she waits till I'm in bed, but tonight she was right here when I got home. And she was mad."

Good grief! Cotton had sprung the main spring. Clearly, medical attention was in order.

"Listen, dear, you are simply having an emotional reaction to your mother's death," I said as I put my arm around her shoulder. Through the thin fabric of her shirt I could feel her trembling. "I'm not going to argue with you anymore because I can see it's upsetting you. I've come here because Ms Lowerby and I were worried about you. She said you haven't been to work for a few days. Are you feeling okay?"

Cotton pulled away from me. "I'm fine," she said in a low voice. "No reason to be concerned."

Boy, how I wished that were true. "Would you like to come home with me?" I asked, forgetting that I was temporarily residing at Ben's. "I hate to leave you here alone."

"How many times do I have to tell you, I'm not alone. Ma is here."

"Right. I was just thinking a real live human might offer more company. You know, someone who could fix you a cup of tea."

"No."

I changed the subject. "Say, your mother hasn't seen Peter's yacht on the island, has she?" I watched her closely for any reaction.

She didn't hesitate. "Well, of course. It's here all the time. Ma says Peter is a bad man."

"Where is it, exactly, when it's here all the time?"

"I'll have to ask Ma."

"But you just said..." I gave up. "Your mother has talked more about Peter?"

"I don't want to discuss it now. I'm too upset."

"It's important for me to know, Cotton."

"Tell you what I'll do. We can have a séance here and talk directly to Ma. She can answer all your questions. Will you come?"

What did I get myself into? And would I never learn to keep my big mouth shut.

"I guess so, if you promise me you won't talk to others about Peter."

"I promise," she said. "It will take a while to arrange."

"Take as long as you need. No hurry. And if your mother doesn't feel up to it, I'll understand."

I'd babbled enough. It was time for me to go. "Before I forget, Cotton," I said with my hand on the front door, "whatever happened to those wonderful necklaces you had at Fashion Court? I'd love to buy another one."

Obviously impatient for me to leave, Cotton drummed her fingers on the top of the box marked *Gems From The Other Side*. "I returned them to the owner."

"I thought you didn't know where they came from."

"A man came to the back door of the shop and said he'd left them there by mistake, so I gave them back. Honestly, Maggie, I don't know why you're making such a fuss about some dumb beads. Will you please tell Ms Lowerby I'm not coming back to Fashion Court."

"Why on earth not? You're not upset because I asked about the necklace, are you?"

Tears bubbled in her eyes. "No. I just don't want to work. I have too much to do for Ma. I have to go to bed now."

There was nothing more I could do. Vowing to get medical help for her tomorrow, I slapped my tote bag over my head and raced out the door and down the steps. Before I got into my car, I combed my hair with my fingers and brushed off my clothes. I didn't feel anything crawling so I assumed I was spider free. I figured a critter that significant would make a definite thump on the skin. Yuk!

CHAPTER 16

▼

"We would be so pleased if you and that handsome man of yours could come to our little party on Friday. Nothing fancy. We'll do lobsters around the pool."

I stifled the urge to tell Janna Maletesta we'd just done lobsters around the pool in Marrakech. And I desperately did not want to do this. Hobnobbing with the Maletestas and their pals was my idea of boring. But you never knew where you'd meet your next customer, and I couldn't afford to turn business opportunities away.

"Perhaps you could convince your friend, Lucy Rotblumen, and her husband to join us. I'd love to get to know them better."

So that was her purpose. She wanted to crack the Rotblumen inner circle. "I'm afraid I can't speak for Lucy. It would be best if you asked her yourself. I'm afraid I can't even speak for—as you call him—my handsome man."

"Oh dear," she sighed. "I had so hoped…"

"I will be happy to accept your invitation," I told her. And Ben would, too. He just didn't know it yet.

"Well," she said unenthusiastically, "that will be fine. Jake will be disappointed if the others can't come. He specifically asked me to invite them."

"We all have our crosses to bear."

"Excuse me?"

"I said, we all have moss on our stairs. Such a problem, don't you think? If you'll excuse me now, I must go scrub mine."

She was still sputtering when I hung up the phone.

*   *   *   *

My house was cleaner than I had ever seen it. The windows sparkled, the floors smelled of lemon polish and every shard of glass and porcelain had been whisked away. There were even fresh sheets on my bed. It was beautiful. And I had absolutely no intention of staying there. Not without a large army to protect me. My dogs were great companions, but I had a feeling they would sleep through a war. And as for actually biting someone or growling defensively, I could forget it. They were lovers, not fighters.

I collected some underwear and clothes and stuffed them along with my hairdryer into an old canvas bag. From the kitchen I took the dogs' dishes and a full bag of dry kibble.

I realized I longed to come home. The marsh, washed in sunshine, was familiar and comforting. At high tide small boats raced down channels that were otherwise not navigable. Herons and egrets swooped low over the water, looking for food. I chided myself for being a weak-kneed female, hoping the stern lecture would stiffen my spine and convince me to once again occupy my house. It didn't work. I would live here when the folks responsible for the break-in were behind bars. I was scared—and even if I'd never admit it to my friends—I couldn't fool me.

Ben intended to be away all day. He was acting very aloof, but I was too wrapped up in my own problems to pay much attention to him.

Back in his villa, I searched the phone book for a good psychiatrist for Cotton. I called Dr. Leonard Fisher's office and spoke to his nurse. "You'll have to get her to come in and see doctor," she told me. "There's nothing we can do for your friend over the phone."

"What if she won't do that? She doesn't believe there is anything wrong, so I doubt very much if she would agree to an examination. Isn't there something you can suggest? Or some drug you can prescribe? I'm genuinely worried about her." I noticed my voice was a few octaves higher than it should have been.

I could feel the nurse pursing her lips. "You must get her to agree to see doctor. Would you like an appointment for yourself?"

"For me? What on earth for? There's nothing the matter with me," I screeched. I could hear her rustling papers.

"Could you give me your name again and a telephone number where we can reach you? I'll have doctor call this evening."

I gave her my maiden name—Magnolia Meadows—and Ben's phone number. The doc could leave a message. I wanted to help Cotton, but I didn't want anyone rummaging around in my psyche. I liked it just fine the way it was.

After that I felt a little at loose ends. I left Ben's villa and wandered around Harbour Town, trying to calm my jittery nerves. I'd tried to entice Lucy into meeting me for coffee, but she had an appointment with her masseuse. "I'll see you tonight for dinner," she said. "Try to stay out of trouble." Why did everyone feel compelled to tell me that?

I intended to try on clothes at Bradford's but changed my mind when I caught a glimpse of my reflection in the toy store window. There were visible gray roots in my chestnut brown hair with blond highlights. I was overdue for a touch-up. I rounded the corner at Bailey's and headed to the Harbour Town Beauty Shoppe, thankful that Lydia, the proprietor, accepted walk-ins.

She was busy. She waved cheerfully, told me to have a seat and she'd be with me in a few minutes. I sat down in a wicker chair, picked up a magazine and idly thumbed through it while I watched Lydia expertly cut a customer's hair.

The magazine, *Boats of New England*, featured page after page of yuppies with expensive sweaters tied around their necks holding onto the rails of boats big enough to haul passengers across the Atlantic.

THE BEAUTIFUL PEOPLE

Skip Marconi and Liz, his lovely wife, are ready to sail away on Good Times, *their 150 foot luxury yacht. Yes, Chip and Liz, we can imagine the good times you'll have on that beauty.*

Bitsy and Ted Lincoln love lounging on their magnificent sailboat, Lucky Run. *Last year the Lincolns sailed through the Panama Canal to Los Angeles with a stop in Costa Rica on the way. We'd certainly call that lucky.*

Looks like Boston lawyer, Peter Bloom, shown here on the Legal Pad, *is about to tie the knot. And we're not talking about the piece of rope he's holding in his hand. Take a peek at the rock his fiancée, Petal Rose, is wearing. Way to go, Peter!*

What! I read it again, not believing me eyes. A beaming Peter leaned against the rail of his Grand Banks trawler with the prerequisite sweater draped over his shoulders. He had his arm around a tall blond with very tan legs, skimpy shorts and a halter top. She held out her left hand, displaying a diamond big enough to choke her if she happened to swallow it. Quite different from the miniscule chip he'd given me when he was a law student and I was working at Filenes to help pay his tuition.

But this obvious injustice was not what made me jump to my feet and yell, "Oatmeal, sausage, clotted cream. Clobber me with jelly beans!"

Lydia was understandably alarmed. She dropped her scissors and hurried over to me. "What's wrong? If you're having some kind of fit, I can call 911, but if you're okay, could you cool it? Yelling gibberish isn't so good for business."

"Look at this," I screamed, ignoring her admonition. "Look at that woman."

Lydia peered at the picture. "So what? Typical older man, younger woman thing. The trophy wife."

"No, it's not." I snatched the magazine out of her hand and waved it around the shop. The customer in the chair, her hair cut on one side only, removed her smock and collected her purse. "This woman," I said as I tapped the page, "this woman is an imposter. "She is not Petal Rose, fiancée of Peter Bloom, She is Fleur Durand, duplicitous thief and what's more, she is here on Hilton Head. Willow took a bite out of her butt."

That did it for the customer. She bolted from the shop as if someone had set fire to her Guiseppe Zanotti sandals. I was right behind her, running as fast as I could in my Nike tennis shoes.

I had to wait until dinner to share my news with someone. Ben left a message on my cell phone saying he'd meet me at six thirty at Stripes, our favorite restaurant on the island. At 6:50, I sat by myself at the bar sipping a glass of excellent chardonnay. At 6:54, Ben, Lucy and Julius Rotblumen strolled in together. I hadn't expected Lucy's husband. Behind the Rotblumens, Ben shrugged his shoulders indicating he was also unable to explain Julius' presence. Julius did not attend social events. He disliked empty chitchat and encouraged Lucy to attend functions by herself.

He was a serious man. He seldom smiled. The only time Julius exhibited the remotest expression of pleasure was when he gazed at his wife. Then his lips moved ever so slightly at the edges of his mouth and his stern eyes softened. There was no doubt about it—he adored his Lucy.

The three of us tried valiantly to sound intelligent, but while we talked about terrorist activity in Afghanistan and the falling dollar on the overseas market, I was bursting to tell them about Petal/Fleur. Unaware of my imminent implosion, Julius folded his tiny fingers into a teepee and listened intently, as if he expected us to disclose insider trading tips or the winner of the tomorrow's trifecta at Pimlico.

The conversation halted when our appetizers arrived. I dug into the fantastic crab bisque as if I hadn't eaten for a week. With my mouth full, I wouldn't be able to talk. Over the main course—which for me was a shashimi tuna to die for—Julius explained, in excruciating detail, seven possible hedge investments against inflation. Even Lucy's eyes glazed over, and she was used to him.

When his cell phone rang, we almost applauded. He pulled it from his pocket, frowned at the caller ID number displayed on the front and bounced to his little feet. "I'm sorry, but something very urgent has come up. I must contact Hong Kong immediately. Lucy, perhaps one of your friends would be kind enough to see you home."

"I will," Ben and I answered in unison.

Julius planted a kiss on his wife's forehead and trotted out of the restaurant. At least one of us had the good grace to look embarrassed. Lucy touched her bright pink cheeks and said, "That was a bit difficult, wasn't it. He's such a fine person, but the poor dear doesn't realize not everyone wants to hear about the fiscal health of Malawi. I think another bottle of wine is in order."

I couldn't have agreed more. While we waited, Lucy said, "Okay, Maggie. Tell us what has you just about bursting out of your skin. It's been obvious all evening."

Yahoo! I whipped the page from the magazine out of my bag, put my hand over the caption and held it in front of their eyes. "Take a gander. Who do you think this is?"

Ben spoke first. "It's that woman from Morocco. Fleur something or other."

I removed my hand from the writing. "That Fleur something or other managed to get herself engaged to Peter. Which I don't understand. It certainly looked like she and Henri were a couple in Morocco. Read what it says. Her name is Petal Rose and that's my ex-husband she's standing with."

Peter gazed at the photo. "So that's what he looks like."

"What? No, no. Don't bother about him. Honestly, Ben, we have a real conundrum here and you're still worrying about Peter." I pulled a paper and pen out of my bag. "Let's write down everything we know. Maybe we can find some connection."

Debbie, the owner of Stripes—along with her husband, Steve—set down a bottle of California chardonnay and three clean glasses. She glanced at the magazine picture on the table. "I've seen them before," she said as she poured wine in my glass."

"Where? Which one."

"Him. And her." She pointed to Peter and Petal/Fleur. "They've been here for dinner, but I don't think they were together. It seems to me she was with another man."

"Would you possibly remember when?" This was too much. Everyone in the world had seen these people but me.

She smiled. "Let's see, I remember she wanted salmon grilled with no sauces or side dishes. And only ice water to drink. But when? I'm sorry, Maggie, but I really can't remember."

Petal/Fleur was an idiot. No one in her right mind passed up sauces or side dishes at Stripes. Debbie left to bid goodbye to departing guests and I began to write. "Let's see. We might as well start at the beginning. I found Peter's business card in Otis's hand and the card had a Moroccan address. Unable to find Peter anywhere in the United States, we went to Morocco to hunt for him."

Lucy took up the story. "There we met Fleur Durand, a woman with ties to Peter. Someone tried to shoot Maggie and ram her car off a cliff. We also met Maggie's friend, Islane Kettani. Islane's ex-boyfriend, Henri, was involved with Fleur—at least it sure looked that way. If Fleur is connected to Peter, is Henri also connected?"

"Maybe we should talk about Cotton Duncan," I said. "I know she's wacky, but she keeps mentioning Peter and how he was involved in Otis's death. I don't for a minute believe she's receiving information from the Great Beyond. I do think she does a fair amount of snooping. She might know more than she's told me."

Ben drained his glass of wine. "Maybe we should get a little tough with her—tell her she can't withhold evidence, and if she knows anything about Peter, she has to tell us."

I shook my head. "She'd too fragile to threaten. There is one thing we could do, though." I told them about the séance. "It would be good if you both went with me. Three heads are better than one."

"We're off track, here," Lucy said. "We can talk about the séance later. Let's finish sorting out the events. What happened after we returned from Morocco?"

"The sheriff is actively looking for Peter and no one at his office has seen or heard from him," I said. "Then I spot his yacht, the *Legal Pad*, on Hilton Head. Some folks sitting at this table didn't believe it was his boat, but the photo proves I was right."

"Maggie's house is broken into and thoroughly searched," Lucy said, ignoring my comment. "Conclusion? Someone is looking for something. Was the same person looking for the same thing in Otis's house? This is puzzling, since neither Otis nor Maggie have anything of value to steal."

"Very funny. But it's the truth. What in the world would someone be looking for in my house? Let's go back to the *Legal Pad* for a moment. Where is it? It has to be docked somewhere. I should think it would be awfully difficult to hide a boat that big." And where was Peter. But I didn't say that out loud.

Ben cleared his throat. "I've been doing a little investigating the last few days. It occurred to me that a boat is not invisible. When it enters and leaves harbors or stops for fuel, folks are bound to notice it. So…I went to all the marinas: Shelter Cove, Palmetto Bay, South Beach, Skull Creek and, of course, Harbour Town. It is amazing the number of people who saw the boat. And it is equally amazing the number of people who couldn't tell me who was on it. Several saw Petal/Fleur.

They were able to describe her quite well. Their cognitive abilities were less accurate when it came to her male companion."

"Don't you just love it when he talks that way," I said to Lucy. "It comes from all those years with the New York Times."

He frowned at me and consulted a note pad he'd pulled from his pocket. "The *Legal Pad* never stayed in a harbor overnight. Which led several boat captains in Harbour Town to suggest the yacht anchors out on Broad Creek at night. By the way, the *Legal Pad* has been spotted as far south as Palm Beach."

I gave Ben a big hug. "You are wonderful. Can't we have the Coast Guard stop it? After all, the police are searching for Peter."

"That we could," he said. "First we must find it. And it seems to have disappeared. I think we scared Petal/Fleur. I also discovered some interesting facts about Otis."

"How did you do that?" I asked, amazed he had done so much snooping.

"Otis had an office in Bluffton. I happen to know the person who cleans the building at night after folks leave for the day. She let me have a look around."

"And you didn't think to mention it to me?"

"You weren't home last night. Do you want to hear this, or not?"

"For heavens sake, Maggie, stop being so scratchy and let the man talk," Lucy interjected. "Would anyone like an Irish coffee?"

Ben and I shook our heads.

"I believe I'll have just a tiny one—and then we must go home. We don't want to overstay our welcome here. Perhaps I'll taste some of that excellent chocolate mousse, too." I must have looked surprised because she said, "Chocolate is good for you. It lowers blood pressure and releases feel-good hormones."

I laughed. "I'm sure whoever said that didn't mean a huge portion of rich dessert."

There were still customers at two tables. Debbie cheerfully brought the coffee and mousse and told us not to worry about leaving. "I'll toss you out when we want to go home, but that won't be for a while."

"Otis kept careless records," Ben began. I found documents concerning the infamous land purchase, but they were straightforward legal papers. Believe it or not, some were coffee stained. Two years ago his bank account had a grand total of $2387.56. The day before he died he made a deposit of $10,000, which brought his checking account total to $389,000.12. I wasn't able to find any other bank record, but I'd be willing to bet he had other accounts. His house is worth well over two million dollars, according to a recent appraisal. However, there was no sign of a deed."

"I wonder how he got all that money?" I mused.

Lucy licked whipped cream from her lips. "Simple. He was involved in something extremely dishonest." She shuddered. "I always knew the man was a thug."

Ben took a credit card out of his wallet and put it on the table. "Allow me. It's not often I take two lovely ladies to dinner."

"Can the compliments, Bub. What else did you find?"

"Well," he began, smiling broadly, "I found that Otis had a passport, and in the course of one year he entered Morocco four times."

I felt extremely befuddled. "So what does all this mean? Otis had a connection to Petal/Fleur as well as Peter? And this connection resulted in heaps of money? I have a headache."

"You have a headache because you inhaled over half a bottle of wine," Lucy said. "Taste this mousse. It's exquisite."

I dipped a spoon into the creamy dessert. "Peter, Petal/Fleur and Otis were involved in some scheme, and since Peter's calling card said import/export, can we assume they were importing something into the United States?"

Ben nodded. "I forgot to add that earlier today I searched for a current import/export license issued to Peter S. Bloom." He covered my hand with his. "The issue date was nine months ago. He used the Sudbury address."

"Alrighty then," I said, trying to keep the tremor out of my voice. It's not easy to hear your ex-husband is a crook. I swallowed a delicious bite of chocolate, hoping it would release feel-good hormones. I sure needed them. "I just have to say one thing and I promise I'll never mention it again. The Peter S. Bloom I married is not capable of criminal activity. I don't care how much evidence there is to the contrary. He may have taken our marriage vows lightly, but he would never break the law."

"We believe you, sweetie," Lucy said. "But facts are facts. We can't afford to be blind. She pushed the empty dish away and wiped her mouth. "We're still missing something. Why is Petal/Fleur on Hilton Head and where is Peter's boat?"

"And where is Peter," I said softly. Since I was convinced he couldn't commit a crime, and I knew he would never neglect his work, I had to conclude something terrible had happened to him. I didn't want to be married to him, but I didn't want anyone to harm him, either. That would be my job, if I ever managed to find him.

CHAPTER 17

▼

My house still gave me the creeps, but it was time to go home—partly because I missed my own space and partly because Wally was systematically destroying Ben's villa. This morning he completely devoured the arm of a wicker chair. I also had to admit Ben and I weren't getting along especially well. The specter of Peter was always between us.

I still felt violated. The thought of someone rummaging through my drawers, examining my underwear and inspecting my jewelry made me queasy. I imagined some oily crook roaming around Hilton Head telling all his pals Maggie Bloom wore cotton Jockeys. He couldn't know that the holes in them were the results of Wally's teeth, not overuse.

I tossed some unidentifiable moldy food out of the refrigerator, read my mail and folded clean clothes. On an impulse I turned on my computer and scanned the picture of Peter and Petal/Fleur into an e-mail to Islane. In the text box, I wrote, *Can you believe this? The woman gets around.*

For the next half hour I searched Google for any information about a Petal Rose or Fleur Durand. As I expected, there was nothing. When the phone rang, I let the machine answer. "Yoo hoo, Maggie," came Islane's unmistakable voice. "*Tu est là?*"

"Right here, I assured her as I picked up the receiver. "Isn't the photo amazing?"

"She is—how you say—a whore, *n'est pas?*"

"I don't know about that, but she does seem to be having an identity crisis. I forgot to mention she is here on Hilton Head and all kinds of weird things have happened."

"Henri has also disappeared. He returned to Marrakech from Ouarzazate, but no one has seen him for days. My sources at La Mamounia tell me he took all his things from the hotel and does not intend to come back."

"He might be with Petal/Fleur," I suggested. "Some folks have seen her with a man."

"I am coming to Hilton Head," Islane stated. "Not because of Henri—because I am not a fool. I know he wanted my money. I feel—how you say—responsible because he is a very large snake and his girlfriend is an equally repulsive reptile."

"I can't argue with you about that. You can stay with me." It would be great to have Islane at my house to help me deal with the demons.

"*Merci, cherie*, but I will be at Lucy's. She and I have been doing the e-mail every day and she has asked me to come."

Well, my goodness. Once again, no one told me anything. But I shouldn't have been surprised by Islane's news. Both were flamboyant, warm, independent women. Why shouldn't they like each other. "Call me when you have you reservations," I said. "I'll pick you up at the airport."

"Be very careful, Maggie," she warned me. "Henri is a dangerous man. These are not nice people."

"Don't worry. I'm not feeling very nice myself." It sounded good, but it was pure bravado. A jellyfish had more spine than I did.

Cotton called just as I was leaving the house. "It's all set, Maggie. Ma can't wait to talk to you. Can you bring Mrs. Rotblumen, too? Ma has a message for her."

Nuts! I'd hoped Cotton would forget all about communicating with Mom. "I'm not sure about Lucy. She has a very busy schedule. When did you want to do this?"

"Ma said this afternoon at four o'clock. That is the best time for crossing back and forth between the Other Side and here. They open more traffic lanes."

A mental image of spirits gliding silently along highways of clouds to the worldly realm sprang into my mind, and I shook my head to erase it. One loony person was enough. "I don't suppose you'd come with me to visit Dr. Fisher. I think he could make you feel much better."

"What are you talking about? There's nothing the matter with me. Will you come this afternoon? And try to bring Mrs. Rotblumen?"

I sighed. There didn't seem to be any way to avoid this. "I'll do my best," I told her. "But don't be disappointed if I arrive alone." I'd get Lucy to come with me if I had to hogtie her and throw her in the trunk of my car. There was no way I was going to talk to the dead by myself.

Lucy greeted me at the door dressed for a carnival. She wore a bright yellow full skirt, a pink frilly blouse, a green satin belt around her waist and a orange, scarlet and purple turban on her head. "Come in, she said cheerfully. "I'm cleaning some things out of my closet."

I followed her up winding marble steps to the spectacular master suite that encompassed the entire second floor of Lucy's oceanfront home. Cardboard boxes filled every bit of floor space in the luxurious sitting room. In one of the boxes I noticed several pairs of Manola Blahnik shoes and an elegant Escada silk evening gown with the price tag still attached.

"I've saved the good stuff," she said, indicating several colorful skirts made of parachute material and piles of sequined, spangled and beaded sweaters. "I don't know what to do with all these things I bought in Morocco. They didn't look quite as impressive in the house as I'd imagined they would."

I could explain the reason. She had placed the silly carved figure souvenir next to a genuine Rodin. The pink, green and blue rug she'd purchased in Marrakech looked like a doormat amid the silks and satins in one of the guest bedrooms.

"This jewelry isn't nearly as attractive as I thought it was," she said. "Look at this beaded necklace. I tried to wash off a bit of dirt and it disintegrated in my hand."

I laughed. "What did you expect? You paid the equivalent of $1.75 for it."

"I have a good mind to write to the Moroccan government. Those folks should know their vendors are selling shoddy goods. She held a pendant on a chain to her nose. "I don't think this is silver, either. It doesn't smell right."

I hadn't raced to her house to discuss jewelry sniffing. Time was a wastin'. I had to be at Cotton's in three hours. "Say, Lucy," I said, fingering a nightgown made entirely of black lace, "I have a great idea for this afternoon."

Lucy interrupted me. "I'm going to Wanda's. She's going to touch up my roots. She also might have time to take a look at the leaves."

Wanda was Lucy's 'spiritual advisor.' When she wasn't reading tealeaves and tarot cards, she did ladies' hair in the kitchen of her Bluffton home. I suspected Wanda was one of Lucy's friends from the 'good old days' when they danced together in the club.

"This is perfect. I think I can promise you a more satisfying experience. Cotton has invited us to her house to have a chat with her mother."

Lucy had her head in a box, so her reply was muffled. I pretended I heard her answer in the affirmative. "That's great. I'll pick you up at three forty."

Lucy's head shot out of the box. "I said no. I'm going to Wanda's. I'll get my hair done, we'll chat, she'll tell me my life is wonderful. I don't need news from a whacko."

"Please, Lucy. I don't want to go alone."

"Take your dogs. They'll scare off any unfriendly spirits."

I realized I'd have to pull out the big guns. "Remember when you bought—sight unseen—that piece of property in Florida and it turned out to be a half acre of swampland? Wisteria predicted that would happen a month before you bought it, but you wouldn't listen."

Lucy scowled. "That deal cost me a lot of money."

"It was your own fault. You should have paid attention. Did I forget to mention Cotton said her mother had a message for you?" I asked sweetly. "Have you bought anything expensive lately?"

"That's a dirty trick Maggie. I'll go, but you have to do something for me."

"Anything," I replied gratefully. Nothing she could think up would be as bad as facing Cotton and her deceased mother alone.

Boy, was I wrong. Two hours later, my hair was so big, I could hardly get my head in the car. Wanda had washed it, given it a henna rinse, backcombed it until my roots hurt and sprayed it with so much lacquer, a hammer couldn't dent it.

Lucy chuckled all the way to Cotton's. "You look good, Maggie. You needed a little zip."

I opened the window to let out some of the overpowering odor of hair spray. "That wasn't fair, you know. Why do you look perfect and I look like a freak?"

Lucy inspected her face in a mirror she pulled from her purse. "Oh, my goodness, I wouldn't let Wanda touch my hair. Once a week I go to Charleston."

"But you said—I mean, I thought…"

"I lied. When I go to Bluffton, Wanda and I gossip and she reads tealeaves. She'd not even very good at that, but she'd my friend so I pretend she's right on the money with her predictions."

We rode the rest of the way in silence. I had to close the window because I was attracting bees.

CHAPTER 18

▼

Cotton's clapboard house was far less intimidating in daylight. It sagged a bit and could have used a coat of paint, but there were flowers blooming by the front door and chickens scratching in the dirt. I covered my head with a scarf I'd brought with me and hugged the right side of the steps.

"What on earth are you doing?" Lucy asked as she marched ahead. "Please don't go goofy on me."

"Wouldn't think of it, dear. Would you mind moving a little to the left." So what if the spider stepped on her head. It didn't eat humans.

The arachnid was busy devouring an insect and didn't even look up as Lucy sailed past. I entered the house backwards, keeping my eyes peeled for sudden movement.

Cotton met us at the door wearing a white, flowing garment probably meant to resemble an astral robe but looked suspiciously like a bed sheet. A *Cannon* tag peeked out of one corner. A curtain tieback served as a belt and a white bath towel doubled as a turban on her head.

Cotton's appearance was strange enough, but the inside of her house was even more disconcerting. There were lit candles everywhere; in holders, stuck on plates, stuffed into canning jars and swimming in water. She had arranged four chairs in a circle so that when we were seated, our knees touched. Feeling foolish I said, "Is this going to take long? Lucy has an appointment."

Cotton folded her hands as if she were saying a prayer and smiled at me benignly. "We can't hurry the spirits. You are so lucky because Ma has promised to come personally and speak to you."

Lucy tapped the face of her Cartier watch. "Maggie is right. We do have to go soon. Perhaps you could give us the message from your mother. It would be a shame to disturb her if she's busy Over There."

Cotton clapped her hands gleefully. "But that's the thing. I don't know what Ma wants to say. She told me to get you here and she'd do the rest."

Lucy and I eyed each other uneasily. The room suddenly seemed extremely hot and uncomfortable.

"We need to be real quiet now and hold hands," Cotton said. "I think she'll come."

"Anything to get this show on the road." Lucy sounded brave, but she didn't fool me. She was as nervous as I was.

We linked hands, spanning the chair between Cotton and me. "Why the empty chair?" I whispered. "Is someone else coming?"

"Silly. It's for Ma. She likes to sit when she visits. Poor thing is still having trouble with her feet. You'd think that once you cross to the Other Side, you could at least have your feet taken care of."

"Etgay emay outay ofay erehay," Lucy said under her breath in Pig Latin. "This is bizarre."

Cotton seemed to go into a trance. She closed her eyes, sniffed a few times and let her head fall forward. Suddenly she jerked upright. "Are you here, Ma? I can smell your cooking."

I stuck my nose into the air and inhaled delicately. Sure enough, I detected a faint odor of apple pie. This was ridiculous—or a well thought-out scam. I did not believe Wisteria's quarters in the Great Beyond contained cooking supplies and an oven.

Cotton's face broke into a happy grin. "I knew you'd come. I knew you'd come." To us she said, "Say hi to my Ma."

Lucy and I both mumbled a greeting.

"I won't tell anyone about this if you don't," I whispered. Lucy nodded in agreement.

"Ma doesn't want you to talk," Cotton interrupted sternly. "She wants you to listen. Go ahead, Ma," Cotton said as if she were a telephone operator connecting a call. "Pay attention, now. And get your purse off that chair, Mrs. Rotblumen. Ma doesn't have enough room."

Lucy snatched the offending object and pressed it to her chest.

I felt the hair stand up on the back of my neck. She began to speak; her voice warm and low as I remembered it. I could almost picture her sitting in the chair next to me, wrapped in the chenille bathrobe she liked to wear to the market. I glanced at Lucy, who had turned the color of paste. We both stared at Cotton. Her eyes were open but instead of being slightly vacuous, were alert and cunning. Her hands, which had been curled in her lap, moved rapidly as she spoke, punctuating the air for emphasis. And her voice was Wisteria's. If I hadn't known better, I'd have sworn Cotton's mother was in the room.

Wisteria's first remarks concerned a recipe for gooseberry pie and the secret for baking fluffy biscuits. While she spoke, I surreptitiously searched the room for wires or a tape recorder or anything that could be broadcasting her voice. There was nothing, and there was no table between us to conceal trickery.

I was flummoxed. Since I am certain audible speech with folks on the Other Side is impossible, there had to be an explanation. On second thought, who was I to determine what is ethereally possible and what is not. From the look on Lucy's face, I figured she and I were thinking alike. I watched as she stealthily stuck out her foot and moved it in front of the empty chair. Excuse me—Wisteria's chair.

Her action elicited an immediate response from Wisteria. "Please don't do that, Lucy. My feet don't feel too good. All that tromping around Heaven is killing me." She laughed—an eerie cackle that made my skin crawl. "Get it? It's killing me. I made a funny."

Good grief! A spirit comedian.

126   A String Of Perils

Wisteria's voice suddenly hardened. "Otis told me who done him in." She clucked disapprovingly. "Weren't necessary to kill him, you know. He wasn't going to do it again."

"Do what again?" I ventured timidly, but Wisteria was off on another topic.

"Your Peter is a bad boy."

"He's not my Peter," I protested.

"It certainly seems that way. Why do you keep sticking your nose into things that don't concern you? Folks don't like that."

Lucy nudged me with her elbow and inclined her head towards the window. I stifled a gasp. Outside, a shadowy shape melted into the trees and disappeared. Every instinct I possessed warned me to get out of Cotton's house immediately. I grabbed my bag and started to my feet.

"Sit down, please," Wisteria commanded. "I'm not finished."

"I think we are, though," I said. "Come on, Lucy."

"I'll give you a clue. And listen, you two. What happens if you use baking soda for glue? All this has nothing to do with you. Get lost. Stay away. Or else...Boo!"

"That doesn't make a bit of sense," I blurted out.

"Yes. It does. I'm getting tired now and it's time to go. We're having corned beef and cabbage for dinner. That whole group from New York refuses to even try grits and red eye gravy. By the way, Lucy—that new desk you bought and paid a fortune for and think is a priceless antique—it ain't. Lucas Brolin and his brother made it out of composition board, paint and varnish. You was taken. Toodle."

Cotton's head fell forward for a few seconds. Then she sat up, patted the towel on her head and smiled at us. "Wasn't that just perfect? I love it when Ma comes for a visit."

For once Lucy was speechless. When she regained the use of her vocal chords, she positively sputtered. "Your mother is as nutty as a candy bar. In fact, she's nuttier. I'll have you know, that table I bought is a genuine Louis XIV. I have a certificate authenticating it."

Linda S. Clayton   127

"I have no idea what you're talking about," Cotton murmured, "but if Ma said something is a fake, you'd better believe her."

"Let's go, Lucy," I said, grabbing her arm. "You can worry about the table later."

I totally forgot about the spider as we flew down the steps and jumped into my car. My heart was beating so fast I could hardly breathe. "Crazy as a loon," Lucy muttered. "I'm going to call the sheriff."

She could call the FBI for all I cared. All I wanted to do was get away. I tossed my tote bag onto the back seat and put the key into the ignition. It was then that I felt something fall on my hand. When I looked down I saw the furry black and yellow spider—almost as big as my fist—crawling slowly up my arm.

CHAPTER 19

▼

Lucy said I fainted. I'm sure I didn't. I may have had a temporary lapse of consciousness, but I wouldn't call it fainting. More like a swoon brought on by extreme stress. I do know that both of us screamed as if our hair was on fire and tore out of the car. I banged my arm on a tree and waved it in the air, but the spider was long gone.

"I'm not getting back into that car until you show me its dead body, "I said. "A thing that big should be easy to find."

"You certainly are a prissy little girl." Lucy poked around the front seat with a stick. "It wouldn't hurt you. It prefers more tender meat."

"You can be flippant because it didn't walk all over you. Do you see it?"

"No, but I'm sure it's not here. The way you flailed your arms, a bat wouldn't have survived. Would you like me to drive?"

I would, indeed. Let it crawl up her arm and see how she reacted. Before I got in the car, I looked under the seat, in the backseat and in the beverage holder between the seats. I flipped the keys to Lucy. "It's not that I can't drive, you understand. I'm still a bit shaky from the surprise, that's all."

Lucy put the car in gear and backed down the driveway. "Righto. No problem. We have to do something about Cotton," she said as she turned onto Hwy 278.

- 128 -

Linda S. Clayton 129

"I've spoken to a doctor, but if she won't allow herself to be treated, there's nothing we can do."

"Yes, medical attention would be beneficial, but that's not what I meant. How do you think Cotton is getting all this information? Does she spend her days snooping? I have to tell you, I am quite annoyed about that table." She glanced at my face. "You don't believe you were talking to Wisteria, do you? Do I have to worry about you now?"

"Of course not, but you have to admit, the voice sounded exactly like Wisteria. How did Cotton do that?"

Lucy shrugged. "She certainly knows her mother's voice. Perhaps she's a good mimic. Some folks have a talent for that sort of thing."

"But Cotton—and forgive me for saying this—isn't a quick witted person. Would she be clever enough to invent the conversation we just witnessed? What does she want?"

"I don't know. Could she be seeking attention?"

"I think she's gone over the edge," I said. "Living all alone in that spooky house can't be healthy. There's something else I think we should discuss. How did that spider get into the car?"

"That's easy. You brought it in with you."

I shook my head. "Nope. I remember seeing it out of the corner of my eye when I put the key in the ignition. It just didn't register until I saw it on my arm. I think we have to conclude someone put it in the car to scare me."

"Well, it sure worked. But people who live around here know that banana spiders won't hurt you. If someone really wanted to frighten you, why not put a copperhead on the front seat? That would do the trick."

"Maybe the person wasn't trying to give me a heart attack," I yelled. "Think about it. Let's say whomever we saw slinking about the property scooped up the spider and put it in my car. When you don't expect to see something like that, it can give you quite a fright. It was very effective."

"Obviously. I still don't understand the reason."

"I think I have something that someone wants and I also think someone is following me. The awful thing is, I have no idea what or why."

Ben and I arrived at Janna and Jake's party punctually at seven o'clock. Ben looked super in tan slacks and a pale blue shirt. He also smelled terrific. I wore a blue and yellow short Lily skirt, blue Lily top and white sandals. I put the beads I'd bought at Fashion Court around my neck and added a colorful Angela Moore bracelet. I tried to undo Wanda's work on my hair but only succeeded in making it worse. Now it lay flat on top and stuck straight out at the sides. It had the texture of a horse's tail.

"Did you lose your comb?" Ben asked as he gave the car keys to a valet.

"Of course not. This is a new style I'm trying. Don't you like it?" I said, daring him to say no.

"No. I'm afraid I'll poke my eye out if I get near you."

Willa Beth Montrose burst between us, hooking each arm with her claw-like fingers. Willa was about one hundred and twenty years old, had skin like tree bark and a voice like a bullhorn. "So," she boomed, "what have you two been up to? Haven't seen you on the beach lately. Understand your ex-husband is remarrying, Maggie. Seen him around here with that girl. Awfully cheeky of him to flaunt her in your neighborhood. But then, young people these days have no social tact. My father would have taken a horse whip to any man who disrespected me."

When she paused to take a breath, I jumped in. "First of all, may I ask how you know it is my ex-husband who is flaunting her? And where, exactly, have you seen them?" This was beginning to infuriate me. Everyone on this island knew more about Peter's business than I did.

"Why, on his boat, of course. No, that can't be right. I heard he has a boat, but I've never seen it. It seems to me I met him at a restaurant in Beaufort. Now I can't remember who it was, but someone we both know was with them and he introduced us. Yes, that's right. I distinctly remember the person saying the awfully good-looking young man with him at the table was Peter Bloom. I just assumed he was your ex-husband. Can't be that many Blooms around."

"Is that right? It would be really helpful if you could remember the man's name. Was it Otis Murbaugh?"

Willa Beth considered this question. "What man are we talking about?"

"The one you said you saw with my ex-husband. Could it have been Otis?"

"Were we talking about Otis?"

"No, you mentioned Peter Bloom in a restaurant in Beaufort and…"

"Why didn't you say so, girl. Don't rightly know. Could have been Otis." She peered through round glasses at my face. "Best you forget all about your ex-husband. Men are always looking for sweet young things. It's no reflection on you. It's simply the way they are." She looked at Ben for confirmation. I watched him struggle with a smile.

"Afraid I don't agree with you, Willa Beth. This is the only girl for me, even when her knees sag and her hair falls out."

Willa Beth looked unimpressed. "Humph. You say that now, but wait until she's so fat she can't see her own feet anymore." She pinched me in the mid-section before I could suck in my stomach. "Already running to a bit of flab. Mark my words, Maggie. Get yourself a good hobby. That way, your twilight years won't be so lonely. Excuse me children. I must greet that lady over there—Constance something or other. You wouldn't happen to know her family name, would you?"

Ben shook his head. I simply shook—with rage. "Come on, Maggie. Let's get a drink. Or do you want to stand here and discuss your expanding waistline?"

I tried to grab a handful of fat around his middle but came up empty. He had abs like rocks. "That's because you don't have the female fat producing hormones," I said as I sailed ahead of him into the house. "Everyone knows that. And if you mention this one more time I am going to tell everyone you wear a toupee." Which was a ridiculous notion. It was obvious his beautiful hair was his own.

Drinks in hand, Ben and I wandered through the crowd of sixty of the Maletestas' closest friends. "Do you know many of these people?" Ben asked.

"This isn't my crowd. But I noticed Janna is using the pitchers I painted, so this could be good for business." Actually, I don't have a crowd, but it sounded good. Tonight Ben and I were getting along well, which was a relief, but I knew it was because we hadn't mentioned Peter. "I suppose I should thank you for coming."

"That would be nice," Ben said sweetly. "But you don't have to. As always, it's a pleasure."

"Thank you," I mumbled. "Let's eat."

We lined up at a buffet table loaded with plates of tomatoes and mozzarella, chicken salad, steamed shrimp, smoked salmon and tender asparagus spears. In the center were platters piled high with lobsters. As we picked up our plates, a smiling waiter tied plastic lobster bibs around our necks and directed us to places at a table on the lawn. For the next half hour we ate and made forced conversation with the folks around us. The man on my right was more interested in the lady on his right so that worked out nicely. I could eat in relative peace.

Ben, however, was not as lucky. Cynthia Loveday, well into her fifth martini, was so taken with him that she practically licked his face. "Darling," she slobbered, "you simply must come to a little gathering I'm having on our boat next week." As Ben shook his head she said, "Oh, please don't say you can't. That would be so hurtful."

I noticed she had lipstick on her teeth. Ben put his hand on my knee and squeezed, which I assumed meant *get me out of here right now*. It couldn't have meant anything else—we were in a public place.

Linda S. Clayton 133

I stood up and took Ben's hand. "So sorry, he's with me and we're leaving."

Unfortunately, Janna stood up at the same time. She tapped a fork against her glass to get our attention. Others took up the tapping and for a few minutes it sounded like an out of sync bell choir. When order was restored, Janna beamed at her guests and said, "I hope you all enjoyed our little picnic." Everyone applauded. A few even whistled and stomped their feet. "Good. Now don't anyone tell me you are too full to move because we have a special treat planned for y'all." Much groaning and laughter. "We are going to play a game. Jake will give you the rules."

Jake put an arm around his wife's waist and said, "How about that? I get to make the rules for a change." Great hooting and cheering. "Seriously, folks, Janna and I have concocted a little entertainment which requires you all to participate—so sit down, Maggie and you others who thought you'd sneak out early. You have to pay for your food."

This time the laughter was not quite as hearty. "Do something," Ben whispered in my ear. But I couldn't. We were stuck.

"What I want you to do is this," Jake continued. "We'll form four groups. There is a colored dot under each coffee cup. If your dot is red, you're in the red group, if it's yellow, you're in the yellow group. And so forth. There are four colored flags on the patio. You line up under your color. There is also a large box next to each flag. You reach in, pull out a piece of paper, find what is written on the paper and deposit it in the box. The winning team receives a case of excellent wine."

"So it's a scavenger hunt," someone called out. "How are we supposed to find things in the dark?"

Maletesta's house was sandwiched between a lagoon and the Atlantic Ocean. Beyond the lawn, I could hear waves crashing on the beach. Colorful Japanese lanterns lit the party area, but otherwise there were no lights. "These people are crazy," I said to Ben. "We can't play games out here at this time of night."

"You don't have to worry," Jake called. "Everything is easy to find. Janna arranged the teams and hid the items, and y'all know she isn't clever enough to think up something difficult. Just kidding, honey," he said as he kissed her head.

Cynthia Loveday, a red dot pasted to her forehead, lurched over to Ben. "Isn't this wonderful? You and I are going to be together. Where is this flag we have to find?"

Ben did indeed have a red dot. I had a green one. "There must be some mistake. We're at the same table. Surely we would have the same color dot."

Ben shrugged his shoulders as Cynthia hauled him away. Reluctantly, I made my way to the patio and lined up under the green flag.

I didn't know anyone on my team, but they all seemed to know each other. They laughed and joked as they pulled papers out of the box.. Jake suddenly appeared at my side. "Janna told me to be on this team," he said. "Hope y'all are good at this game. I'd like to keep the wine." He winked at me as he put his hand in the box. "Oops, I drew out two. Here, Maggie. You and I are the last ones."

I took my paper and moved to a corner of the patio to read it.

It's green and it hops and it likes to eat bugs. It may not be moving. Be careful, don't croak.

What kind of a dumb clue was that? A six year old child could figure this out. I was obviously looking for a frog, and it was most likely some type of figurine or outdoor decoration. Since inside the house was out of bounds, I knew I should confine myself to the garden area. There was absolutely no way I was going to stick my hand under a bush at night. If the frog wasn't in plain sight, I wasn't going to play. I noticed that most of the other players moved to the beach where spotlights now illuminated the search area. I didn't see Ben.

I roamed around the patio, hoping to trip over the frog. Finding nothing, I hesitantly moved along the path rimming the house. Although it was lit by ground lights, I still had difficulty seeing. It was brighter on the lagoon side. I was able to make out beds full of blooming roses and daisies.

Using the flashlight on the end of my key chain, I played the weak beam over the ground near the water. Every person with an ounce of sense knew not to walk close to a lagoon, especially at night when alligators liked to move onto the grass, and here I was creeping around the bank as if I were immune to gator bites. I decided to count to fifty—very fast—and then go back. At thirty-eight, my flashlight picked up an object on the ground near the lagoon.

Closer inspection revealed a green bronze frog about the size of a loaf of bread perched on a rock. As I bent down to touch it, something brushed my shoulder. Alarmed, I swatted vigorously, afraid a bat had decided to build a nest in my hair. I felt nothing, so I returned to the frog. It looked heavy and slimy and would certainly ruin my skirt if I tried to carry it to the house. Enough of this game. I would somehow find the car and go home. Cynthia could take care of Ben.

There it was again. Something was definitely attacking me. Gloved fingers reached for me from behind, trying to grab my body. I swiped at my throat, trying to remove whatever was clawing at my neck. To my horror, I lost my balance and fell on my *derriere* into the lagoon. I landed with a splash and a scream loud enough to wake any snoozing amphibian. Terrified I'd soon be gator bait, I struggled for a foothold in the muck and water. Relieved to find I was able to stand, I waded to the bank and crawled out, dripping water, mud, algae and lagoon debris behind me.

Folks stared as I stalked across the patio in search of Ben, but I didn't care. I wasn't even interested in a conversation with Jake. I wanted to go home. I found Ben standing by the pool with Cynthia attached to his neck. I'll have to admit, he looked extremely unhappy. His face brightened considerably when he saw me. His look of joy turned to concern and then disbelief. "I don't know what to say. Are you okay?"

"Do I look okay?" I peeled wet leaves off my arm. "Thank you so much for a lovely party, Janna," I said to our hostess, who had rushed over. "Ben and I have to go now."

On the way out we met Willa Beth. When she saw me, she clicked her dentures. "You're going to lose him for sure if you don't do something about your wardrobe, dear. You should have dressed more carefully. Made sure your clothes were tidy."

I grabbed Ben's arm and hauled him out the door. "Get out of my way, you crazy old bat."

She cupped her ear. "What did you say?"

"I said, *you know what they say, for church wear a hat.*"

She smiled and waved, but I heard her tell Janna she feared not only was I aging poorly, I was also unwell.

I was a mess. Even Wally and Willow thought so. They licked unenthusiastically at my legs, then jumped onto my bed and burrowed into the pillows. Too tired to do anything but wash my face, I undressed, tossed my clothes in the hamper and joined the dogs. That night I dreamed I was being chased by a two headed Petal/Fleur and a chenille bathrobe clad crazy woman with no feet. One ran, one streaked through the air like a motorized ghost.

CHAPTER 20

▼

The next morning I assessed the damage. My legs had scrapes and cuts but seemed to work. There were no visible bruises on my neck, making me wonder if I'd imagined the incident at the lagoon. My skirt had a huge grass stain on the back and a series of small holes on the hem. I threw it in the trash. Likewise my new sandals, which now sported a broken strap and heel.

I wet a tissue and dabbed at spots on my beaded necklace. I'd only been immersed up to my waist in the water, but my shirt, necklace and bracelet had been splashed with muck. The bracelet cleaned up nicely. The necklace, however, seemed to get smaller the more I rubbed. I removed the tissue and looked carefully at the beads in my hand. They were soft and sticky. Thinking I'd used too much soap, I held a section of the necklace under the faucet to rinse it.

Something clinked into the porcelain sink and washed down the drain. Two beads had disappeared. I quickly put the stopper in the drain and examined my necklace. Three more beads disintegrated in my hand. I had some kind of pasty substance on my fingers—and to my utter astonishment—three diamonds in the sink. They were partially covered in the white goo, but there was no mistake. The florescent light in the bathroom picked up the cut facets of the gems, making them blink like strobes of light in my washbasin.

- 137 -

Hello? Convinced I'd hit my head in the lagoon and was now experiencing some sort of visual disturbance, I contemplated lying down until it passed. Instead, I went to the kitchen, poured a cup of coffee, ate three doughnuts and practiced deep breathing. Feeling calmer and fatter, I returned to the sink. The diamonds were still there. This time I carefully washed them until there was no white stuff left and put them on a clean washcloth to dry.

Unwilling to trust the drain to remain closed—after all, I had already lost two diamonds—I emptied the dogs' water bowl in the toilet, washed it out and filled it with clean water. Then I counted the pearl-like beads. There were forty five. Next—my heart tap dancing in my chest—I submerged the necklace. And waited. Within minutes the coating dissolved.

I raced into the kitchen, scattered pots and pans all over the floor until I found the strainer and tore back to the bathroom. Half an hour later I sat in a chair at the kitchen table drinking a glass of wine. There were forty five immaculate, sparkling diamonds in the strainer in front of me.

I couldn't wait to call Ben. I reached him on his cell phone just as he was pulling onto I 95 on his way to Columbia. His voice was incredulous. "You found WHAT in a necklace? There's so much static, I can hardly understand you."

"You heard me right," I screamed. "I found diamonds—lots of them—and they look very expensive. They were hidden in the beads. Just imagine! I've been running around with a fortune hanging on my neck. Where do you think they came from? I wish you were here. I don't know what to do."

I listened for his response. When none came, I said, "Ben, are you there? I'm babbling, and you're not saying anything."

"That's because I'm worried. I'm turning around and coming home. In the meantime, put those diamonds in a safe place. You're sure they're diamonds. They couldn't be some sort of cubic zirconium?"

"How would I know that?" I yelled. "They look like diamonds. If you wish, I can scrape one against a window and see if it cuts glass."

"Sit tight. I'll be there soon. Don't do anything stupid."

"Everyone has to stop telling me that. Hurry home. I'm about to explode."

As soon as he hung up, I hunted for a hiding place. I let the gems run through my fingers as I dumped them into a plastic bag and put it in the freezer. Twenty minutes later I took the bag out. The first place a crook would look for "ice" would be the freezer. There had to be a better place. My eyes fell on a carved, wooden pelican I'd bought when Peter and I went to Costa Rica many years ago. It had many little secret drawers and compartments. I carefully placed several diamonds in the beak and divided the rest into the little drawers. Then I boldly replaced it on the mantle. The diamonds were hidden in plain sight, but no one would bother with a wooden pelican. Or at least I hoped not.

After that I couldn't sit still. I was afraid to leave the house for fear someone would break in and discover my hiding place, and I was too full of adrenalin to accomplish anything productive. So I played with the diamonds. I spilled them out onto a velvet cloth I found in my silverware drawer and arranged them in different formations.

At 12:05 when Ben arrived I had just formed the words *All For Me.* "I'm rich," I yelled as I opened the front door He brushed past the dogs and me as he burst into the living room.

"I bought a jeweler's loup. Thought it might help us."

Wally pawed Ben's leg, hoping for his usual pat on the head. When this elicited no response, he jumped up on Ben. Ben absentmindedly pushed him away. I watched my puppy casually lift his leg against the cuff of clean khaki pants and release a tiny stream—not enough to soak the fabric but sufficient to show he was miffed. Ben didn't notice.

"Where are they? I hope you've put them in a safe place. I've been thinking about this, and I find the possibility that they could be genuine gems extremely remote."

"Now you are babbling. Come with me." I led him into the kitchen and showed him my stash. "What do you think about that?"

"*All For Me?*" You can't keep these, Maggie. They obviously belong to someone."

"Possession is nine tenths of the law. Don't get so close. You might breathe on them, and I have them all nicely polished."

"Do you realize you have sort of a maniacal gleam in your eye. Let me repeat, these are not yours."

"Back away from the table, Sport. Momma's getting mad."

"Listen to yourself. You're crazy. At least let me examine one under the loup."

"What will that prove? Do you know how to recognize a genuine diamond?"

He looked offended. "Maggie, I'll have you know that during my stint with the New York Times, I spent many weeks researching a variety of subjects. Now, in diamonds, you have to have the 4 Cs—carat weight, cut, color and clarity."

"I know all that," I told him. "What I don't know is how to recognize a good color from a bad. Do you?"

He pulled the loup out of his pocket and put it to his eye. "Not really. With your permission I am going to check for occlusions. May I?"

What the heck. I figured he didn't know any more than I did. He just sounded better. But it couldn't hurt for him to have a look. He picked up one of the diamonds and scrutinized it closely. Several seconds passed without a sound in the kitchen. Finally he put the loup away and rubbed his eye. "I don't see any occlusions. This looks flawless. That means we either have a perfect piece of cubic zirconium or we have a perfect diamond." He looked at the array of gems spread on the cloth. "And that would mean the rest of these are either fake—or amazingly genuine. I have to sit down."

"What do you think we should do," I asked excitedly. "Shall we take them to a jeweler and have them appraised?"

"Maggie, Maggie." He patted me on the head. "It's a good thing you have me around. We can't scoop up the gems, put them in a bag, march off to a jeweler and say, 'take a look at these, will you, and let us know if they're real.' That would prompt all kinds of unpleasant questions. Let me think a minute and then I'll tell you what we should do."

I waited. He fondled Wally's ears. Sniffing intently, Willow circled Ben's pant leg, apparently unable to believe her nose.

"What we'll do is this. We'll take one diamond to a jeweler in Beaufort. We'll say I bought it at an estate sale and want to have it set. I estimate the weight of each stone to be approximately a carat. The jeweler will examine it and either tell me I have a lovely diamond or suggest I have it set in sterling silver because it's a fake. What do you think of that? We'll pretend we're buying an engagement ring."

"Works for me," I said casually. "One thing though—until someone officially tells me differently, these rocks are mine. I will be happy to lend one for authentication purposes, but I want it back."

"Fine with me. We won't actually go through with having it set. We'll find out if it's real and what it's worth and then say we've changed our minds."

"That's a plan, Stan. When do you want to go?"

"No time like the present. Unless you have something else to do."

I put the leashes on Wally and Willow and led them to the door for a short walk. "Nothing I can't cancel," I called. I could clean out the refrigerator later.

Half an hour later I had changed into a short, apple green linen dress suitable for ring shopping and we were on our way. Ben put the top down on his snazzy Indigo Ink Pearl Lexus sport coupe and let her rip down Hwy 278. "You know," he said over the roar of the wind, "these diamonds, if they're real, have to be the reason folks have been stalking you. Someone wants them back."

My hands flew to my throat. "I took it to Morocco. And last night at the party—I didn't imagine someone grabbed at my neck. A person was trying to retrieve the necklace. I was wearing it last night."

"Which means a guest at the party is involved."

"Not necessarily. He could have entered the grounds without being invited. I was at the back of the house all by myself."

"This isn't good, Maggie," Ben said as he turned onto Hwy 170. "After we talk to the jeweler, we have to talk to the sheriff."

I pretended I didn't hear him. "I've been thinking. I got my necklace from Cotton at Fashion Court. She said she'd found the box with the beads at the back door and didn't know where it came from. As I recall there were several strands. She was going to put some on display until I advised her not to. When I asked her about them, she said a man came to the shop and told her they had been left by mistake. She says she gave them back."

"Do you suppose she knew what was in the beads?" Ben asked.

I considered this question. "She'd have to wet them to discover the coating dissolved in water. What reason would she have had to do that?"

"But let's suppose she did," Ben insisted, "and realized she had a fortune in her hands. Would she have given them back? She could be lying to you."

This was true. "Maybe we should be talking to Cotton instead of racing to the jeweler. If she kept them, she could be in danger. I have only one necklace but there must have been at least twenty in the box."

"First things first. We chat with Cotton after we know if the gems are genuine."

We found a parking space on Bay Street. While Ben put quarters in the meter, I broke two teeth on my comb trying to detangle my hair. I gave up and joined him on the sidewalk. "Do you have the diamond?" he asked.

"Sure do. It's in a ring box wrapped in tissue in this jewelry pouch."

"Good job," he said admiringly. "We can't be too careful."

"I also have these." I showed him another black velvet pouch. "I couldn't leave them at home. Too risky."

Ben's face turned an unattractive shade of red. "Do you mean to tell me you have ALL the stones with you? They are in that thing you are waving in my face?"

I nodded. "Like you said, we can't be too careful."

"But, Maggie, what happens if we have an accident and you get thrown out of the car and the diamonds scatter everywhere?" he sputtered.

"Is that what you worry about? Let me remind you, they are my diamonds. Therefore, if I scatter, so do they. By the way, it's nice to know I would come in second to a handful of stones."

"That's not what I meant," he protested.

"Hah!" I flounced. "That's exactly what you meant.

The atmosphere between us was decidedly chilly as I pushed open the door and stepped into the cool interior. A pleasant man with a round face, balding head and wire rimmed glasses looked up from his desk at the back of the room. "Good afternoon, folks. What can I do for you today?"

"I'm interested in having a diamond set," Ben said, taking the pouch out of my hand. "I bought this stone at an estate sale, thinking it would make a wonderful ring for a special person." He put his arm around my waist and tried to pull me towards him. I stretched my lips across my teeth in a semblance of a smile that must have frightened the jeweler because he said, "Is there something I can do for you, Miss? Do you need a glass of water?"

Ben nudged me none too gently in the ribs. I responded by tromping on his toe. While we behaved like children, the jeweler examined the stone. Suddenly Ben and I became quite still. We forgot to breathe as we waited for the verdict.

"Well, folks. You have quite a stone here. Mind telling me where you got it?

"It was in Pennsylvania," Ben lied. "My Aunt Talia's best friend lived in one of those huge houses that no one can afford to keep up anymore. When she died, all her possessions were sold at auction."

"I see. When was this? Do you happen to remember?"

Ben rubbed his forehead and closed his eyes, indicating he was thinking. "It has to have been four or five years ago. Let's see. Aunt Talia's been dead for three years and the auction was at least a year before that."

This explanation seemed to satisfy the jeweler. "It's a mighty fine diamond. I'd say it has no occlusions, is about one carat, E color. It's worth between $11,000 and $12,000. What kind of setting were you thinking of?"

"Whoopee!" I yelled. "Smoke me some oysters and fry me some cod. Mama is going to be richer than God."

"I beg your pardon."

Ben slapped his hand over my mouth before I could utter a second stanza. "You'll have to excuse my friend. Sometimes she has an uncontrollable urge to blurt out nonsense." He lowered his voice and leaned over the counter. "It's a condition that requires medication."

"Give me your pocket calculator," I demanded.

"Not now, Maggie." Ben smiled weakly. "You can wait until we get home." He took one look at my face and handed over the requested item. While he and the jeweler chatted about precious metals and settings, I figured out how much the diamonds were worth. Forty eight diamonds at—let's say $12,000—apiece. That came to $576,000. Was that right? I calculated again. Yep. I had over half a million dollars of diamonds in a pouch in my pocket.

"Oh, Benny?" I said sweetly.

He looked at me warily. "What?"

"That's okay if you keep the thing I told you to return. You just go right ahead," I said magnanimously. After all, if I could wash two diamonds down the drain, I could give one to good old Ben. However, I vowed to take the sink apart as soon as I returned home.

"I think," the jeweler began, eyeing my finger, "yellow gold should be the metal we use. I'd like to see three channel set diamonds on either side of the center stone. Unless you folks have other ideas or would prefer platinum. What size ring do you wear," he asked me.

"Don't you have something generic, like one size that will accommodate several people?

"That's not the way we usually sell rings. Oh dear, have I made a mistake thinking the ring is for you?"

"Of course not," Ben said briskly. "Step up, darling, and tell the man what you want. Remember what we said we were going to do."

He meant, of course, that we were going to cancel the order. For some reason, which I honestly couldn't understand, I felt extremely upset. "I like the channel setting idea," I said with tears in my eyes. "That would be just fine."

The jeweler beamed. "I'll need your ring size." I defiantly stuck out my digit and allowed him to measure it. "Size 8. You have chubby little fingers."

Wonderful. Now I had to worry about fat hands.

"It will take two or three weeks to find suitable diamonds for the channel settings. I don't keep such stones here in the shop."

"I understand completely," Ben said, pocketing the velvet pouch. "I'll give you a down payment and bring the diamond back when you're ready to set it. I'd feel better keeping it in the safe deposit box."

The jeweler nodded his head. "Very wise."

While they completed their sham transaction, I wandered out to the car and wiped my eyes with a tissue. I certainly didn't want Ben to know I'd been crying about something so stupid. I needed a vacation. Or more sleep. Or a gun to shoot someone.

CHAPTER 21

▼

That night I made a new necklace. I had a plan. I would set myself up as a decoy. Since I didn't think the crooks would come after me for my nubile body, I had to have something for them to steal. As luck would have it, I found an *ersatz* string of pearls in my jewelry box. It was one of those "free, expensive gifts" you get for ordering a subscription to a magazine. I'd meant to throw it away, but innate thriftiness prevented me from actually tossing it in the trash. The plastic pearls were nearly the same size as the ones on my diamond necklace.

I thinned a mixture of white and blue acrylic paint with water until it was the consistency of cream. Then I rubbed the fake pearls with sandpaper to make them rough enough to accept color. Next, I dunked the beads in the paint and swirled them around until they were completely coated. Satisfied with the color, I put them on a paper towel to dry.

While I waited, I poured a glass of wine and thought about Petal/Fleur and her connection to Peter. Would my ex-husband stoop to stealing? In my heart, I didn't believe so, but what was he doing with Petal/Fleur? The answer had something to do with the diamonds. Every time I thought about them, my eyes shifted uneasily to the pelican on the mantel. I couldn't keep the stones with me and I didn't have a safe deposit box. The pelican seemed to be the best solution.

Linda S. Clayton   147

Wally pawed my leg for attention. When I tried to put his leash on him so we could go for a walk, he ran into the hall, barking loudly. This upset Willow, who was sleeping next to me. She jumped off the couch and growled at him. Wally does not recognize rejection. He danced on his hind legs, ecstatic to have our attention. I soon found out why. While I was busy with the beads, Wally had amused himself by dragging toilet paper from the powder room, through the living room and dining room into the front hall and sunroom. In other words, he had teepeed the house.

I didn't have time to worry about that, however. I had to finish my necklace. I selected three paintbrushes with very fine tips and mixed up several pastel shades of colors. Sitting at the kitchen table, I painted flowers and leaves in delicate shades of pinks and greens on the dry beads. It was tedious work and took longer than I'd anticipated, but in the end, the result was acceptable. I'd be able to fool the crooks.

Somewhere close to morning, I dreamed a baby sat on the couch in my sunroom playing with a bag of colorful diamonds. He fed some to Wally, who swallowed them instantly. When I tried to take the stones away, the child shot me in the shoulder with a gun he retrieved from his diaper. I woke up in a cold sweat, wondering if I should consult Dr. Fisher myself.

*   *   *   *

"It's very simple," I said to Lucy as we walked through the Mall at Shelter Cove. "Unknown folks—although I'll bet Peter's fiancée is involved—want to steal my necklace. I'm going to let them. In other words, I'll be the bait. When the perps attempt to take the beads, either you or Ben swoops in and captures them. Then we turn the crooks over to the sheriff."

"The perps? What have you been reading? And how do you propose to set yourself up as bait when you no longer possess the necklace? Also, does this mean I have to follow you around waiting for someone to accost you? I have things to do, Maggie. This is an insane plan, and I'll bet you haven't run it by Ben."

"I wish I had a better suggestion. But how else are we going to smoke these people out? We don't know where Peter's boat is—or Peter, for that matter—and we have no idea where Petal/Fleur and her friend are hiding. We have to get them to show their hand."

I stopped at a shoe store and looked in the window. "That reminds me, I need new sandals. I wrecked my white ones at Janna's party."

Lucy wasn't interested in shoes. "Even if I agreed to go along with your scheme, how are you going to get another necklace? You said Cotton returned the box to the owner."

"Observe," I said smugly, as I removed my sweater and showed her the necklace. "I made it last night. No one will be able to tell the difference."

We moved past the shops and into the food court in the center of the mall. I stepped out of the way as a young couple with a baby stroller bore down on us from the opposite direction. The wheel of the stroller skimmed my ankle as the woman shoved me.

"Really," Lucy said indignantly. "They had the entire center of the mall. You'd think they could have avoided hitting you."

I rubbed my ankle, glancing at the retreating backs of the couple. There was something familiar about the woman, who was now almost running towards Belks. "Jumping toads and heavy metal," I yelled. "That sprinting woman is the lovely Petal."

Lucy, who was used to my poetic outbursts, said, "Huh?"

"Right there," I yelled over my shoulder. "She was after the necklace. These people are relentless. Come on."

I was proud of my friend. She hiked her lavender broomstick skirt around her hips and, knees high, took up the chase. Several men, unable to believe they were seeing a tall, sturdy woman with flaming red hair and scarlet lace panties streaking through the mall, joined in. They veered off when Lucy pulled a nightstick out of her black boots and waved it menacingly.

Linda S. Clayton   149

"You amaze me," I yelled.

"Jolly good," she called.

Our quarry charged through the Better Women's clothes section and tore out the door into the parking lot. A customer headed to the dressing room with an armful of clothes blocked our path, making us stop. Lucy assisted the woman by grabbing the pile of clothes and heaving the garments into the dressing room.

By now we had attracted the attention of the department store security. An armed guard strode down the aisles towards us.

"Start running, Lucy. Petal is probably heading for a car. Oh, and you might want to pull your skirt down once we hit the outdoors. Wouldn't want you to cause a traffic accident."

The bright sun blinded us as we burst out the door. To our right and several rows down, the fleeing woman jumped into a brown Saturn. At that moment a Ford Expedition backed slowly out of a space in front of the vehicle, cutting off its exit. We reached Lucy's Porsche Carrera before the Saturn could get away. My feet weren't totally inside the car when my friend wheeled out of the lot towards Petal/Fleur.

The chase was on.

"She won't turn left," I screamed. "To do that she would have to wait at the light. She'll turn right towards Sea Pines."

"And the Cross Island Expressway," Lucy reminded me. "We won't catch her then."

"I don't know why not. The speed limit is a very firm 55mph. And you know what happens if you drive too fast on Palmetto Bay Road. The police are waiting for you."

Lucy looked disgusted. "It is fairly obvious you have never been a crook. People who break the law don't care about speed limits."

"You mean she'll speed on Palmetto Bay Road?" No one ever did that.

"Fasten your seat belt. I see her up ahead."

Unfortunately, Hwy 278 was full of cars at this time of day. A mini van with New Hampshire plates crawled along the left lane at a sedate 30 mph, forcing all traffic to pass on the right. "It doesn't look like she's going to the Cross Island," I said. "She doesn't have her turn signal on."

At that moment the Saturn turned right at the Sea Pines traffic circle and headed onto Palmetto Bay Road. It zoomed down the left lane, leaving us far behind. "Our only hope is the police pull her over," I said as Lucy accelerated. I grabbed the armrest and held on. "What are you doing? You're going too fast."

"Do you want to end this or not? Shall we get her, or do you want to give up?"

"When you put it like that—let's see what this baby can do. Wow wee!" After all, I wasn't the one who would get the speeding ticket.

"You don't get out much, do you?" I heard Lucy say. I didn't reply. I was too busy watching the Saturn ahead of us.

Petal/Fleur flew past the Gumtree Road exit at 80 mph. We were right behind her. "She's going to have to slow down on Hwy 278," I said. "There will be too much traffic for her to drive that fast."

I was wrong—not about the traffic—there was plenty of that. I was wrong about Petal/Fleur slowing down. Undeterred by two solid lanes of cars, she simply pulled to the right and raced down the bicycle path. Lucy applied the brakes. "I can't do that. I'm afraid I'll hit someone."

"No, you won't," I yelled. "They'll get out of the way. We have Petal/Fleur running interference."

"This probably will attract the attention of the police," Lucy murmured as she drove onto the path in pursuit of the Saturn. To my utter astonishment, several cars behind us followed.

"They're not allowed to do that," I said.

"This could be good," Lucy replied. "Now we're in the middle. If the police stop the other cars, we'll be able to get away."

One thing was certain; they sure weren't going to stop Petal/Fleur. The distance between us was growing greater. "You've got to catch her," I yelled. "She's getting away."

Spying a gap in the traffic on Hwy 278, Lucy pulled into the right lane and stepped on the gas. When the Porsche drew even with the Saturn, I rolled down my window and—in the best tradition of law officers everywhere—yelled, "Pull over. I'm making a citizen's arrest."

Petal/Fleur stuck her middle finger in the air.

"That was quite impressive, Maggie. Did you really believe she would stop?"

I leaned out and waved my hands. "Rude gestures won't get you anywhere, missy. Pull that vehicle off the road." I held my cell phone—which was not turned on—to my ear. "I'm calling the police as I speak."

Both cars sped down the highway, but at least one of them was in an actual traffic lane.

"She doesn't seem to be listening to me," I said. "Can't you do something?"

"If you mean ram her ugly Saturn with my beautiful Porsche, the answer is no."

This time I leaned out the window so far, I was afraid I'd lose my balance. "Now see here, Petal/Fleur or whatever your name is, I have had about enough," I shouted. "Stop this instant."

In reply, a bullet whizzed past my shoulder and landed with a thunk in the red metal of Lucy's car. I threw myself onto the seat before she could get off another shot. "You'd better duck, Lucy," I said. "She has a gun."

I peeked between my fingers at my friend. Lucy clutched the steering wheel with both hands, her eyes blazing with fury. "I'll teach that little whore to shoot holes in my car." To me she said, "Either sit up or get on the floor. Your butt is bouncing against the gear shift."

I opted for sitting. The floor was too cramped for human occupancy.

"Open the glove compartment, Maggie. I think I put a gun in there."

"Excuse me? You want me to pick up a weapon?"

"You don't have to if you don't want to. The next time our friend over there shoots at us, you can roll down the window and politely ask her to stop."

I opened the glove compartment and extracted a tiny gun with a white, mother-of-pearl handle. "What should I do with this?"

"Think of something. And do it fast. I'm running into another traffic jam."

Quaking in my tennis shoes, I turned towards the Saturn and pointed the gun at the driver. "Do you see this," I yelled in a high-pitched, scrawny voice. "Stop."

Petal/Fleur reacted quickly. She suddenly yanked the steering wheel violently to the right and, barely keeping control of the vehicle, careened down Squire Pope Road. Unable to make the turn, we lost her. Lucy slowed the Porsche to 45 mph and mopped her sweaty face with a silk hankie. "There's no point going back. She can turn into Hilton Head Plantation or park anywhere on Main Street and get away."

I shoved the gun back into its hiding place. "I'm glad I didn't have to shoot her. I would have, though. She needs to be taught a lesson."

"You can shoot her the next time you meet, but not with that gun. It isn't loaded."

"You mean to tell me I faced an armed opponent without any means of defense? We could have been killed. What if she'd decided to pop off a few shots at us instead of turning off the highway?"

"But she didn't. I told you before, I don't like loaded weapons."

A loud siren interrupted her words. Behind us, officers in a police car used a bullhorn to urge several cars on the bike path to stop immediately. "Humph," Lucy sniffed. "Some folks have no regard for traffic rules. It's no wonder driving has become such a dangerous activity. So many crazies on the road."

I looked at her to see if she was laughing. She wasn't.

CHAPTER 22

▼

The next morning Janna called before I finished my first cup of coffee. "I love the glasses with the magnolias, Maggie. Do you think you could do three dozen more?"

"You mean three dozen more than the order you just gave me?" What was Janna doing? Tossing the stemware on the floor instead of washing it?

"Yes, please, if you don't mind. Cindy Burkett wants some, too. I told her to give you a call."

Good news! If I ever got this mess with Peter and the diamonds straightened out, I intended to work like a demon.

"A thought just occurred to me," she said. "I'm having a few of the girls to the boat on Wednesday for lunch. Cindy will be there. If you could come, you could talk to her then. I know she'd appreciate it."

Yuk. I hated doing lunch and I hated a gaggle of women—but business is business. "I'd love to come, Janna."

"Super. The boat is in Harbour Town. You won't have any trouble finding her."

That's because it was the biggest yacht in the marina. Everyone on the island knew who owned the *Lazy Lady*. I hung up, regretting I'd accepted the invitation. But it could work out nicely. I'd drum up more commissions, and I'd wear my necklace. You never knew what kind of scum you would find until you dredged for it.

*　　　*　　　*　　　*

"Tell me again what we're doing?" Ben strode through the mall beside me, his long legs setting the pace.

"We're trolling for crooks. They were here yesterday so if they're following me, they may come back today. That's what you're here for. When they try to snatch my necklace, you grab them." My creation looked spectacular. I deliberately wore a scooped neck, blue top, which set off the painted beads nicely.

Ben stopped. "I'm not doing this, Maggie. Frankly, I'm more than a little worried about you. I have no intention of grabbing anyone, and I'm not going to assist you with any of your crazy schemes. If that's why you wanted me to come with you, I'm going home."

"You know, Ben, I'm tired of your preaching. You're beginning to annoy me."

"I've noticed that. We haven't been getting along very well, have we?"

"What's that supposed to mean?" I felt blood surge to my face.

"It means maybe we should take a little vacation from each other. You're too consumed with your ex-husband to think about anyone else."

This couldn't be happening. Ben wanted to break up with me. And in the mall, of all places—although the more I thought about it, the shopping center was a perfect place. I couldn't throw a hissy fit with so many people around. Yes, I could. Much to my horror, tears welled up in my eyes and spilled down my face.

"You're horrible," I shouted. "You haven't cared anything about Peter from the beginning, have you. What's your motive for hanging around with me? Are you going to steal the diamonds?"

Several people stopped to stare, shake their heads and murmur to each other in hushed tones as they hurried past.

"You are completely unbalanced," he said. "And you are absolutely right—I don't give a damn about your ex-husband. I was trying to help you, but you are way too self-absorbed to recognize that."

"I certainly am not. I'm putting myself out there as a decoy to attract the crooks so we can end this mess and get on with our lives."

He guffawed. He also looked totally disgusted. "Don't give me that crap. Normal folks would have called the police a long time ago. You enjoy this unbalanced behavior. It gives you some kind of thrill. But I'm done. You can run around the island behaving like an escapee from a mental institution, but you can do it without me. I'm through."

"You already mentioned that," I said defiantly. "No need to be redundant."

"There's also no need to be a smart ass. You just can't admit you've gone overboard. I pity you, Maggie." He turned and walked away. I watched all the way to the exit, not believing he would actually leave me in the mall. How did he think I was going to get home?

*   *   *   *

I spent the rest of the afternoon lying on the couch in my sunroom. For some reason my stomach refused to accept food. I sipped beef broth and nibbled on toast, waiting for whatever virus had invaded my intestines to leave. The next day I still felt terrible. I wandered around the house in my terry cloth robe eating chocolate ice cream with butterscotch and hot fudge sauce. Both dogs had brown snouts from licking my empty dishes. At six o'clock I didn't feel any better, but I couldn't neglect my Decoy Plan any longer.

I'd made a chart with possible locations of perps and taped it to the refrigerator. The trip to the mall had turned out badly. I hadn't strolled leisurely as I'd intended. After Ben left, I called a taxi and went home. Tonight I planned to visit two restaurants and walk through Harbour

Town. I'd also planned to have Ben accompany me, but since that was no longer possible, I'd have to do it alone.

He'll be back, I told myself as I dressed in a DNKY red and black skirt and black top. The skirt felt a little tight but I convinced myself I looked alluring. When I looked in the mirror, I realized the beaded necklace didn't match my skirt. I changed to white Capri pants and a yellow top.

Once in my car, I decided to visit Harbour Town while it was light enough for folks to see my necklace. Feeling extremely self-conscious, I parked the car in the lot and crossed the oyster shell path to the shops.

The joint was jumping. A guitar player singing old Willy Nelson songs vied with a steel band for an audience. The aroma of grilled hamburger and French fries hung in the air. A loudspeaker at the Crazy Crab announced, "Branson, party of five, your table is ready." People milled about, laughing and talking and enjoying the summer evening.

This was perfect. I stuck out my chest and walked through the crowd, watching for anyone who made eye contact. Several men showed interest, but when I accidentally caught my reflection in a shop window, I understood why. I had my upper body thrust so far forward, I looked like a drum major leading a band.

I assumed a more normal posture and made the circle past the shops and the lighthouse, around to the long pier and back to the harbor. No one paid any attention to me. Not even in the bar of the Crazy Crab, where I sipped half a glass of chardonnay and checked the crowd. When a hand reached out to touch my necklace, my heart began to beat wildly, but it was only a tourist from Ohio. Beer in hand, the lady rolled the beads through her fingers. "Mighty pretty. Where do you buy something like that?"

"I don't know," I told her.

The woman turned to her husband and said, "Honey, give her some money. Five bucks should do it. These locals are happy for anything." She emptied her glass and motioned for another.

"Excuse me," I said. "In case you hadn't noticed, I'm right here, so I can hear what you're saying. And these aren't for sale. And the locals are not happy for anything.

It may have escaped your attention, but this is a premier resort community. We do not depend on the charity of tourists from the Midwest."

"Well," she huffed. "No need to be insulting. "Come on, Fred, I'm not staying where we're not welcome."

"You do that," I said to her retreating back. Lately I'd been chasing a lot of people away.

*   *   *   *

My next stop was Stripes. The restaurant was full. I took a seat at the bar and ordered another glass of chardonnay.

"I'm surprised to see you here tonight," Debbie said as she gave me a hug.

"I'm doing some evening investigating, so I thought I'd drop in for some liquid refreshment."

"Well, good. Drink up."

Debbie seemed nervous—quite different from her usual cheerful, relaxed self.

"Is something wrong? Do you need this bar stool?" I joked.

"Actually, I do. Would you mind finishing your wine in the courtyard? Or better yet, I'll give you a plastic cup and you can take it home with you."

"Excuse me? You're kidding, aren't you?"

She wasn't. She had already moved behind the bar to search for a plastic container.

I leaned over the counter and tapped her on the back of her ruby red top. "What's going on? Since when can't I buy a glass of wine? What's the matter with you?"

Debbie looked positively miserable. "I don't want you to get hurt, Maggie. He is the scum of the earth and you deserve better."

"Excuse me?"

She pointed to a table in the Open Kitchen Room. "Maybe it's better you see for yourself. I tried to get him to go to another restaurant, but he insisted they wanted to eat here."

"Say again?" I still didn't get it. But when I followed her finger, I did. I suddenly felt so ill I thought I was going to throw up.

Ben, looking smashing in a white shirt and navy sport coat, raised his glass to the person with him. Cynthia Loveday held her glass in her right hand. Her left possessively covered Ben's hand on the table. She wore a strapless, totally inappropriate, silver dress that barely contained two melon-sized breasts. Diamond earrings the size of Christmas tree ornaments hung from each ear.

"I'm going to be sick."

Debbie put her arm around my shoulder. "You poor thing. What in the world happened? I thought you two would be together forever."

"So did I." Good grief? What made those words fly out of my mouth? The thought never occurred to me.

"And with Cynthia Loveday," Debbie continued. "That woman is awful. But she has a lot of money."

"Ben wouldn't be interested in money."

"Rumor has it, she is so rich she doesn't know exactly how much she has."

"Ben is different. He doesn't care about material things." For heaven's sake, who was I kidding? Of course he did. He was human, wasn't he? My dogs and I couldn't compete with that. "I'm just going to go over there and say hello," I said to Debbie.

"Oh, dear. Do you really think you should?" She looked around at the full restaurant and then back at my face. "Go get him, Maggie. Let me know if you need a butcher knife or something."

"Please," I said as I swept over to Ben's table, "I am not that kind of a person." I didn't need a weapon. I was mad enough to tear him apart with my bare hands. Steve, Stripes marvelous owner/chef, gave me a thumb's up as I passed the open kitchen.

"Cynthia, how marvelous to see you again," I said, ignoring Ben.

His companion stared at me blankly. "Do I know you?"

"Silly. We met at Janna's party. You probably don't remember me because you were swilling martinis." Did I say that out loud? Judging from the look on Ben's face, I guessed I did, but Cynthia didn't seem to notice.

"Nice to see you again." She extended a limp hand. "Where did you say we met?"

I had her number. She one of those people who never listened to what anyone said. She'd nod her head at all the right places and smile brilliantly, but she couldn't tell you the gist of the conversation if her alimony depended on it.

Ben was not pleased to see me. "What are you doing here, Maggie?"

"I'm having dinner," I said gaily. "My escort isn't here yet. You don't have a monopoly on restaurants, you know. I do think you could have waited a decent interval, though. The body isn't cold yet."

"Did someone die?" Cynthia asked.

"Certainly not. No one even came close. It's just an expression. Everyone feels just fine."

"I didn't realize I needed your permission to visit a restaurant. And why should you care what I do? You're obviously busy, too. And preoccupied"

"I certainly am. I hope you don't think I'm moping around the house thinking about you. I think this going our separate way thing is a great idea. I had no idea how much fun I was missing." My stomach began to hurt so badly, I had to force myself to stand up straight.

"I'm beginning to be bored, Ben," Cynthia whined. "Isn't this person waiting for someone?"

"The name is Magnolia Meadows Bloom, lady, and what I'm doing is none of your business. Hope it's worth it, Ben. But I forgot. You won't actually have to talk to each other. I don't think gigolos are required to speak."

Ben rose to his feet and put his hand on my arm. I smelled his after-shave and felt my knees go weak. "That's enough, Maggie. You should go home now. I'll ask Debbie to call you a cab."

I shook him off. "For your information, I am perfectly able to drive. I haven't been drinking. I'm just surprised at you, Ben. I thought you had more integrity. Is she still married, or doesn't that matter."

He reached for my hand. "Touch me again and I swear to heaven, I'll clobber you." This was terrible. Tears that I prayed he wouldn't notice streamed down my cheeks. I felt awful, and the look on Ben's face broke my heart. I turned and ran and didn't stop until I reached my car. Then I put my head on the steering wheel and sobbed my eyes out.

CHAPTER 23

▼

"Watch your step. The deck is a bit slippery. The others are in the stern having mimosas," Janna Maletesta said. I followed a woman in a short pink skirt, green and pink top and sunglasses to the back of the boat.

As I passed the salon of the *Lazy Lady*, Jake Maletesta opened the door and waved to me. "Come on in, Maggie. I want to ask you something."

I entered the plush interior of the yacht, marveling at the mahogany cabinets and bookshelves and the luxurious celery green, silk-covered couches. Jake stood in front of a bar filled with heavy Waterford crystal decanters. "Can I fix you something stronger than a mimosa? I find them insipid, don't you?"

Actually, they made me gag. I hated champagne and wasn't crazy about orange juice. As far as I was concerned, the combination of the two should be avoided at any cost. I also had no intention of drinking alone with Jake.

"What did you want to ask me? I should join the ladies."

His face slid into a lopsided grin—designed, I knew, to utterly charm me. Jake had quite a reputation with women. He liked them— married or not—and made no attempt to hide his infidelities. Janna dismissed reports of his frequent liaisons with a wave of her manicured

- 162 -

hand. "Boys will be boys. Jake knows where his home is. He has his fun, but he always comes back."

"What's the rush?" he asked. "You and I never have a chance to talk."

"Why should we, Jake? We don't exactly run in the same circles."

"That's a shame."

Good grief! "Forgive me for saying this, but you're wasting your time. I hate all men right now."

Jake smiled. "You are a blunt little person. Sorry to disappoint, but I wasn't hitting on you. I simply want to ask you about those things that you paint."

"Which things? There are several."

"Those things my wife likes. I want to buy her some more."

"The other day she placed another order, Jake. She probably has enough."

He shook his head. "She loves that stuff. Her birthday is coming and I wanted to get her a complete set of your hand painted dishes—dinner and salad plates, bowls, glasses—everything."

Perhaps I had been too rude. This order would involve a great deal of money—money I couldn't afford to turn down. "Which pattern did you have in mind, Jake? Janna loves the magnolias."

"I thought I'd get something completely different—a brand new design."

"Well," I said doubtfully, "Janna has already started a pattern, but if that's what you want, it's fine with me." Rule number one—never argue with a customer.

He rubbed his hands together. "Excellent. I can come to your house and you can show me the different possibilities."

"That won't be necessary. I'd be happy to bring my brochure to you."

"Nonsense. Next week sometime would be fine. I'll give you a jingle."

Peachy. I would meet him on my front porch, take the order and send him on his way. Of course, if Ben were there, I wouldn't have to worry. But that wasn't possible.

I took a glass of tepid orange juice from a tray and sauntered up to the pack of women in the stern. As I approached, they stopped talking. In fact, they parted like the Red Sea, leaving me in a space all my own. I smiled tentatively at Murphy Adams, a woman I knew slightly from tennis. "Lovely weather today, isn't it?"

She nodded and looked around for help. Finding none, she stepped closer to me and said, "I want you to know, I'm so sorry. I don't know you very well, but I think it's a shame."

Confused, I stammered, "Has something happened I should know about?"

She gave me a pitying look. "You were brave to come here. Under the circumstances, I wouldn't have been able to."

Barbara Wilkins, who had been standing at the edge of our conversation listening to every word, joined us. "Murphy is right. It's awfully tacky. I'm surprised at Janna—although I understand it's so recent, she probably didn't know."

What in the world were these ladies talking about? "Have you all gone nuts?" I managed to say. "If not, could one of you please explain what has happened. You're beginning to scare me."

Barbara took me by the elbow. "Look over there. She's been telling everyone."

I followed her pointed finger to a group of women gathered at the rail. Cynthia Loveday, dressed in a multi-colored chiffon skirt and white tube top, stood in the center, and judging from the smug look on her face, she was mighty pleased about something.

"She's been telling everyone," Barbara whispered. "Is it really true?"

"Is what true?" I watched Cynthia adjust the clip on her blond ponytail.

"That you and Ben have broken up because of her."

"What!" Truly stunned, I felt my legs sag and I gripped the back of a chair for support.

"She's telling everyone. She says she's going to take him to the Bahamas for a vacation as soon as he can get away." Barbara searched my face. "Are you okay?"

"Absolutely," I snapped. "And this is ridiculous. Ben and I have merely had a small difference of opinion. He certainly didn't leave me for her. He didn't even know the lady—and I use the term loosely—until the other night. I think she's consumed one too many vodka beverages and is suffering from brain damage."

Barbara looked doubtful. "She seems awfully sure of herself. Why would she tell everyone if it's not true?"

"How should I know," I snapped. And how could Ben do this. I'd convinced myself that our separation was temporary. Ben said we should take a vacation from each other. He didn't say *let's break up so I can snare Cynthia Loveday*. There had to be a mistake.

Running true to form, I proceeded to make a big one. With the entire horde of women at my heels, I marched over to the lady in question and said, "I understand you believe you are seeing Ben Jakowski. I wanted to tell you, that is incorrect."

Cynthia's lips curled into an unattractive sneer as her eyes focused on me. "You're that little girl from the restaurant. Why don't you find someone in your own league and leave Ben alone. He's not interested in you." Gold bangles on her wrist clanged as she waved me away. The women next to her giggled behind their hands and said things like, *Oh Cynthia. You're so awful.* I calculated how much effort it would take to heave her overboard.

Just as I was about to discuss her surgically enhanced body, plastic, Barbie doll hair and empty head, I felt a hand on my shoulder. Jake Maletesta hugged me possessively and said, "Hate to interrupt, but I need to steal you, Maggie. There's a call for you in the salon. I think it's that Jakowski fellow. Cynthia, why don't you have another drink.

I'm sure you could use it. Goodbye, ladies. Carry on." He took me by the arm and firmly led me into the yacht. There was silence behind us.

"Is there really a call from Ben?" I asked as he released my arm.

"Nope. But I overheard the conversation and thought you could use rescuing." He shook his head. "That is one vicious woman."

"Thanks for your help, but she doesn't bother me." We both knew that was a lie. "I do think I'll go home now. Will you tell Janna I had a lovely time?"

"Don't worry about Cynthia. She isn't worth it." He opened the door and led me down the steps. "Jakowski must be an idiot to let you go."

"He hasn't let me go," I called from the dock. "Why does everyone keep saying that?"

I looked at Ben's villa. It would be so easy to mosey over there and see if he was home. Maybe even talk to him. But I didn't. I ran to the parking lot, jumped in my car and drove away.

I called Cotton, hoping we could have a chat about the beads, but she didn't answer. In fact, there was a cryptic message on her machine; *I have my hands over my ears. I'm not listening. I'm not listening.* I assumed she and her mother had another disagreement.

Day Two without Ben ended pleasantly. I washed my hair, all my underwear, some old sweaters I found on the top of my closet, and the cushions on the kitchen chairs. I paid all my bills, joined the Book Of The Month Club and ordered a pipe cleaner for clogged drains from the shopping channel. I took the dogs for a walk, watered the geraniums on the front porch and put birdseed in the feeder. At ten o'clock I called it a day. It wasn't until I went into my bedroom that I noticed my necklace was still on my bedside table. Some sleuth I was. I'd forgotten to wear the bait.

The next morning I cleaned the lint trap in the dryer, scrubbed the heart of pine floors with Murphy's Oil Soap and rearranged all the canned goods in my cupboard according to color. I brushed and clipped both dogs and gave them baths with lavender shampoo I'd brought from La Hotel Mamounia in Marrakech. Then I went for a jog. I ran down Governor's Road to Greenwood, turned right on Plantation and followed it across Lighthouse Road. Ben's Lexus was parked in front of Cynthia Loveday's house. I knew it was Cynthia's because I looked up her address in the phone book. As I passed the residence for the forth time, Ben opened the front door and stepped into the bright morning sunshine. I consulted my watch. It was 9:24. He didn't see me. He waved to someone inside and bounded down the stairs.

So…I guess that was that. What possible explanation could he have for visiting at this hour of the morning? Cynthia Loveday didn't strike me as someone who eagerly greeted the light of dawn each day. Therefore, I had to conclude he arrived last night and was now going home—no doubt to get some much needed sleep. I hid behind a tree and pretended to tie my shoelaces as he got in his car and drove away. Oh well. Easy come, easy go. I was glad I hadn't made a commitment to Ben, because if I had, I'd be really upset by now.

CHAPTER 24

▼

I lost my lust for sleuthing. As far as I was concerned, Peter could go to jail and take Ben with him. Men were snakes. I preferred dogs. They were cheerful, grateful and most of all, faithful. You wouldn't catch Wally sniffing around some fancy French poodle when he had Willow at home. Well, maybe you would, but that's only because Willow didn't like a cold nose on her private parts. What I should have said was the dogs were loyal to me. And best of all, they never criticized or told me I was irresponsible or tried to control my life. They simply loved me.

And I loved them. To prove it, I attached their leashes, put them in my car and drove to the Forest Preserve for a walk. Not only would the dogs enjoy a brisk stroll down their favorite paths, but I also hoped the lovely woods and wildlife would have a tranquilizing effect on me. I was fresh out of Xanax.

I left the car in the Greenwood Drive parking lot and took the path along the Old Rice Dike. The branches of live oaks, decorated with leaves and Spanish moss, rose like arms through the water, their roots submerged. We startled an egret sitting on a rock. It soared high above our heads, much to Wally's delight. He bounded around tugging at his leash as he tried to chase the bird.

Deep in thought, I allowed the dogs to proceed at their own pace, sniffing the bushes and trees. As I walked, I concocted a plan. I needed to get out of town. I would use some of the diamonds to finance some fancy travel. First, I'd take the QM2 to England, spend a week shopping in London, then hop on the Chunnel train to Paris, do more shopping, after which I'd fly to Italy and recuperate on the Amalfi coast. By the time I got back, Peter, Ben and the whole mess would be thing of the past. Or, perhaps I wouldn't return. I'd buy a chalet in Pontresina and an apartment in London and become a decadent jetsetter.

Fortunately, reality intruded. Wally had wrapped his leash around a bush and required untangling. When I looked around, I realized we had walked farther than I intended. Dark clouds blew off the ocean, indicating rain was on the way. Should we retrace our steps or take the more scenic, shorter route through the woods? I opted for the shorter route.

Since I could get lost in a bathroom, I carefully studied the directional signs and chose a path I believed would take us to the car. For a while the dogs and I strolled briskly, enjoying the unfamiliar surroundings. We were alone. The weather had chased other wanderers away. Indeed, the first drops of rain plopped through the canopy of trees onto my head.

When I heard the sound of crunching straw behind me, I figured it was an animal scurrying for shelter. There were plenty of deer and raccoons in the woods. I walked faster, hoping to reach the car before the rain intensified.

There it was again. When we turned right on a trail, the noise behind us followed. *An animal wouldn't do that, would it?* We stopped. The noise stopped. We walked. I heard branches snap. I turned around to see what was behind us. Nothing.

Uneasy, I increased our pace until we were nearly running. Wally protested. He sat down, refusing to go any farther. I listened for more sounds and heard a faint rustling to the left. *Don't be paranoid,* I warned myself. *There is nothing wrong.* "Ha, ha, ha, silly me. I see ghosts in every tree," I sang loudly, feeling foolish. "Come on, Wally. Let's go get a dog biscuit." He flopped down on the ground and put his head between his paws. There was no way I was going to allow a recalcitrant little puppy to slow us down. I picked him up, yanked on Willow's leash and ran.

Behind us branches crashed. *I wasn't imagining it. Someone was chasing us.* I heard the muffled sound of feet running on pine straw as twigs snapped under the person's feet. My heart banged in my chest and the air tore out of my lungs. Running full tilt while dragging one thirty pound English cocker spaniel and carrying another is not the most efficient way to elude a pursuer, but there was no way I was leaving my dogs behind. Pure panic propelled me forward, giving me a strength I didn't know I possessed. I stumbled down the trail clutching my precious cargo and gasping for breath, hoping I'd be able to outrun the danger behind me.

I couldn't. Before I knew what was happening, I fell to my knees on the dirt path. Wally flew out of my arms. I saw a bright light and some vividly colored stars.

And then nothing.

CHAPTER 25

▼

I was on a roller coaster. It plunged and rose, making me feel sick to my stomach. I was also dizzy. *If I could just see where I was I'd feel better. It's so dark.* I wanted to wet my lips but couldn't seem to open my mouth. Panicked, I tried to get to my feet. *Get off the roller coaster. Now.* My feet didn't work. Neither did my hands. Something was holding them down. I opened my eyes.

"You're awake, I see. I'd hoped we could do this while you were— shall we say—asleep. I might have to hit you again."

My eyes wouldn't focus. The roller coaster bounced and I bit my tongue. My fingers felt stiff cord wrapped around my wrists. *Focus. Try to see where you are.* I saw gray clouds. *That can't be right. Why am I bouncing? I can feel tape across my mouth.*

"There's no point in struggling. You're not going anywhere—except down."

I turned my head—which ached unbearably—towards the voice. Petal/Fleur smiled at me as she pointed out the window. "Look down there. The sharks are waiting. Too bad you had to be so nosy."

I was in a plane. I squinted at Petal/Fleur, not believing my eyes. A gun dangled from the forefinger of her left hand. "This is for insurance. I won't need it because you are a pushover. Of course, I could shoot you now and be done with it, but that wouldn't be any fun. I want to enjoy myself." She reached over and ripped the tape off my mouth. "I'd like to hear you whimper. It would make up for all the trouble you've caused."

My lips burned and I longed to rub them. *Think. Try to think. What has happened?* I remembered walking in the woods. "My dogs," I whispered.

"Your dogs are history. They are probably road kill on Greenwood Drive by now. I would think you have more immediate problems than the fate of those pests."

I shook my head, causing the pain in my skull to vibrate like a banjo string. *Don't let her see you're scared.* That was a tall order. I was petrified. I looked out the window of the plane, trying to get my bearings. I saw the Harbour Town lighthouse receding rapidly as Petal/Fleur turned the plane away from the coast and out to sea. There wasn't much I could do to stop her. I was trussed up like a Thanksgiving turkey.

"I suppose, before you are eaten by sharks, you deserve to know how close you came to learning the truth. By the way, let me introduce myself. My name is Ruby Wolochik from Jersey City, New Jersey. Educated at the Sorbonne in Paris. I speak five languages including Moroccan Arabic. And you are welcome to your ex-husband. I had no intention of marrying him and I have to say, you deserve a medal for putting up with him for as long as you did."

"Arrgh!"

"I hear you. He's somewhat dull. And tight with his money." She stuck out her left hand and displayed the ring I'd seen in the magazine picture. "Can you believe I had to supply my own diamond?" She laughed; an unpleasant sound that made me wish I could cover my ears. "He had no idea what we were doing." A shadow flitted across her face. "It's too bad. He was sort of nice in his own boring way."

A cold shiver ran through my body. What did she mean? For sure— something bad had happened to Peter. *Do something. This person is unbalanced.* But what? For the next few minutes she concentrated on gauges on the instrument panel. Satisfied, she leaned back in her seat. "We're on automatic pilot now. I need both hands free to shove you out."

"Why do you want to do that? I didn't do anything to you." *Keep her talking. And think.*

"We don't need anyone interfering. You were becoming an annoyance with all your meddling. You kept getting in our way. You don't have any ideas about the diamonds, do you?"

"What diamonds?" I asked carefully.

"It doesn't matter now so I can tell you. The diamonds in the beads. I know you didn't find them because you've been wearing the necklace. Where is it, by the way?"

"You let me out of this plane and I'll tell you. Let me rephrase that. You let me out on the ground, and I'll give you the necklace."

"No can do. We'll search your house more thoroughly tomorrow when we can take our time. We'll find them," she said smugly.

"Maybe not. Maybe I found them and put them in a safe place. You'll never know where."

She shrugged. "A pity. But not the end of the world. There are others."

"Maybe I gave them to the police."

"And maybe you didn't. I don't think you found them. The necklace was intact the last time I saw it."

At least I'd done a good job of duplicating the beads—not that it mattered now. "You've been following me all over Hilton Head. Was it you who put the spider in my car?" Or grabbed my neck at the party?

"My associates assisted me. We had hoped to frighten you enough to make you want to leave the island."

"It didn't work." I glanced out the window and saw no land. We were over open water. I hoped she wouldn't notice. She did.

"It's party time," she said. "I can't say it's been a pleasure knowing you."

I tried to kick her but only succeeded in nearly upending myself. At least my askew position would make it more difficult for her to dispose of me. She wouldn't be able to simply lean over and push.

Undeterred, she reached across me and opened the door. Hot air raced into the airplane. Powerless to stop her, I braced my feet against the instrument panel, determined to give her as much of a fight as I could. She put her hands on my backside and pushed. I tried to wedge my upper body into the space by the door, but she grabbed my hair and yanked. The next thing I knew my head was dangling two thousand feet above the Atlantic Ocean and the lady from New Jersey was effortlessly trying to get the rest of my body to join it. Below me, angry white caps ripped the water.

I refused to give up. Aside from being the most terrified I'd ever been in my life, I was also extremely angry. People just didn't push innocent folks out of an airplane off the coast of Hilton Head. It wasn't civilized behavior. I heard her grunting, indicating she was having a harder than anticipated time removing me.

One second I felt her strong hands on my body, intent on sending me to a watery grave and the next second her hands suddenly relaxed and dropped away.

"Are you okay? Do you need some help?" a timid voice asked.

"Does it look like I'm okay?" I screamed to the ocean. "A little help down here would be good." *Did I actually hear that or had I started to hallucinate?*

"I'll try, but I may not be strong enough. Your butt is pretty big. Ma always said you should go on a diet."

Cotton!

She pulled on my hips enough to allow my head to zip back into the plane. Cotton sat in the backseat of the aircraft. She held the business end of a hammer in her hand. I could only stare.

"I hit her with this," she said unnecessarily. "I hope I didn't whack her too hard. She looks kind of bad."

"Could you please untie my hands? We can discuss Petal/Fleur later."

"Is that what she's called?" she asked as she worked on the knots. "Such an unusual name. Ma would like that."

As soon as my hands were free, I untied my feet and rubbed the circulation back into my aching limbs. Then I checked on the condition of our pilot. I found a steady pulse. Cotton looked relieved when I told her. "I just meant to tap her a bit to make her let go of you."

"And that you did quite nicely. She's out cold and there is a nice lump forming on the back of her head."

Cotton smiled broadly. "I'm so happy. I sure didn't want to hurt her permanently."

"I wouldn't cheer about anything too soon. You have clonked, as far as I know, the only pilot on this plane. Or do you know how to fly?"

"Me?" She looked startled. "I don't know nothing about flying."

"That leaves us in a bit of a predicament because I don't either— and it doesn't look like our friend here is going to wake up any time soon."

"You mean we have to stay up here forever?" She grabbed my shirt. "I can't do that. I have to get home to Ma."

This was like dealing with a child. She had obviously forgotten that planes are powered by fuel and when fuel runs out, planes fall out of the sky. I scanned the instrument panel for a gauge. There were several dials. The only one I recognized had blue in half of the dial, which I assumed was meant to be sky.

"That there is the attitude indicator," Cotton informed me.

"Excuse me? Do you know what these dials mean? I thought you said you didn't know anything about airplanes."

"I don't. Otis used to take me flying. This is his plane, you know. He used to say, 'As long as that blue color is on the top, we're okay.' He was teaching me the names of things—like this here attitude indicator."

"Would you happen to know how to use the radio? Or do you know where the radio is?"

Cotton looked doubtful. "I don't reckon I do. I don't think Otis ever used it."

We had to do something because time was a wastin'. I sure didn't want us to do that falling out of the sky thing. Which meant one of us was going to have to fly the plane. "Here's what I think we should do, Cotton. We'll use this cord to tie Petal/Fleur wrists and feet together. That way, if she does wake up, she can't harm us. I also think we should save any irrelevant chatter for later when we are both sitting at a bar having multiple drinks. I certainly am interested in hearing how you happened to be hiding in the backseat of a plane that was carrying me to a horrible fate, but now is not the time for explanations. I have to concentrate."

Cotton leaned over the seat and bound our captive's wrists while I attended to her feet. She was still unconscious, which made our job easier. Now I had to figure out how to fly the plane. How hard could this be? I mean, Otis managed to take off and land without catastrophic incident, and he was a nincompoop. I should be able to do this.

I rubbed my sweaty hands together. My heart suddenly began to race as I examined the gauges. We had fuel, but if I read it correctly, not very much.

I fiddled with the dials on a box that resembled a radio in the middle of the instrument panel and was rewarded with lots of static—and a human voice.

"Hello," I screamed. Can anyone hear me? May Day! May Day!"

"I think you have to talk into this," Cotton said, handing me a microphone. "You have to press this little button to talk. And let it out when you want to hear what someone is saying"

I released the button. "Identify yourself, please. What's the nature of your emergency?" The voice was calm and deliberate—as if it weren't dealing with a loony woman flying on autopilot.

"My name is Maggie Bloom and my location is somewhere over the ocean and my problem is that no one knows how to fly this plane."

"Say again?" The voice suddenly sounded interested.

"You heard me," I screeched. "Tell me how to get this thing on the ground, preferably in one piece."

I thought I'd lost the connection because there was an extended silence. Then another voice said, "Maggie, this is Arnie Blake at the airport. You've been patched through to me. First of all, tell me exactly where you are."

I looked out the window. We were flying due east. If I didn't get this plane turned around and headed back to Hilton Head, we'd be in France before anyone could help us. That wasn't entirely accurate. We'd get very wet before we'd have a chance to say *Bonjour*, but I didn't want to think about that.

"We're going to Europe," I said. "We passed South Beach a while ago."

"Use your compass. Can you find it?"

"I think it's that thingy," Cotton offered, pointing to a dial. I quickly read him the numbers.

"That can't be right. That reckoning would put you somewhere over the Red Sea. Try again."

"I don't want to do this," I yelled. "I just want to get down. Can't you get someone to come up and tow us?"

"It doesn't work that way. You have to turn around and fly back to Hilton Head and to be able to do this, you have to turn off the autopilot."

"I don't think so." I looked down at the water. It didn't seem that far away. "I'll just get out now and swim for it."

"Come on, Maggie, don't lose your nerve now. You know you like a challenge," a strong, familiar voice admonished me. In spite of the serious situation, a happy grin spread over my face.

"Ben! Is that you? What are you doing there?"

178   A String Of Perils

"I just got in on US Air from Charlotte. Arnie saw me and filled me in on what was happening. Do as he says, Maggie."

For some reason I felt much better knowing he was on the radio. He didn't know how to fly either, but he was worried about me—not Cynthia Loveday.

"Okay, ready?" Arnie said. "Disengage the autopilot. Then we'll tell you what to do."

This seemed fairly straightforward because there was a red button on the yoke marked *autopilot*. All I had to do was push it. And then what?

I'd watched Otis fly. He used the yoke like a steering wheel and pulled back on it when he wanted to climb. That's what I would do. I'd watch the attitude indicator to make sure we stayed level, and I'd pretend I was driving a car. Piece of cake.

"Look out there, Maggie," Cotton said. "You can see the rain coming down."

Good grief, she was right. A dark gray band of rain spilled out of the clouds into the ocean directly ahead of us. We had to turn around. Right now.

I closed my eyes and pressed the *autopilot* button. The plane lurched immediately to the right. Panicked, I grabbed the yoke and pulled back. Too much. The Cessna climbed until it felt like we were going to tip over and a horn began to squawk. I knew what that meant—we were going to stall. I pushed the throttle forward and the nose shot down, sending the plane far too fast towards the ocean.

"Woweee! Are we going to die?"

I was too busy to answer her. This time I pulled back gently on the yoke and the Cessna wobbled to an upright position. I waited for a horn to clang or squawk, indicating another problem, but the only sound I heard was my own ragged breathing. And Cotton talking to her mother. "Can you see us, Ma. We're up here right close to you.

"Maggie, Maggie, what in the hell are you doing? All I told you to do was disengage the autopilot."

"Sorry about that," I yelled. "It's not as if I'm doing this stuff on purpose."

"Be calm. See the attitude indicator? Try to keep the blue line straight."

"Hey, I just happen to know where that is." I adjusted the yoke slightly and—miracle of miracles—we were flying straight.

"Very good. Now check the fuel gauge. How much fuel do you have left?"

"Stop telling me to check things. I'm busy up here." My fingers were wrapped so tightly around the yoke, I figured I'd never be able to pry them off. But if I made it out of here alive, I'd gladly carry the yoke around with me for the rest of my life. I mean, how inconvenient could that be compared to being dead.

"Ben?" I could hear my voice shake. "I could use a little reassurance right now."

"Not to worry, babe." His voice was low and tender. "I promise you'll be fine. There are some things we have—that is, I wanted to tell you…"

"Maggie, listen to me," Arnie interrupted. "We'll guide you through the landing, but you want to have an airspeed of about 70 knots. Do you know where to find the airspeed indicator?" The radio crackled with static

I wasn't interested in airspeed at the moment. "Let me talk to Ben. Where did he go?" This was absolutely not the time for this conversation, but I had to hear what he was going to say. It was suddenly the most important thing in the world.

"We can talk when you're on the ground," Ben said as his voice faded.

"What? I can't hear you. You're breaking up."

The radio was dead. I yelled into it, I shook it, I pushed buttons and I pleaded, but it was no use. The atmospheric conditions must have knocked out our only means of communication. We were on our own.

"Ma says we had better do something soon. There are big storm clouds ahead."

"I don't need your mother to tell me that," I grumbled. "I can see as well as she can." What was I saying? *Get a grip, Maggie.*

"Ma says this is all your fault. If you didn't have an evil ex-husband, we wouldn't be here and I wouldn't be in danger."

"Tell your mother I'll talk to her later, but now is definitely not a good time." So far, so good. There was one thing I had to find out from Cotton. "How did you happen to be in the back of this plane?" I asked, keeping my eyes glued to the attitude indicator.

"I was looking for something. I told you, me and Otis went flying and I thought maybe I left something of mine in the plane. I was looking around when her—she pointed to Petal/Fleur or Ruby or whatever her name was—and a real good-looking guy brought you to the plane. I hid under a tarp so they wouldn't see me. There was no way I could get off."

"This good-looking guy—was he Peter Bloom?"

"Ma says no."

"What do you say? I'm assuming you saw him."

"I didn't get a real good look, but I don't think it was him. How soon till we are home again? I have to go to the bathroom."

"Too bad, toots. You'll have to suck it up for a little while."

I turned the Cessna gently to the left and tried to guide it back to the island. To my astonishment, I saw the shoreline in the distance. Buoyed by the sight of land, I let out a happy whoop. "Would you look at that! Maybe I'll be able to do this after all." Pointing out the window, I said to Cotton, "I think that is Daufuskie Island. All we have to do is fly down Calibogue Sound, follow Broad Creek for bit, line up over Pineland Station and we'll be on the landing path for the Hilton Head airport."

Cotton looked at me curiously. "How do you know that?"

"The other day I was shopping in Pineland Station. The US Air plane flew very low over my head as it turned onto final approach. That's what we'll do."

"Does this mean you know what you're doing?" she asked timidly.

"Look at it this way. We're still in the air, so I must be doing something right." But I couldn't guarantee how long my luck would last.

My plan sounded good. All I had to do was execute it. I kept my eyes glued to the horizon, trying to recognize familiar landmarks. When a small plane appeared beside me, I assumed someone from the airport had come to guide me back. I stuck my hand out the window and waved, then gave them the old thumb's up.

"We're going home, Cotton. See that plane? All I have to do is follow it."

Cotton frowned. "Why is the pilot wearing a ski mask? Don't you think that would be hot in the summer?"

"Huh?" I looked again. He was, indeed, wearing a black mask that covered his entire face. He was also pointing a gun at us. My newfound flying skills did not include evasive maneuvering, but I gave it my best shot. As we approached the Cross Island Parkway bridge, I banked to the right and lost altitude, hoping the plane would fly over. When I didn't see it ahead of us, I turned in my seat and looked behind. Nothing. Excellent. Whatever I had done seemed to have worked. The plane was nowhere in sight.

"We lost them," I yelled to Cotton. "You can relax now."

Cotton screamed and pointed. As we flew over the highest point, the plane suddenly appeared from under the bridge, roaring up and banking sharply in front of us. I could clearly see the pilot and his pistol. It was unbelievable—like a scene from a James Bond movie. All that was missing was the music. And, of course, James Bond. Right at that minute, I could have used James Bond. Since he wasn't there, I closed my eyes and prayed. When I opened them again, the other plane was heading down—and there was no airport in the area.

"He's going to crash," Cotton yelled.

Water sprayed the plane as it grazed Broad Creek. I figured the pilot meant to do a touch and go so he could fly back and scare me some more, but he dipped too low and now sat with his wheels in the water. I watched as a boat stopped for a look.

"Don't worry, Cotton. That plane is done chasing us. All I have to do now is find the airport."

I flew along the Cross Island Parkway until I saw Pineland Station off to the right. I'd taken enough commercial flights to know that planes circled to get into landing patterns. Therefore, I guided the Cessna into a large arc west of Pineland Station and headed back towards the airport. For orientation, I kept my eyes on the duck pond in the center of the mall.

"How do you know there isn't another plane out there? Maybe US Air is landing now too. We could be squashed like a bug."

"Why don't you ask your mother? I'm sure she'll be able to tell you." I instantly regretted my flip answer to Cotton, but I was too terrified to be polite. I considered it a virtual impossibility that I would be able to put this aircraft on the ground with any part of it intact.

We were too high. I pushed the yoke forward and we plunged towards the earth, but when folks shopping at Pineland Station flattened themselves on the ground, I knew I'd made a mistake. I pulled hard on the yoke, sending us soaring up over the treetops.

"What are you doing? Cotton screamed. "That's not how you land. I want to get off."

I managed to get control of the plane and steer it into another circle. This time I decided to make the descent gradually. I found the lever marked *Throttle* and pulled it out slightly. Our airspeed slowed. *That's better. Now slowly lose altitude.* The only way I knew to do that was to push the nose down, straighten out and repeat the maneuver. "Do you see any dial indicating airspeed?" I asked Cotton.

She was busy talking to her mother. No doubt they were both having a good chat about me. I found the gauge myself. *Airspeed 90 knots.*

Too fast. I throttled back. The plane responded by shuddering. *Too slow. More airspeed.*

The runway was ahead of me, but it looked so little. It would be like threading a needle. *I can't do this. You have to. You can't stay up here forever.*

"I can't land, Cotton. I'm afraid I'll hit the buildings and the trees."

Cotton looked out the window. "But we're there. Look at those people waving. Please, Maggie."

The landing gear! I'd forgotten all about the landing gear. Somewhere I'd seen a lever marked gear. While I fumbled with dials on the instrument panel, the runway vanished behind us.

As I saw it, I had two choices; I could turn around and fly back, hoping I could dodge all the houses and trees between me and another shot at the runway, or—and I favored this option—I could fly out to the ocean and land on the beach. Either way we were going to splat, and sand sounded softer than concrete.

I banked to the left and descended until we were skimming along the water. Fortunately, the tide was out. Ahead of us was a vast expanse of sand. And lots of people. There were kids flying kites and throwing Frisbees and folks sitting in chairs with their toes in the surf and others jogging or exercising dogs.

"I can't land on the beach, either," I told Cotton.

She put her head out the window. "Look, Maggie, the water is so close. I could jump out. Shall I?"

I stuck out my hand. "I think not. That would be extremely dangerous." Even Cotton laughed at that remark.

Where should I land? Think. Somewhere without people or buildings. Eureka! I knew just the place.

"We have been cleared for landing. Please make sure your seatbelt is securely fastened and your seatback is in the upright and locked position. It will be necessary to turn off all electronic equipment at this time."

"Why are you talking like that, Maggie?"

"Fasten your seatbelt and put your head on your knees. We are landing now."

I flew down Calibogue Sound parallel with Harbour Town. Far to right, I could see my house in the distance. I pulled even with Buck Island, banked to the left, came around and began to descend. *Airspeed 90, 85, 80, 70.* I put the landing gear down. I saw a lever marked flaps, but since I had no idea how pulling the lever would affect the airspeed, I decided to ignore the flaps.

The shoreline of Daufuskie Island was ahead of me. And it was empty. No people. Nothing. All I had to do was put this plane down. I was terrified and sweating so badly, water ran down my face and into my eyes, making it hard to see.

We were over the coast and we were low enough, but we were going too fast. Water raced past my eyes as I tried to get the wheels to touch the sand.

"Do something." Cotton screamed as she grabbed my hand. "We're going to go into the ocean."

She was right. We were rapidly running out of beach. I could think of only one thing to do—I turned off the power. For a few seconds we hung silently in the air. Cotton stared at me, her eyes huge and frightened. Then the plane fell like a stone, burying its nose in the sand. I felt the tail of the aircraft flip up as my head banged against the yoke. I tasted blood on my lips. We'd forgotten to secure Petal/Fleur, who careened in her seat like a ping-pong ball. Suddenly there was sand on the windshield. We were upside down.

"Are you okay, Cotton?" Receiving no answer, I got on my knees and looked in the backseat. Cotton, head down, was in deep conversation with her mother. I tapped her on the shoulder. "We have to get out of the plane now. You can chat later." I pushed the door open and crawled out onto the hot sand. For a few minutes I patted the ground rejoicing that all my parts seemed to be working. I'd actually landed a plane. Well, landing might be a bit of an exaggeration. It was fortunate

Otis wouldn't be needing his Cessna any time soon. But I did manage to put it on the ground without killing anyone.

"Let's go, Cotton," I called. "I have to find a phone and call the sheriff."

Cotton scrambled out of the plane. "Ma told me not to go anywhere with you. She said I was very close to being with her while we were up there. I'm not ready to do that yet, Maggie." Was it my imagination, or were her eyeballs spinning in their sockets. "I'm taking off by myself. We've got kin here. They'll take me back home." She started to sprint across the beach.

"Don't do that, Cotton," I yelled. "You should be checked out in case you have an injury."

Too late. She was gone.

I surveyed the wrecked Cessna. Since there wasn't much fuel left, I didn't think there was any danger of fire. Petal/Fleur would be safe enough while I went for help. I started across the dunes in the direction of the Daufuskie Island Resort.

I thought the bump on my head was causing me to hear things when a voice said, "Maggie! Maggie Bloom! Wait a second."

CHAPTER 26

▼

Jake Maletesta ran over the sand, waving a golf club over his head. When he reached me, he sank down on one knee and tried to catch his breath. "Whew! I'm out of shape. I need to work out more. Are you okay? I was playing golf and saw the plane coming in low. I knew somebody was in trouble but never figured it was you."

"Jake, do you have a cell phone? It's too complicated to explain right now, but I have to call the sheriff."

"Already taken care of."

"Huh? Why did you call before you knew what had happened?"

"Maggie," he said as he extended a hand to me, "when you see a plane fly that low over the beach, you can assume the flight is going to end badly. I was afraid it had landed in the water. Where's the pilot, by the way."

"That's the part that's difficult to explain, and I'd just as soon not do it now. But the pilot is okay. You're sure the sheriff is on his way?"

"Positive. Follow me. We'll get you cleaned up and find you a stiff drink. You can rest at the club while I finish my round of golf. Is that blood on your face?"

I licked my mouth. "I bit my tongue during the landing. If you don't mind, I'd just as soon call Joey Archer and ask him to bring the Moondancer over to pick me up." At least I hoped he would.

- 186 -

"You're in luck," he said as we strode along the beach. "The *Lazy Lady* is docked at the Freeport Marina. Tell you what—I don't need to play any more golf. Wasn't having that good a day anyway. Let me collect my gear and we can be on our way. My golf cart is over there." He pointed to the cart path. "Hop in."

What could I do? He was kind to offer me a ride home, and he had already notified the sheriff. However, I still needed to make a call. "Could I use your cell phone? I'm afraid something may have happened to my dogs."

Concern flooded his face. "That's terrible. Of course you can. It's in my golf bag." He rummaged through the pockets of the bag, tossing out towels and golf balls. Finally, he withdrew his phone. "Here you are. I knew it was in there somewhere."

With shaking fingers, I punched Ben's number and waited for an answer. When the machine picked up, I said, "Hi, it's just me wondering if you had Wally and Willow under control. Talk to you soon." I longed to say more, but I didn't want to reveal too much in front of Jake. Next, I tried Lucy. "She is not here, Miz Bloom," Emerald informed me. "I think she went to the airport."

I was stuck with Jake. That wasn't fair to say. He was being extremely solicitous and kind. I'd accept a ride with him, find my dogs—and my heart lurched every time I thought about them—and then locate Ben and Lucy. I was sure by then the sheriff would want to chat with me.

I waited outside while Jake retrieved his things from the locker room of the Daufuskie Island Resort and Breathe Spa. The back of my head ached from the blow I'd received. My lips felt raw and my mind felt like it was about to unravel. Too much stress. Way too much stress. I longed to lie down with my dogs next to me and sleep forever. My dogs. Were Wally and Willow safe? How could they be? They wouldn't know how to get home from the Forest Preserve. Tears sprang to my eyes and rolled down my cheeks.

"There you are," Jake said heartily, ignoring my wet face. "Let's get going. This is my golf cart, so we can take it to the marina."

I sank down beside him and surreptitiously tried to wipe my eyes with the back of my hand. "This is awfully nice of you. I'm sorry your golf game is ruined."

"Don't be silly. I'm always happy to help a lady in distress."

"You've sure got that right. I'm in distress," I bit my lip to stop more tears from spilling.

"Want to talk about it? I'm a good listener."

I shook my head. "I wouldn't know where to begin. All I want to do is go home and make sure my dogs are okay."

He reached across the seat and patted my hand. "Don't worry. I'm sure whatever is bothering you can be fixed. I just want you to know, I'll do anything I can to help you."

I felt like a heel for having misjudged him in the past. He was genuinely a nice guy. So what if he liked the ladies. That wasn't any of my business. I was grateful he was with me now. I inhaled deeply and tried to relax as we bounced down the dirt road. Within minutes we passed the general store and the restaurant and arrived at the marina. The *Lazy Lady* was the only boat at the dock. The tour boat, which brought visitors from Hilton Head to Daufuskie, was not due for another hour.

"Go onboard. I'm going to park the golf cart and I'll be right there," Jake said.

I clambered up the steps and made my way around the deck to the bow of the boat. I looked behind me and saw Jake above me at the helm. Thinking I should attempt to be sociable, I joined him. "Don't you have a captain to drive this thing? It seems awfully big for one person to manage."

He smiled. "I do. But it's a short trip to Daufuskie and she handles extremely well. Just like a willing woman."

I glanced at him quickly. What was that supposed to mean? I couldn't read anything from his face. *Let's not invent trouble,* I chided myself. *It was an innocent remark.*

Linda S. Clayton 189

"You know, Maggie, I could probably help you if you confided in me."

"There's nothing to confide. I've just been having a bit of a problem with Ben. But you already knew about that."

"You and I both know that's not what we're talking about."

"We do?" Suddenly uneasy, I looked towards Harbour Town, trying to calculate how much further we had to go. Was I imagining it, or had we veered slightly to the left.

"Are you sure we're headed to Harbour Town? Maybe you do need that captain, after all," I said, trying to make a joke.

"I know where I'm going. Why don't you sit down."

"We are going home aren't we? Because I absolutely have to get back right away. Ben is expecting me."

"I thought you and Ben were finished. Janna told me he and Cynthia were going away together. I believe he's moved in with her."

"That's not true," I said hotly. "I know it because I just…" I stopped talking. A basic instinct told me something was going wrong.

"Why didn't you ask him about your dogs when you spoke to him from the plane?"

"How do you know I didn't? Or that I spoke to him? What's going on here, Jake? Whatever it was, I don't like it. Maybe you should take me back to Daufuskie and I'll find my own way home. You're acting kind of strange."

"Why the change of heart? You were happy enough to accept a ride from me a while ago."

We were definitely not headed to Hilton Head. I had to turn to my right to see the famed Harbour Town lighthouse. Panic began to ripple through my body. "Where are we going, Jake? Why aren't you taking me home?"

"Don't worry, little one. You'll be home soon."

Jake turned the *Lazy Lady* away from land and towards a series of uninhabited islands. "Answer me," I yelled with as much bravado as I could muster. "Why are you acting like this? Have I done something to offend you?" The *Lazy Lady* glided majestically through the deep blue water. A bright sun blazed in the sky, all traces of the rainy weather gone.

He turned to face me. "You're right. An explanation is in order. I want you to see something I'm very proud of."

Relief flooded through me. He only wanted to show off. No nefarious plot. I was such a silly idiot. "You had me really alarmed. I'd love to see whatever you want to show me, but not right now. I've had quite a day and all I want to do is get home."

"Please, Maggie. It won't take long. This is my finest accomplishment and I'd like you to see it."

"You're being so mysterious. What is it? A secret harem? An island hide-away?" Even to my ears my laugh sounded shaky. "How long is this going to take? I have a dinner appointment."

He slowed the boat as we approached an island. I tried to determine where we were, but I had never visited this area before. "This will do nicely," he said as he dropped the anchor. "We'll take the dinghy. You'll have to get your feet wet, but I'm sure that won't bother you."

I summoned all my courage and said, "Enough is enough, Jake. I've been going along with you but I really don't have time for nonsense. If you have some romantic interlude in mind, I have to tell you I prefer a bit of foreplay. This seems rushed."

He snorted. "You're not my type, lady. Don't worry your pretty little head about that. Now, if you wouldn't mind, start walking. I want to get out of here before the tide comes in."

I had no choice. I stepped off the yacht into the rubber dinghy. Jake fired the motor and we raced to shore. I waded through the surf and, in spite of the heat, stood shivering on the beach. Jake took my elbow and led me across the sand. "This is a prime piece of real estate," he said conversationally. "I picked it up years ago for a song. Wouldn't be able to touch it today. I come here often."

"Do you bring Janna," I asked.

He scowled. "She doesn't know about this. It's mine."

That didn't sound very good. It also meant no one knew where we were. "Could I use your cell phone again? I have to call Ben." And beg for help.

"Won't do you any good." I must have looked alarmed because he added, "There's no reception here. I'm going to have to change my cell phone company. Well, here we are. What do you think?"

We stood before an enormous, half-built house. The foundation rose at least sixteen feet above the ground. There were three turrets at the very top. The front door and palladium window encompassed two stories. Built in an L shape, there was a three car garage attached to the house. "Why did you build that, Jake? You can't drive over here. Or do your vehicles operate on water?"

"It's for the boats. Also house equipment. Come and look around. I want you to see everything."

I had to admit the house was fabulous and I'd have enjoyed the opportunity to explore such a magnificent dwelling if my uneasiness hadn't returned in full force. Something was definitely wrong. Jake had changed from the concerned, helpful person he was when he found me on the beach. Now he seemed coiled like a snake, cautious and polite but ready to strike.

"This elevator will bring me to the upper level," he said, pointing to an empty, box-like area. "It will service the kitchen and the second floor." He led me up concrete steps into the cavernous interior of the house. "There will be a great room, a library, a billiard room, large country kitchen and an indoor pool. Three guest suites on the second. My bedroom will be in the back of the house."

"I can imagine Janna will love this," I said timidly. Although I wasn't sure how thrilled she'd be when she found out he'd kept the construction a secret.

"She won't be coming here."

That remark nearly scared the socks off me. What did he have in mind for Janna? Was he going to leave her and hide out here? She certainly hadn't seemed like a woman on the brink of divorce.

"Why are you so curious about Janna?"

"I'm not curious. Just wondering—and understandably so—why she doesn't know anything about this magnificent house and why she won't be coming here?" Someday I would learn to control my mouth, but today obviously wasn't the day.

He reached for my hair and gently twisted an unruly lock between his fingers. It was an intimate gesture that revolted me. I longed to slap his hand but I was afraid that action might cause the snake to strike. "Maybe I intend to send her on a long trip. Or maybe I'm going to disappear—I'll stage an accident and make everyone think I'm dead. Then I'll hide out here until they all forget about me."

I began to shake and prayed he wouldn't notice. "Why are you telling me this? If you disappear, I'll know what happened and where you are."

He focused his eyes on my face and laughed. "Did you believe that silly story? Honestly, Maggie, you know me better than that. I was just having a little fun with you. Come on. There's more to show you."

I was relieved when we left the house and walked around the grounds. He stopped at a peculiar looking circle of wood about ten feet in diameter lying flat on the sand. On closer inspection, I saw the top of the wooden cover was crisscrossed with slats and was hinged in three sections.

"This was supposed to be my hot tub. I thought it would be relaxing to sit out here and watch the ocean." His face turned dark. "But the idiots building this made a mistake. Unfortunately, it's a fatal flaw. Here, let me show you." He folded back one third of the cover, leading down into a deep, dark hole. A shaft of sunlight lit the space directly below us. I could smell the ocean. "Watch you head. Go on down. It's easier to turn around and grip the sides of the ladder, but it's up to you."

I didn't want to. Every fiber of my body screamed, *Get out of there right now. Start running and don't look back. This guy is nuts* I tried to back up, but he pushed me forward. "Don't be shy. There's someone down there you might want to see. Or maybe not. It doesn't really matter."

What was he talking about? I pressed my hands against the cold cement walls on either side of the stairs, determined to resist as long as I could.

"There's no point in doing that. You are—if you will forgive a bit of melodrama—doomed. There is no way out, and I am stronger than you are."

"Why are you acting like this, Jake? What did I ever do to you?"

"Don't flatter yourself. You're insignificant. But you've become annoying with all your snooping. Tell me, Maggie, where are the diamonds? I'll find them, of course, but it would be so much easier if you would help."

"I don't know what you're talking about," I whispered. "What diamonds?"

"Don't play games. I don't like games," he said roughly.

I gave up. "I can't believe you're involved in this, Jake. Do you work for Petal/Fleur? Why would you do something like this? It doesn't make any sense." And indeed it didn't. Jake Maletesta, one of Sea Pines leading citizens, involved in some sort of sordid diamond deal? No one would believe that.

He laughed. "I work for no one. Stop talking now."

We were at the bottom of the steps. I struggled to see beyond the darkness, but the slatted cover effectively blocked most of the light from above.

"You just stay where you are for a minute. I'll be right back."

"Now see here," I yelled. "You can't treat me this way. I won't stand for it. Maybe you can behave this way with Janna but it won't work with me." I made my fist into a ball and socked him as hard as I could in the stomach. I felt a satisfying squish as I heard the air whoosh out of him. While he clutched his stomach, I tried to race past him on the ladder.

A hand grabbed my hair. "Not so fast. You're not going anywhere. Get back there and be quiet." Then he did a very ungentlemanly thing—he smacked me across the face. Recoiling from shock—I mean no one has ever hit me, except maybe Lucy when we were kids in the third grade—I fell backwards onto the floor. The beam of sunlight disappeared as he replaced the cover. From the darkness, a voice said, "Maggie? Is that you?"

CHAPTER 27

▼

"Peter?" I'd know that voice anywhere, but I sure didn't expect to hear it now.

"Maggie, it's me. You'll have to come over here. I can't move. The bastard has me chained to the wall."

As my eyes grew accustomed to the darkness, I saw a figure in the corner.

"How did you get here, "Peter," I asked as I felt for his hands. They were tethered behind his back with cord and attached to a hook on the wall. They were also ice cold.

"He brought me here a few hours ago. They've been holding me prisoner on my own boat. And the funny thing is, until a few days ago I had no idea what they were up to. This has been terrible."

"Well, before you start feeling all sorry for yourself, I think you should know a lot of folks have gone to extreme amounts of trouble to find out what had happened to you."

"Is that right? Bless Angel. That girl has a good head on her shoulders. I knew she'd try to rescue me."

"If you are referring to the empty headed Bambi living in your house in Sudbury and who believes Switzerland and Marrakech are on the same continent, I'm going to have to disappoint you. No, she did

- 195 -

not try to help you. In fact, she packed her peroxide and took off—no doubt to hook up with Ken."

"Do you have to be so caustic? You never have been able to carry on a civil conversation."

I sighed. "You know, Peter, if you could just once stop thinking about yourself first, you would be a much more sympathetic person. I, for instance, am locked in this stupid spa because I tried to protect you, but you don't hear me whining." Believe me, I wanted to.

"I am not whining."

"Well, whatever it is, it's very unattractive. I'd prefer we put our heads together and figure out how to get out of here."

"Unless you have a hacksaw, I think that's impossible." Peter kicked at something. "I think there are rats in here. Every once in a while I feel something run across my foot."

"Well, of course there are. There are always rats around the water on Hilton Head. We locals don't worry about them." I stood on tiptoe and danced around a bit, just in case one decided to climb my leg.

"Tell me everything, Peter. That way, we can figure out a plan of action. For instance, how long have you been here?"

"As far as I can tell, about two hours. He was in a hurry—made me get off the *Legal Pad*—that's the new name of my boat—and go with him."

"Speaking of your boat, where is it? I saw it once in South Beach, but no one has been able to find it since."

"They've kept her in open water during the day. At night we've anchored in Broad Creek—right off your house."

"Excuse me?"

"They want something that you have, so they've been watching you with binoculars. I told them you didn't have anything valuable—unless you counted that stuff you paint, which I guess some people pay good money for, but…"

"Shut up, Peter. I'm sorry I tried to help you."

"You're impossible to talk to. You always have been."

"My inability to converse is not the reason we divorced. It was your inability to keep your pants on."

It was his turn to sigh. "I believe I apologized for that—more than once."

This was ridiculous. A madman locked us in a spa on a deserted island and we were worrying about ancient history. "If we intend to get out of this predicament, we need to stop this." I heard the gate above us open. "He's coming back, I whispered. "Let's pretend we're not afraid."

"I'm certainly not," Peter said.

"Of course you're not, dear. That's why your voice is quivering. Maybe you should let me do the talking."

"You really know how to cut off a man's…"

"Shh. Save that for later."

We listened as Jake clattered down the ladder. Unless he had four feet, there was someone with him.

"I'll let you all get to know each other," Jake said. "Lady and gentlemen, this concludes our relationship. Since I'll never see you again, I want you to know that you really will have died in vain. Your amateur interference will remain what it always has been—a nuisance. But when I sit on the deck of my lovely home, enjoying the sun and a lovely lady, I'll cast a fond thought your way. You will—after all—be the first people to use my new facilities. Goodbye."

"You are a nut case," I called as he went up the rungs. You'll never get away with this."

At the top he turned and said, "You disappoint me, Maggie. Such a cliché. Surely someone as creative as you could come up with a more original protest. By the way, I suppose I should cancel the order for the hand-painted dishes."

His evil laugh made the hair on the back of my neck stand up. Slowly, the lid of the spa descended, plunging us into total darkness. When he was gone there was silence in the cell—as I'd come to think of our prison.

Then a male voice said, "Maggie?"

"Ben?"

"Who's Ben?"

"Who's that?"

"Peter's here"

"Your Peter."

"He's not my Peter."

"Excuse me. I'm here, you know."

"Ben, meet Peter."

Could it get any worse? My current love, who was very mad at me because of my involvement with my ex-husband and my ex-husband and I were trapped together in a small dark cell. Life wasn't fair.

I groped for Ben's hand. "It's good to see you—even if I can't. Can you believe it? Jake Maletesta is a bad guy.'"

His fingers did not enthusiastically grasp mine. In fact, they felt limp and cold. "Are we still not speaking? I thought maybe things were okay with us again. You know, when I heard your voice on the radio and you said we needed to talk?" A cold chill ran over me. Did he intend to say he was dumping me for Cynthia Loveday? Surely not.

"I don't think this is the time or the place, Maggie."

"I don't either," Peter said. "I don't know what is going on with you two, but I really don't care. My main concern is getting out of here. I want to get as far away from all of you as I can get."

"Don't you just love it, Ben? We've risked our necks to protect him and he can still only think about saving his own skin."

"I agree with Peter. We need to concentrate on our predicament." His voice sounded cold and distant. "What do you suppose Maletesta thinks he is going to accomplish by locking us up in here? We may miss a few meals, but the construction crew will find us tomorrow when they return to work. I don't get it. He must know we're going to run to the police."

I cleared my throat. "I believe he mentioned something about us all being doomed."

"Like I said, I don't think we'll starve to death before tomorrow," Ben said, "but I'd just as soon get out of here. Let's check this thing for a possible way out."

"I can't move. My hands are tied to something," Peter said.

"Then we'll just have to leave you."

"Maggie, that is not helpful," Ben muttered in a low voice. "Try to work with me."

Ben and I checked the perimeter of the spa but could find no opening. I'm sure the folks who built this intended to install a regular hot tub with benches and water jets, but for some reason, Jake's spa was unfinished. It was a round, deep hole in the ground.

"There has to be a way out," Peter said, his voice tinged with panic. "I can't stay here much longer."

I touched Ben's arm. "Maybe we should try to push the cover off."

Ben bounded up the ladder and shoved as hard as he could against the wood, but it refused to budge. "We'll have to think of something else."

The space began to feel confining. Suddenly, I couldn't breathe. The men had used up all the oxygen. I clutched my throat and gasped.

I felt Ben's hand on my shoulder. "What's the matter with you, Maggie?"

"I am oxygen deprived," I wheezed. "There's no more air. That's what Jake meant. We are all going to suffocate." I sank to the ground. "Goodbye, Ben. We'll never know what could have been, will we?"

"I knew it! We really are going to die"

"Be quiet, Peter." I arranged myself in a comfortable position on the ground.

Ben nudged me with his foot. "Before you go, I'd like to point out that air is coming through the lattice work on the roof. He pointed to the ladder and the wooden slats beyond. "It would be impossible to suffocate, but if that's what you want to do, have at it."

"That's what you think. I can't breathe."

I felt a hand fumble with my face. "That's because you have your scarf over your nose. Would you like me to remove it?"

Peter snickered.

"No, thank you," I said. "I'm using it to filter noxious fumes. By the way, Peter, if it hadn't been for your Moroccan business card we wouldn't be in this mess. Did you know we went to Marrakech?"

"You did?" Peter sounded incredulous. "I had no idea."

"That's why you shouldn't be so condescending," I said from my position on the floor. "So talk. We've earned it."

"There is no import/export company. At least I don't own one. Petal used my good name to start a phony business. All those times she wanted to take the *Legal Pad* and cruise to Palm Beach and Miami, I thought she wanted to be with me. You have to believe me, I really am in the dark about what she was doing. And I've never seen Jake Maletesta before in my life. We cruised up to Hilton Head from Palm Beach because Petal said she wanted to visit an old friend. That friend was Maletesta. He commandeered my boat and kept me a prisoner in my own bedroom."

"Ah, the lovely Petal. Did you know her real name is Ruby Wolochik and she tried to kill me this morning? She was planning to push me out of a plane in the middle of the ocean. Creative, don't you think?"

"That can't be," Peter whispered. "Petal wouldn't do that."

I guffawed. "You don't know your girlfriend very well.

"I think these people set up a dummy company in Morocco and used my boat to distribute whatever they were 'importing'."

"You don't have to be a rocket scientist to figure out they were smuggling diamonds," Ben said.

"Diamonds?"

"Nothing you need to know about," I told Peter.

"They imported the necklaces with the gems into the United States," Ben continued. "What I can't figure out is—what did they intend to do with the diamonds? If they owned the stones, why not keep them? And where did they get the diamonds?"

"TELL ME WHAT IS GOING ON."

We spent the next five minutes bringing Peter up to speed.

"So," Peter said in his best lawyer voice as soon as he'd heard the story, "this is fairly obvious. Petal—I can't call her Ruby—and Maletesta smuggled diamonds into this country using a phony company—Peter S. Bloom Import/Export—as a cover. The bills of lading would have read *Moroccan beaded necklaces*. The interesting question is—who received the merchandise on this side of the Atlantic"

"You don't have to be a brain surgeon to figure that out," I said scornfully. "Jake Maletesta.

"I don't think so. I don't know anything about the man, but it would be far too risky to send them to a home or business address. Someone could look in the box by mistake."

"That makes sense," Ben said. "Jake is married. His wife might have opened a package if it came to the house. Or at the very least, she would have asked him about the contents. A Moroccan postmark arouses curiosity. And," he added, "We also don't know what size package we're talking about."

"I saw the wooden box that held my necklace. It was about the size of a loaf of bread. A small loaf. The beaded necklaces were individually wrapped in bubble paper. Otherwise, I can't remember any special packing," I told them.

"But you don't know if the box your necklace came in was a single shipment or part of a larger one."

"How could there be a larger one? Do you know how many diamonds that would be?"

Peter shuffled his feet—no doubt chasing away more rodents. "Diamonds may not be their only export item. There is also active drug traffic in Morocco. We have no idea what these people were up to."

I sat on the floor listening to them talk. Under the circumstances, Ben was being very civil—not at all as I imagined the first meeting between him and my ex-husband would be. Of course, if he didn't care about me anymore, he wouldn't care about Peter either. I longed to ask him how he felt about our relationship, but that wasn't something you discussed in front of your ex.

My shorts were wet. I'd been so engrossed in the conversation, I hadn't noticed, but they were definitely wet. I moved my hand across the floor and found water there, too. I stood up and wiped my clothes. "There must be a leak in here," I said. "I'm dripping. Probably water seeping in from underground."

Ben's feet made a squishing sound as he walked over to me. "I hadn't noticed it either, but you're right. Water is coming in from somewhere. Look here. It's coming through cracks in the cement. How odd."

Water splashed on my head. "Hey," I called. "My hair is wet. It must be raining outside." But the water came in surges, not steadily like rain.

"Maggie," Peter said, "do you happen to remember where Maletesta anchored the boat when he brought you here? Was it close to the shore, or did you anchor and walk through surf? In other words, was the tide coming in or going out?"

I tried to think. "We took the dinghy to the beach. I'd have to say the tide was out, but I don't know if it was low tide."

"When he brought me, the tide was coming in. I remember he was in a hurry to get out to sea," Ben said.

"Hmm."

"What is that supposed to mean?" I asked.

"I think the tide is coming in. That means we might be in a bit of trouble."

"How do you figure that? Honestly, Peter, don't be so mysterious."

"I see where you're going with this, Bloom. In other words, this isn't ground water on the floor."

"Right."

Linda S. Clayton 203

"So what's wrong with that? There isn't much we can do to stop the tide."

Silence.

"Somebody answer me. What does the tide have to do with our problem?"

Ben took my hand. "Maggie, I don't want to scare you, but you should be aware of what we might be facing. Look. The water is already up to our ankles. If it keeps rising…" His voice trailed off.

"Go on. If it keeps rising?"

"It could very well put this little chamber under water," he finished.

"Get out of town!"

"Well, I could be wrong, but I don't think Maletesta would have left us here simply to cool our heels until tomorrow morning. Unless he is planning to run—in which case this temporary incarceration makes perfect sense. By the time we get back to the island, he would be long gone. But I don't think that was his plan. Didn't he say something about us not getting out of here?"

I gulped. "I remember his words—*You are doomed.* Do you think this is what he meant? We're supposed to drown? That is sick!"

"I'm shackled to the wall," Peter reminded us unnecessarily. "I'd sure like some help." Even though he was trying to hide it, I could hear the fear in his voice.

I slapped myself on the forehead. "We haven't been thinking. All we have to do is untie the rope around Peter's wrists." I stuck my hand behind my ex-husband's back and felt for the knot. "This isn't easy. I can't get a good grip. And the rope is pretty thick."

"Will you please try?"

"I am, Peter," I assured him. "But I don't think I can do it."

No one mentioned the water that now reached my mid calf. "How high do you reckon the tide will be?" I asked, trying to appear nonchalant.

"I figure a little over seven feet," Peter answered. "Could be higher."

"And—ah—how high is this place?"

"It's about eight feet high, but that doesn't matter. Imagine a glass buried to its rim in the sand. When the tide comes in, the glass fills up. The water doesn't recede. By the time the tide reaches its highest level, the glass has long since disappeared."

"So this is the structural flaw Jake was talking about. It's a lovely spa, but it was built too close to the shore. At high tide it's under water."

Panic clawed at my chest, and once more I felt like I was going to suffocate. "What are we going to do?" I whispered.

Ben put his arm around my shoulder. "We're in this together," he said in a soft voice. "We'll think of something."

But what? The water had crept up to my knees.

"I noticed a few rocks in the corner," Ben said. "If we can hammer the wooden slats enough to make a hole, we might be able to crawl out." Ben and I took turns slamming the rocks against the wood. I clawed at the slats until my fingers were raw and my arms ached, but to no avail.

"I'm not having much luck," I said. "At this rate I'll have a hole sometime next year." No one laughed. I didn't think it was funny, either.

"Ben, the water in at my waist. We don't have much time."

"I know that. Don't worry."

How could I not worry? My shorts and tank top billowed as the water poured into my clothes. I clutched Ben's arm.

"Go stand on the top rung, Maggie. I'm going to work on Peter's knots. If we can tread water, we may be able to press our noses against the cover and get some air."

The water had reached my armpits and I felt my feet float off the ground. "I think I'll just do that," I said. "I'm having trouble standing. I don't want to leave you two, though." And that was the truth. I suddenly realized I didn't want to save myself if Ben and Peter died. "I'll stay with you."

Linda S. Clayton   205

Ben lifted me off my feet and deposited me on the ladder. "Stop being silly. Stay up there. We'll be okay."

"How would that work? You're not going to be okay. We're all going to be dead." I stuck my nose through the slats and yelled. "Help! Somebody come and help us. May Day! May Day." I shouted until I was hoarse. When I turned around, Ben and Peter stood in water up to their chins. "No!" I stepped off the step and dog paddled over to them. "Put your head up. I love you, Ben. I have to tell you that." I didn't care if Peter heard. He wasn't going to live to taunt me about it."

"Don't give up, Maggie. And get back on that step. Do it now." The tone of his voice shocked me into action. I swam up the cover and tried to scream some more.

"Good grief," a voice said. "Don't get your shorts in a knot. Do you have any idea how hard it was to find you?"

CHAPTER 28

▼

Who said that? Now I was seeing things. I could have sworn Lucy, wearing a fuchsia wet suit and orange goggles, wiggled her fingers through the lattice. My poor, about to be drowned eyes, were playing tricks on me. "You look so much like my good friend," I said to the mirage. "You even have her gaudy taste in clothes. Whoever heard of a hot pink wet suit?"

"You know, I'm tempted to leave you here. Could you please get out of the way. This thing has a padlock on it. I have to shoot the lock."

That sounded too much like my friend to be a mirage. Lucy was always shooting something. "Is it really you?" I tried to reach her face. "Let me touch you."

"Lordy! Is there anyone else in there," she yelled.

"Two of us," Ben called. "And if you have a solution to this mess, you'd better hurry. We also need a knife."

Another figure, wearing a sensible black wet suit, materialized next to Lucy. "*Bonjour, ma petite*"

"Islane?" Now I was sure I was going crazy. Islane was in Morocco.

"*Oui. C'est moi.*" Do you require your tools, Lucy?"

"Please. I'll need the big gun and one of those sharp knives. Better make it a big one, too."

- 206 -

Islane reached into a canvas bag she was carrying and handed the requested items to Lucy.

"Listen, Maggie. Get a grip. Can you take this knife to Ben? And make sure you stay out of my line of fire."

I grabbed the knife, put it between my teeth like a commando and dove into the water. I surfaced immediately, sputtering. It isn't easy to swim with a knife in your mouth. I also nearly sliced my tongue off.

"Give it to me," Ben said. "I'll cut him loose."

"Nope. I'll do it."

"Don't let the blade slip accidentally," I heard him say before I held my breath and stuck my head under water. I wiggled over to Peter, reached behind him with the knife and sawed at the rope. Just as I thought my lungs were going to burst, the taut rope slackened and fell away. Peter was free.

I missed the boom. Peter said it sounded like Lucy shot a cannon through the cover. But it was effective. It created a crater-sized hole. We wasted no time scrambling out. "We're on the back side of this island," Lucy called as we ran. "Do you think you can make it?"

"Do you think I want to stay here?" I called as I blew past her. I noticed Peter and Ben were running as fast as I was.

"The *Legal Pad* is anchored out there," she said pointing to the water. "I'm afraid you're going to get wet."

"Not funny, Lucy."

Twenty minutes later, wrapped in warm blankets, I still shivered. I simply could not make my arms and legs behave. Peter, however, was delighted to have his boat under his control. He immediately took over the helm. "Tell me again where you found this, Lucy."

"It had gone aground on the Redneck Riviera. The fools didn't know about the sandbar."

In spite of my misery, I had to smile. The locals knew there was a large sandbar in the May River outside of Bluffton. At low tide folks took their boats there for picnics and parties. They dug holes in the sand, filled them with charcoal and grilled hot dogs, burgers or a Lowcountry boil. Boaters who didn't know about the sandbar went aground and spent an enforced eight hours enjoying the amenities of the Redneck Riviera until the tide came in and allowed them to leave.

"Did you find Petal?" Peter asked.

"Nope. I'm guessing she hitched a ride on a boat that was anchored off the sandbar. The *Legal Pad* was abandoned."

"No, she didn't," I told them. "Petal piloted the plane I was in. Cotton clonked her over the head. That's when I had to take over. Someone else must have been driving Peter's boat."

Ben, who up until now had been quiet, said, "How did you happen to spot the *Legal Pad?*"

Lucy expertly mixed a batch of Bloody Marys. She stuck a celery stalk in each glass and filled it with the beverage. "It's a bit of a story. Sure you want to hear it now?"

Ben nodded. "We're safe out here. I told Bloom to stay out in the open water for a while—until we know what's been happening. No point in running right back into more trouble."

"Amen to that," I said.

"Well, it started at the airport. I went there to pick up Islane. She arrived on the flight after yours' Ben. Anyway, I overheard two men talking about a woman who had called for assistance landing a plane. She said she didn't know how to fly and apparently wasn't interested in listening to any instruction."

"That's not true." I felt my face flame.

"I'm not making this up, Maggie. I'm just repeating what they said. When they mentioned the name *Maggie*, and said she had nearly put the plane in a stall, I knew who they were talking about."

"Really, Lucy, I don't find this at all humorous."

"It's not meant to be. I was terrified. Especially when the man at the airport mentioned he had no idea where you were. Then Islane arrived, and we tried to decide what to do."

"By then Maletesta had already offered to help me find you, Maggie," Ben interrupted. "I ran into him at the airport. He said he was looking at a Cessna he considered buying. I was so upset, I told him about you flying the plane. He seemed very concerned. Offered to take me out on his boat to find you."

"He is a snake. Yes?" Islane asked.

"Yes, indeed. Go on, Lucy."

"Islane and I agreed the easiest way to find you, if you had crashed, was to hire a plane and get an aerial view. It would be much quicker than trying to go by boat or car. It only took a few minutes to rent a plane and start looking. That's how we found the *Legal Pad*. The pilot flew low enough over the sandbar for me to read the name on the back of the yacht. Then, since I'd been clever enough to rent one of those planes that lands on water, he pulled up next to the boat and we climbed on. Attracted quite a crowd, too. And luckily, the keys were still in the ignition. Whoever had run it aground had decided not to stick around. After that, it was a piece of cake."

I eyed her skeptically. As far as I knew, Lucy's skills did not include running a boat.

I hoped Peter wasn't listening when I said, "How'd you get the *Legal Pad* to the island, Lucy? You can't even competently drive a car."

My friend folded her arms over her chest and scowled at me. "You know, the next time you're in trouble, I'm going to stay home and eat chocolates. Or go on a trip. Or have my legs waxed. You are an ungrateful wretch."

"I repeat, how'd you manage to find us?"

"Islane is an extremely competent boater. Did you know that she and Hassan used to keep a little yacht on the Mediterranean? She had no problem with the *Legal Pad*."

I smiled admiringly at my Moroccan friend. She certainly had hidden talents. "But how did you know to come to the island? I have to tell you, I've been cruising around these waters for years and I didn't know it existed."

"We found the crashed airplane on Daufuskie. Islane and I were both relieved not to find you. There was also no trail of blood, which was a good sign."

"Did you find Petal? Or Cotton?"

"There wasn't anybody there."

Even though Petal/Fleur/deserved to be pushed under a speeding train, I was secretly relieved to hear she hadn't expired in the crash. Someone else could do the dirty work.

"So," Lucy continued, "we simply cruised around. I think fate brought us to the island." She looked slightly embarrassed. "From the water, we saw the half finished house. It looked intriguing—you know, like who would build such a magnificent structure on an empty island. We had to investigate."

"So let me get this straight. Even though you very concerned about me and weren't sure if I were still alive, you decided to temporarily suspend the search in order to check out a house."

"We didn't plan an extended stay. Just a quick look. Then I heard you screaming as if your tail feathers were on fire. I'd call that mighty lucky for you."

I'd call that mighty lucky, too. I turned to Ben. "What did Jake do with you after he offered to help?"

"We got on his boat in Harbour Town and headed out to sea. When we were far enough away, he pulled a gun and told me to get below. He tied me up and put tape over my mouth. I guess I was there the whole time you were with him on deck."

I shook my head. "He is a cool customer. He told me he was playing golf on Daufuskie and saw me fly low over the island. He knew beforehand I was in the plane." I remembered something Cotton told me. "Petal didn't put me in the plane by herself. There was another man with her. Cotton said he was very good looking. It wasn't Peter and it wasn't Jake, because Cotton knows Jake. I wonder who it was."

"Another reptile, perhaps," Islane offered.

"Indubitably. But who?"

"That doesn't matter right now," Lucy said. "We need a plan of action. We can't float around out here forever."

"I suppose we should call the sheriff. He can go after Maletesta."

"No, Ben. Peter still hasn't had time to learn everything that has happened. The sheriff would devour him before he had a chance to defend myself."

Ben glanced at my ex-husband who kept his hands on the wheel as his eyes scanned the water. "I see. You're still worrying about Peter."

"I'm not worrying about him. Things are moving too fast, that's all. And Peter doesn't know half what we do. Let's give him a chance to come up to speed."

"Whatever you say." His voice was noncommittal. "Let me know what you decide to do."

Lucy squinted her eyes at me. "You are aware that you're wrecking any chance of a happy relationship with that man, aren't you? Why are you so stubborn about Peter? He's a big boy. He can take care of himself."

"I am not stubborn," I said as I stomped off to the stern. I sat on the deck and wrapped my arms around my knees. I was about to run out of steam. One more incident that involved me in a life-threatening situation and they could cart me off to a nice padded room. In fact, it would be a relief. All I wanted to do was go home and chase Wally and Willow around my house.

"Holy crow and whispering hogs. I have to know about my dogs." I jumped to my feet and raced to the others. "Does anyone know anything about my English cockers? We were taking a walk and someone hit me over the head. Petal/Fleur/told me they were road kill."

"Nonsense," Lucy said briskly. "You couldn't lose Wally if you wanted to. He has the homing instinct of a boomerang. And Willow apparently decided to stick with Wally. They both went back to your house—and I consider this an extraordinary feat since they had to cross Greenwood Drive—and were waiting patiently on your doorstep. Dan Jackson, your neighbor, knew we were good friends and called me. I

212   A String Of Perils

went to get them. That's when I became alarmed. As soon as I picked up Islane, I intended to hunt for you. You can put your mind at ease. At the moment they are sunning themselves by the pool at my house."

I gave her a hug. "You are an angel. I don't know what I'd do without them—or you."

"Yeah, yeah," she said, returning my embrace. "What do we do now?"

"Let's recap what we know. Petal/Fleur/is running around somewhere. Ditto Jake Maletesta. Their import/export company was a front for diamond smuggling. They want my diamond necklace and both are willing to kill me to get it

"I know what we should do," Lucy said. "We should go to Maggie's and get the diamonds. First things first. Peter," she called, "steer this thing to your ex-wife's house. I assume you know the way."

CHAPTER 29

▼

Peter anchored the *Legal Pad* in a channel off Point Comfort. We rowed his inflatable dinghy through the marsh grass to the back of my house. "I hope this is a good idea," I whispered. "What if the bad guys are here looking for the diamonds?"

"I think they are long gone," Ben replied. "What did you do with the fake necklace?"

"It's in the bathroom—in plain sight."

"Good. They may have seen it, picked it up and left, thinking it was the real thing."

We stopped talking as we approached the house. For once I was happy that the marsh myrtle and pine trees had grown nearly eighteen feet high and surrounded the deck. They offered great camouflage. Ben put his finger to his lips and pointed to the doors. "We'll put the dinghy under the house and then one of us can climb up and take a look."

That would be a long climb. The main floor of my house was fourteen feet above ground—a necessity due to flood danger. "There isn't any reason for all of us to go in, is there? One of us takes a quick look around, grabs the necklace—if it's still there—and the other diamonds and gets out," I said. "Then we'll go to Lucy's and implement Plan B."

"Right." Ben picked up a large stick and handed to me. "I assume you know what to do with this since breaking windows is a specialty of

- 213 -

your." He put his hands on my butt and began to hoist me up. "Hey, what do you think you're doing? I'm not going in there."

"Of course you are. You know where you hid the diamonds. Don't worry. I'm going to be right behind you."

"I wish people would stop telling me not to worry," I grumbled. "I can feel my hair turning white."

I threw a leg over the railing and pulled myself up. The stick clattered to the deck, making a sound loud enough to wake up sleeping alligators.

"We could go around and ring the doorbell," Ben said in my ear. "What don't you understand about stealth and the element of surprise?"

I pressed my face against the window and looked into the sunroom. "It looks okay. I don't see anybody. Maybe we could try the front door. I mean, why break glass if no one is here?"

"How would we get in?"

"With a key. There's one hidden in a ceramic frog under the lantana. I called down to Lucy. "Would you mind getting it and opening the door?"

Minutes later we entered my house. There was no sign of an intruder—but someone had been there. The fake necklace was gone.

"How did they get in here," I wondered. "There's no sign of a forced entry."

"I'll bet they have your purse—and your keys. Didn't you have them with you when you took the dogs for a walk?" Lucy asked.

That seemed like years ago, but she was right. There was no need for the bad guys to break in. They simply walked up the front steps and put the key in the lock. But this wasn't the time to worry about keys. I zoomed into the family room. The wooden pelican wasn't on the mantle where I had left it. Panicked I swiveled my head around, looking for the wooden bird. I saw it on the table in the sunroom. Someone had picked it up, looked at it and—miracle of miracles—put it down. I opened the secret compartment and diamonds spilled out into the palm of my hand.

Even to my biased ear, my high, shaky laugh quickly took on an hysterical pitch. "Am I going to have to smack you across the face?" Lucy inquired.

"No. And if you hit me, I'm going to whack you back. I'm so relieved. The fools actually had the diamonds in their hands and didn't know it. They're not so smart, after all."

Peter, Lucy and Islane stared in astonishment at the gems. "Those are worth a fortune," Islane said. "I can't believe they came from my country."

"I don't think we can say that with certainty, but my necklace certainly looked like the one Lucy bought as a souvenir. Ben saw the resemblance, too. Where is he, by the way?"

"He's in your bedroom using your computer, "Lucy said. "I'd be happy to put those diamonds in the safe in our house, Maggie. My knees are weak thinking you left them in this wooden thing on the mantel."

"I'd be very grateful. Let's go now."

The look on Ben's face as he walked into the family room nearly stopped my heart. I could not—would not—take any more stress. I flopped down onto the couch and put a pillow over my head. "What is it? No, if it's really bad, don't tell me." I got to my feet. "I'm going up to the roof now and dive off. Y'all have fun."

"Wait, Maggie," Ben said. "It isn't bad. But if I'm right, you're not going to believe it."

"If this news doesn't involve missing or dead dogs, dead bodies, airplanes or drowning, lay it on me."

"Not right now. I don't want to stick around here in case those folks come back. They might be a tinch angry when they realize the necklace was a phony.

"I'm for leaving, but how are we going to get to Lucy's? My car is still parked at the Forest Preserve."

"You folks are not the most resourceful people in the world. If you would follow me, we'll be on our way." Lucy opened the front door. Her blue, Lincoln Navigator—its engine purring, waited in my driveway with Emerald behind the wheel. "I keep this car for shopping and hauling antiques. All aboard."

"But how…?" I asked.

"Called her from your house." She grinned. "This is fun."

"You're sick, do you know that?" But I gave her a big hug anyway.

"Those dogs don't look like they missed you very much. In fact, I think you could say they don't know you're here," Peter said.

"That's not true." I whistled and patted my leg. "Good puppies. Come see Momma." Wally raised his head from his cedar filled, hypoallergenic luxury bed on the patio, and looked at me. Then he rolled over on his back and went to sleep. Willow, wearing a sequin studded, turquoise collar, didn't even wake up. "They're exhausted from their ordeal," I informed the others. "But enough about the dogs. Let's hear your news, Ben."

We sat around Lucy's pool drinking ice tea and eating chicken salad sandwiches. I felt safe for the first time in several hours.

"Don't worry," she promised us. "No one can get into this house. It may look open and vulnerable, but there are security precautions in place that you can't see. Julius is a bit paranoid about his home being his sanctuary. He doesn't like it threatened, and there are people who—if you can imagine this—don't like him. He's in London for a few days, so he won't have to know about this little…ah…incident I'd also like to invite you all to spend the night here. I have plenty of room and I'd sleep better knowing I won't have to haul out at an ungodly hour to save your asses."

Worked for me. The others also nodded in agreement. I stretched out my legs on the chaise lounge and tried to relax. Emerald moved among us, refilling our glasses and urging us to take more food. As she passed the dogs, she slipped each a piece of chicken. I could swear I saw

Willow smile. I sighed deeply. They could enjoy themselves for now. There would be plenty of time for me to reacquaint them with the joys of dry dog food.

Night settled peacefully on the ocean in front of us. Gentle waves lapped at the sand. For a moment I fooled myself into believing life was as calm as the water. But only an idiot would think that. There were people trying to kill us. "So tell us, Ben. What did you find out that is so astonishing?" I closed my eyes and listened as he began to speak.

"The idea occurred to me as soon as I saw the diamonds, but it seemed so preposterous, I dismissed it. I did a little investigating in Charlotte and when I checked my email at Maggie's, my theory was confirmed. I think the diamonds, which are now stashed in Lucy's formidable safe, are part of the biggest jewel theft in history." He paused to let his words sink in.

"Huh?" I was stunned.

"You all know that Antwerp, Belgium is the diamond-cutting capital of the world. During the weekend of February 15/16, 2003 a gang of well-trained thieves broke into the underground vaults of the Antwerp Diamond Center. They cleverly chose a time when the entire city was distracted by the Diamond Games tennis tournament."

"I remember that," I said. "I think Venus Williams won."

Ben nodded approvingly. "Very good. Anyway, the police always believed it was an inside job because the thieves used keys to get in and they were able to bypass the alarm system. They emptied one hundred and twenty three vaults. They had so much loot, they didn't bother with the rest of the vaults. The estimated value of the stolen gems is $100 million."

Peter whistled softly. "Why do you think these stones are part of the heist?"

"Two reasons: we know the box containing Maggie's necklace also held similar ones. Maggie estimated there were approximately twenty. Fifty fake beads on each necklace. That's a heap of diamonds. I asked my sources to check for any large jewel theft in the last two years. Every lead pointed to Antwerp. And most importantly, the gems have never been found. They think a gang of Italians pulled the job, but they have never found any of them. They arrested a man accused of aiding and abetting, but he didn't personally take part in the robbery."

"Fascinating," Lucy murmured.

"Does this mean I can't keep the diamonds?"

Ben laughed. "I'm afraid so. I don't think the Belgian authorities would approve of that. I asked a friend in the State Department to take a closer look at Maletesta. Jake tells people he was born in Teaneck, New Jersey, but that's not true. He was born in Turin, Italy and travels there approximately once a month. He occasionally crosses the ocean in the *Lazy Lady*. He speaks fluent Italian and has had a permanent address in this country for only four years. Authorities estimate the gang spent two years planning the robbery. I think that means Maletesta uses his Hilton Head residence as a hideout. Who would suspect the likeable Jake?"

"But what about Janna," Lucy asked. "Surely she'd not part of this, too."

"She and Maletesta have been married for four years. She probably doesn't know a thing about his other life. He chose her because she lends an upper class respectability to his image. She is a gracious, charming hostess and the perfect foil for Maletesta."

"I can't believe this. No wonder he's trying to kill us. How do the rest fit in?"

Peter, who had been listening quietly, raised his hand. "I think I can help with that. "These folks would have trouble selling the diamonds. Reputable dealers don't buy from seedy people. What do you think of this theory? Maletesta and his cronies somehow manage to get the diamonds out of Belgium. They choose North Africa rather than a European country because it is easier to avoid the law in North Africa. He gets Petal to set up a dummy company. They don't actually send the diamonds as freight because that would be too risky. That's where

Maletesta's boat fits in." He paused. "Do you think he told Petal to hook up with me?"

The man was so naïve. "I think that's a possibility, Peter. When did you meet her?"

"It was kind of funny, actually. It was about one year ago. I got an invitation in the mail for a free, expensive dinner at the *La Table de ma Tante*, which is an exclusive restaurant in Boston. They're booked for months in advance, so I couldn't figure out why they'd be handing out free dinners. But I was curious, so I took Angel—the girl you spoke with on the phone. The meal was fantastic and so was the hostess. She—and you have probably already guessed it was Petal—really came on to me. Do you think it was a set-up?"

"Good heavens, Peter. How vain are you? Of course it was a set-up. Did any of your friends receive an invitation for a free dinner? Did Petal shower other guests with attention? Surely you must have wondered why she had singled you out."

The look on his face told me he hadn't a clue. I didn't feel a bit sorry for him. The man could be the poster boy for stupidity. I wanted to tell him he was a sorry sucker, but I was suddenly so sleepy, I couldn't keep my eyes open. I staggered to my feet. "I have to go to bed. Come on, puppies."

How about that. Both dogs stood up and followed me into the house. I started up the stairs, but they raced past me to the kitchen where Emerald was waiting with a midnight snack.

CHAPTER 30

▼

"Before we leave, I've found weapons for all of us." Lucy had a semi-automatic swung over her shoulder and Islane carried a pearl handled revolver. Our hostess handed an antique cutlass to Peter and gave Ben a Samurai sword. "This is for you, Maggie. You're athletic, so this bow and arrow should work just fine."

"You've got to be kidding," I yelped as we piled into Lucy's Lincoln Navigator. "What am I supposed to do with this?"

"Use it." She patted an arrow in the quiver on my back. "Brings back some good memories."

I shuddered. There was obviously a lot about Lucy I didn't know.

"This is ridiculous," Peter said. "Where did you get this stuff? From a museum?"

"Julius collects antique weapons," Lucy said defensively. "I'll have you know Geronimo once carried that bow and arrow."

"Remember the plan," I told the others. "Don't forget to wear your costumes. I hate to do this to Cotton, but we may have to scare her to get the information we need." I patted the bag next to me, which held stuff I'd found at Lucy's that I thought might come in handy. "Let's get this show on the road."

Lucy drove down Hwy 278 and turned right onto Squire Pope Road. "What we should do is this," I said. "We should leave the car a

- 220 -

short distance from the house and approach on foot, just in case one of the bad guys is lurking about. I don't think there's any reason to alarm Cotton by all of us barging in the front door."

Ben looked amused. "Are we going in with weapons drawn"

"Don't be silly. I'll check it out. If she isn't in the middle of a deep conversation with her mother, I'll make the call of the Piping Plover."

"What?" Peter and Islane said simultaneously.

"The Piping Plover. It's a bird."

Peter rolled his eyes. "Pick something else. It might take all of us quite a while to recognize the sound of the Piping Plover."

We settled on a crow.

"I'm coming with you because you are a nutcase." Ben said. "And I'm bringing my sword."

"Really, Ben. I am quite capable of ringing Cotton's doorbell by myself."

"I'm coming with you."

I snuck a glance at Peter. He didn't seem at all perturbed that a real man was protecting his ex-wife. Although, he wouldn't have recognized a real man if he'd stumbled over him in the dark.

We left the Navigator in a thick copse of trees and palmetto scrub. Ben and I walked over the dirt path to the house. "Tell you what," he said. "Just for kicks, you ring the bell but before you do, give me time to swing around to the back of the house." When he saw the look on my face, he said, "I want to make sure we don't have any surprises. If you see anything that bothers you, forget the crow and yell for Peter. On second thought, call Lucy. I have more faith in her ability to remain clearheaded. That is one awesome woman."

I waited until Ben was out of sight. And then I didn't ring the bell. I peered in the window. Cotton was dressed in her white ensemble, and she was lying on the floor in the middle of the living room, surrounded by her favorite candles.

I tiptoed back to the others. "I may need some help here. Cotton seems…um…unwell. I don't want to deal with her by myself."

"Let's call the sheriff," Peter said.

"Let's try to deal with this by ourselves. But I think we should bring our weapons." I realized a bow and arrow wouldn't do much against folks from the spirit world, but they made me feel better. "We'll fan out," I whispered. "Lucy, you take the left, Peter, you and Islane go around to the right side of the house. Wait until I give the signal and then come on in."

I waited until the others had taken their positions. Feeling about as foolish as anyone wearing a quiver of arrows and carrying a bow while traipsing around Hilton Head Island can feel, I pulled a bright orange wig out of my bag and slapped it on my head. It was a relic from Lucy's more festive days. Her hair could still guide ships through thick fog, but these days she colored it a more subdued shade of flame. I applied a thick layer of bright red lipstick and wrapped one of Lucy's expensive white tablecloths over my shoulders. I looked at my reflection in my pocket mirror. Believe it or not, I resembled Wisteria.

Now, how do I get in the house? Departed souls probably don't ring doorbells. I didn't feel I'd be able to morph through the wall. I settled for a window. I pushed it open and hauled myself over the sill. My foot landed in the toilet. I pulled it out, shook it off and dried it on a black terrycloth towel. I was in Cotton's bathroom. There were several blue bottles on the sink. Each bottle had a label with Cotton's loopy handwriting. *For when you want to stun him. For avoiding people you don't like. For bats.* I edged past the sink and snuck a peek at Cotton. She was still on the floor with her arms folded across her stomach and a beatific smile on her face. I adjusted my wig. It was show time.

"Yoo hoo, Cotton," I said in my best imitation of Wisteria. "I've come to talk to you. No need to open your eyes, my daughter. Just nod your head if you can hear me." Her eyes opened to slits. I felt her staring at me as she nodded her head. "Now you know we've had serious chats before, but this time I want you to tell me the truth."

"I'm always truthful, Ma," she said in a shaky voice. "Why are you wearing arrows?"

"The arrows aren't important. And I know you tell the truth, but this time it's very important you don't leave out any details. I've brought some friends from the Other Side. I'll just let them in." I quickly opened the front door and motioned to Peter and Lucy. When I saw them, I nearly burst out laughing. At Lucy's house, each of us had grabbed things we felt we could use as disguises. We'd moved so fast, I hadn't had a chance to see what the others had found.

Peter, who was supposed to be Otis, had a pillow strapped around his middle. Over this he wore a jellaba Lucy brought back from Morocco. He'd combed some sort of heavy grease through his thinning hair and parted it in the middle. A white silk scarf around his neck and goggles completed his ensemble.

I guess Lucy was supposed to be Daniel Boone. Her flaming hair was completely covered by a coonskin cap. She must have been sweltering in a brown suede, fringed jacket and matching pants.

"I've brought Otis to speak to you," I said. And this is, ah…"

"Davy Crockett. Pleased to meet you. It's good to get to this Side for a change." Lucy spoke in a low, rough voice.

Cotton sat up and opened her eyes. "Y'all came just to see me?"

"You bet, snookums. You're a good-looking broad. Haven't seen a live one for quite a while." I accidentally stepped on old Davy's toe.

"I'll do the talking here," I warned the loquacious Lucy. "So, Cotton. We need two pieces of information from you. First, we need to know who killed Otis. It wasn't Peter, was it?"

Her eyes took on a crafty look. "Why don't you ask him yourself?"

"Good idea." I turned to Peter, who had begun to sweat. Globlets of grease ran down his face. "Otis, did Peter kill you?"

He shook his head, splattering my tablecloth with fat.

"Who murdered you?" He spread his hands and shrugged his shoulders.

"Just as I thought," I said. "Otis is suffering from a very common malady called Crossing Over Amnesia. When a person suffers a violent

224　A String Of Perils

death, very often the perpetrator of said expiration remains an enigma for several months."

"Huh?"

I didn't even understand what I'd just said. "He can't remember who offed him. It's a temporary thing."

"I don't know who killed him." Cotton squinted her eyes. "You know, he doesn't look much like Otis. Are you sure you didn't bring the wrong person?"

Not good. I didn't want her to inspect Peter too closely, so I changed the subject.

"Listen to me, dearie. Ma knows all about the diamonds."

"You do?"

"Yes, indeedy. You must give them to me. I'll take them with me to the Other Side where they will be used only for good—like buying replacement pearls for the Pearly Gate or a new book for Saint Peter. Where are they?"

Cotton's eyes spun in their sockets.

"Shall we play a game? I'll move around the room and you tell me if I'm hot or cold. You like that game, don't you?"

Cotton clapped her hands. "Goody. I like games. Can the big one play, too?" she asked, pointing to Lucy.

"I'm afraid not. The big one doesn't do games. He skins critters and chews tobacco."

The big one pointed to her diamond, Cartier lady's watch and cleared her throat.

"Let's speed this up, my child. Am I getting warm?" I asked as I moved across the room.

"You're cold as ice," she replied gleefully.

I stood in front of a cupboard full of plastic dishes and glasses. "How about now?"

"Still cold, but a little bit warmer."

I touched an old trunk in the corner. "Am I hot?"

"No, colder." Cotton's eyes sparkled.

I backed up. "Now I must be burning up."

"Nope. I'm getting tired of this."

Cotton had the attention span of a turtle. "Are you sure the diamonds are in this room?" I moved to a table covered with junk. There were magazines and old newspapers, an empty pizza box, several framed photos of Wisteria and the box marked *Gems From The Other Side.*

Cotton's eyes widened. "Am I really close now?"

She shook her head.

"You have to tell me, Cotton. Don't keep secrets from your Ma." I moved my hands over the objects on the table. She watched me carefully. I had the feeling she was ready to pounce if I got too close to the gems. "Are they here?" I pointed to blue ceramic jar.

Like an angry child, she stomped her foot and broke into tears. "Go away, Ma. You're not nice to me. I don't want to talk anymore. Otis, you tell her about the diamonds."

"We'd rather hear it from you, if you don't mind." Jake and Petal stood in the open door, and they both had guns in their hands.

CHAPTER 31

▼

I cawed. I cawed and cawed as loudly as I could. A bird in a distant tree responded.

"Stop making that racket." Jake leveled the gun at my stomach. "I don't know how you escaped from my little surprise but it doesn't matter now. Tell me where the diamonds are, Maggie, and then you and your friends get back against the wall."

"You won't get away with this, you know. People know we came here."

"Spare me your threats. I don't believe you."

Cotton looked dazed. "Why are you calling her Maggie, Mr. Maletesta. She is my mother. And that other one is Otis Murbaugh. I forget the name of the big one."

Jake smirked as he ripped the wig off my head. "This is Maggie Bloom. That one dripping grease on the floor is Peter Bloom, her ex-husband. I'm going to assume the lumberjack is Mrs. Rotblumen. Where did you hide your boy friend?" he said to me. "Or have you two had another spat?"

"I haven't seen him," I said, praying the others would keep their mouths shut. And he didn't know anything about Islane—which was good. She had a gun.

- 226 -

"Listen, Bubba," Lucy said, "You lay one finger on me and my husband will cut your balls off. Just so we're clear about that."

Jake looked bored. "Idle threats. I'll tell you what's going to happen here. I'm going to shoot you all and then I'm going to put the gun in Cotton's hand. The sheriff will think you were engaged in some satanic ritual that involved candles and strange clothes. Poor, bewildered Cotton, who lately had been exhibiting peculiar behavior, came unglued and killed you. A good plan, don't you think? You'll be dead and we'll be far away."

"You have forgotten about Ben. He knows you tried to kill us and he knows the whole story of the diamond heist." I watched him closely for a reaction. His eyebrows lifted a fraction of an inch.

"Ben Jakowski won't be a problem. Someone is, ah, taking care of him as we speak."

Fear rippled through my body. That couldn't be true. Ben was outside somewhere. But Cotton said Petal and a good-looking man brought me to the plane. That meant there was one crook missing.

"Petal, I'm not naïve enough to think you really cared about me," Peter said, "but I'd like to know something. Why pick me? There must have been more qualified candidates for your little scheme."

Petal stroked her sleek ponytail. "Not really. You were single and willing and an upstanding member of your community. You had a valid passport. A thriving law practice. And most importantly, you had a boat. And you weren't bad looking. A little stuffy, but bearable. All in all, the perfect candidate. If you opened a little import/export business, no one would suspect you of anything illegal."

Peter's face crumpled. I couldn't feel sorry for him. The man would never learn.

"So let me see if I have this figured out," I said. "You scored big in the Antwerp diamond theft. You had all these gems but no way to get rid of them. So, you somehow got them to Marrakech, had them imbedded in the paste beaded necklaces, packed them up as products of Morocco and brought them to the United States." A thought occurred to me. "Tell me, Jake. Do you have a passport in the name of Peter S. Bloom?"

"Very good, Maggie. You're catching on. But no, I am not the one with the Peter S. Bloom passport. That belongs to another of our colleagues." He paced back and forth, avoiding the candles that still burned on the floor. "It is, as you can imagine, very difficult to sell the diamonds. There are plenty of potential buyers, but we have to be very careful. I've made certain—shall we say acquaintances—in this country who are eager to participate in the dispersal of the gems. That's where Bloom's boat came in. I couldn't very well run up and down the east coast in my own boat distributing diamonds."

"You used the *Legal Pad* for that?" Peter sputtered. "I was with you on those trips, Petal. Why didn't I know this?"

"Because you weren't looking, darling. Remember the times I would go shopping in Palm Beach and Miami. Or to visit an old school friend in Charleston? I simply walked off the boat with the diamonds in my bag, sold them to our contact, returned to the boat and pretended I was enjoying myself with you."

"And Otis Murbaugh? How did he fit in?" I asked. I noticed Jake's pant leg was dangerously close to the flame of one of the candle.

"Otis had a plane, which came in quite handy. He never carried the diamonds, but he sometimes flew Petal and me to meet customers."

"You actually flew with Otis?" I had to ask. "Did he pretend to stall and scare you to death?"

Jake looked at me disdainfully. "He was a competent enough pilot. He would still be alive if he hadn't become nosy."

"Which means?"

"He found out about the diamonds. I had a box of necklaces with me on one of the flights. When I arrived at our destination and looked for it in my hotel room, it was gone. Otis had apparently stolen the box. Which reminds me—I am now going to have a little chat with Cotton."

Cotton put her hands over her face and backed up until she was pressed against me. "I didn't do nothing and I don't know nothing. You leave me alone or I'm going to tell my mother."

Jake stepped across the circle of candles to grab Cotton.

"Jake, look out," I yelled. "Your pants are on fire."

"Yeah, like I'm going to buy that," he snarled. "Come here, you little bitch."

"Look down, you idiot. You really are burning," Petal screamed.

While Jake slapped at his leg, I cawed like mad. When that didn't produce any results, I yelled, "Peter, where's your weapon?"

"Never mind about Peter. I'm here now." Ben exploded into the room, yelling *Bonsai* and waving the Samurai sword above his head. Fortunately, the only thing he managed to decapitate was a vase of flowers.

Lucy pulled the semiautomatic weapon out of her pants and began firing at the ceiling. Plaster, glass from a light fixture and pieces of a plastic duck rained down on our heads. "Get your hands up. I'm not fooling with you people," she shouted. Bullets sprayed the dishes and glasses on the shelves, sending them flying around the room like targets in a skeet shoot.

Cotton threw herself on the floor and implored her mother for divine assistance. Petal surrendered. Jake, however, tore out the front door, pant leg smoking. "Keep her covered," I yelled. "I'm going after Jake."

"I'm right behind you," Ben said. "Call the police, Bloom. And don't let your girlfriend get away."

Jake headed for the dense woods behind Cotton's house. "Where have you been?" I called to Ben as we thundered after our prey. "You certainly took your sweet time coming to help us."

"I was kind of busy. One of Maletesta's goons was wandering around outside, carrying a very large gun. I had to hide."

"Humph!"

"Excuse me?"

This was hardly the time for an argument. "Jake is getting away. Where do you think he's headed?"

"As I recall, there's water on the other side of these woods. It's possible he has a boat nearby. I didn't see any other car at Cotton's."

I wheezed as I ran. "He couldn't bring the *Lazy Lady* in here, could he?" I was so out of breath, I could barely speak.

"Nope. But he could bring in something smaller; the dinghy, for instance."

Ben was right. We burst out of the woods in time to see Jake climbing into a small boat. "I'll get him. You wait here," Ben called as he sprinted across the clearing. He wasn't going to make it in time. Jake was ready to shove off.

I dropped to one knee, pulled an arrow out of the quiver, put it in the bow, pulled back, closed my eyes and let go. The arrow struck a tree about thirty feet to the right of my target. *It would work better if you opened your eyes,* I told myself. I readied another arrow and aimed for the boat. It zinged over Ben's head and landed with a plop in the water. He looked up in the sky, trying to figure out what had nearly parted his hair.

Jake stood up, pulled out his gun and fired at us. Ben dove for cover behind a palmetto tree. A bullet whizzed over my head close enough for me to hear it zing by.

I had to get him before Ben or I spouted holes in our bodies. I tried a third time. I steadied my hand, squinted one eye and took careful aim. The arrow pierced Jake's khaki shorts, narrowly missing his private parts and impaling him to the wooden side of the boat. He turned a ghastly white color and looked like he was going to pass out. His weapon fell overboard.

"Huah!" I yelled as I raced towards him. "I got him. Look Ben, I got him." When I saw how close I'd come to castrating Jake, I ran to the side of the water and threw up.

"Pretty fancy shooting," Ben said admiringly. "Remind me not to get you riled."

"Just keep him covered, will you. I think I'm going to be sick again."

Ben stood my side and held my head. "I hate to bring this up at a time like this, but we don't have a gun or other significant weapon. Jake may soon figure out he isn't injured and free himself from your arrow. I'm thinking he might be in a nasty mood. Therefore, I suggest we get out of here now and let the sheriff handle this."

"That seems like a sensible idea." I splashed water on my face. "Shall we go?"

We turned around to see Janna Maletesta pointing a gun at us.

"What is with you people?" I yelled. "Everywhere we go, one of you is trying to kill us. I'm getting tired of it." Ben put a hand on my shoulder. I knew he really wanted to put it over my mouth.

Janna frowned. "I'm not sure I know how to work this thing," she said, looking at the revolver in her hand.

She looked smashing in pale blue shorts and a mint green and turquoise, sleeveless top. I loved her tan, suede sandals. "Mephisto?" I asked politely.

Puzzled, she patted her hair. "Clairol. Platinum ice. I suppose you should put your hands up. Am I doing this right, honey?"

Color flooded back into Jake's face. He yanked the arrow out of his pants and tossed it away. "You're doing fine, sweetheart. You can shoot them now, and I'll throw their bodies into the water."

She spread her legs and pointed the gun at Jake and then at me. "Should I shoot Maggie first? That's probably the polite thing to do."

I held up my hand. "You can't kill anybody, Janna. You're too much of a lady. Did you know your husband is a major jewel thief? Put the gun down and I'll tell you everything I know."

"I know about his other business," she said stiffly. "What kind of a wife would I be if I didn't keep up with my husband's affairs?"

"Are you going to shoot them or do I have to come over there," Jake called.

"You heard him. Put your hands up and turn around. I'll have to shoot you in the back because I don't like looking at your faces."

I glanced at Ben. He raised his eyebrows and nodded imperceptibly to the left. I followed his glance. Islane, hidden by bushes and palmetto stood at the edge of the clearing. She put her finger to her lips. I watched as she raised her pearl handle revolver, took deliberate aim and fired. The bullet went through the side of Jake's boat. The second bullet tore into the ground beside Janna. She yelped and jumped aside.

"Throw me the gun, Janna. Stop fooling around," Jake yelled.

"Get it, Ben," I yelled.

Ben dove at Janna. She tossed the gun to her husband. The weapon arced gracefully in the air. I performed a *grand jeté* worthy of a prima ballerina as I soared upward with arm outstretched. In one fluid motion, I snared the gun, landed on my feet and pointed it at Jake. "The jig's up. Get your ass out of the boat." I detest vulgar language but the words seemed to suit the occasion.

Instead of obeying my order, which I thought I'd issued with exceptional authority, Jake stuck his middle finger high in the air and dove into the water.

"Shit," I said to Ben. So much for my pristine vocabulary. "He's going to swim away."

"Shoot him," Ben yelled from the ground. "You have a gun in your hand. Use it."

Use it? Pulling the trigger was an enormous step. I might actually hit someone.

Ben scrambled to his feet. "What are you waiting for?

"Maybe if I call him, he'll come back."

"We're not dealing with Lassie." He grabbed the gun, pointed it at Jake and fired. The bullet splatted two feet to the right of the target. Jake immediately ducked his head under water.

"He can't swim like that forever," Ben said as he tried to take aim again. "He has to come up for breath sometime."

Suddenly I felt surprisingly strong arms grab me around the middle and hurl me to the ground. Janna sat on my back and pounded my shoulders with her little fists. "Don't hurt my husband. Really, Maggie, this isn't going to help your painting career. My friends won't buy your little dishes when I tell them what you've done to Jake."

I pushed her off. "Are you insane? Do you understand at all what's going on here? Your husband is an international jewel thief who is in the process of running away. Did you happen to notice he's not urging you to come with him?"

She shaded her eyes and looked across the water. Jake had surfaced and was swimming strongly towards the shore. "Jake? Sweetie," she called. "You forgot me."

Ben pulled a cell phone out of his pocket and flipped it open. "I don't know whether Bloom had managed to call the police yet, but just in case he hasn't, I'm doing what we should have done a long time ago. I'm calling the sheriff. He can pick up Maletesta."

"Jake probably has a car waiting," I moaned. "The sheriff will never get here in time." We watched as Janna's husband stood up and waded through the water to dry land. He turned around and once more flipped his middle finger in our direction, followed by a jaunty, two finger salute. Then he put both hands high in the air. Lucy walked out of a thicket of trees, her sub machine gun pointed at Jake's stomach.

CHAPTER 32

▼

"I found this person lurking in the woods," Lucy said, inclining her head towards a tall, dark haired, good-looking man. "He bears a remarkable resemblance to the man we saw in the tent in Morocco, don't you think? Just wait till we show Islane."

I studied the person who stood sullenly in front of us, his hands bound with heavy cord. "Could this be the infamous Henri?"

"Bitch," he snarled as he tried to head-butt me.

Lucy nudged him with the barrel of the gun. "Behave. Don't make me shoot you, although I must say, you and your friends are a nasty bunch of low life. We'd be doing the world a service if we removed you all from circulation."

Jake spit on the ground. "You people are amateurs. Merely an annoyance—like an ant running up my arm. I could squash you in a minute."

"Shut up, bubba," Lucy said pleasantly. "You seem to forget your hands are tied and I have a gun. That makes me the boss. And I say we march back to Cotton's house while we wait for the sheriff."

Our group was becoming unwieldy. Lucy, Ben and I escorted Jake, Janna and Henri through the woods. Janna's incessant bleating was beginning to drive me crazy. During out ten minute walk, she complained about a broken fingernail, the unfairness of being treated as a

- 234 -

criminal and the plight of her friends, who expected her for cocktails this very minute. Not a word about her husband's attempt to flee without her or the fact that she had been willing to kill me a few minutes earlier. Her behavior convinced me she was either totally out of touch with reality or totally whacko. Either way, she scared me.

Islane was waiting for us on Cotton's front steps. As we approached, she stood up, her hands on her hips. "After you," Lucy said to Henri, pushing him forward. "This should be good."

It was obvious Islane recognized our prisoner. I mean, you don't normally smack a stranger across the face and yell a string of French words I can only assume had something to do with his birth mother and the dark places she would stuff his amputated parts. "Where is my money? I want it back. All of it."

A cruel smile flitted around Henri's mouth. "I feel sorry for you rich, old bitches. You get your money's worth and then you moan when there's nothing left."

Islane's cheeks turned a bright red. "Do not speak to me that way. And do not think you can get away with this. I am going to kill you now. *Au revoir.*" She raised her gun and pointed it at a space between his eyes. "Perhaps," she said, "I will not shoot him. Do you have—how you say—the tweezers in your bag, Lucy? I will either pull out his fingernails or break his fingers. Perhaps both."

Lucy handed her a large wrench. "No tweezers, sweetie. Will this do?"

"*Mais oui*" Wielding the tool, Islane advanced menacingly on Henri.

"Keep this lunatic away from me," he yelled. We turned our heads and studied the ground.

"Where is my money?"

"Ouch! You're crazy."

I lifted my eyes discreetly. I had to see what was going on. Islane had the wrench firmly clamped on Henri's nose. "Tell me."

"I don't have your money. Get her away."

She gave his nose a wicked tweak.

"Enough," he wailed. "There's nothing left. I spent it all, and that's the truth." I was gratified to see he was genuinely terrified. A wet stain spread across the front of his pants.

Islane laughed and threw the wrench on the ground. "You are like a girl," she said. "No, not a girl. A girl has more courage. You are a miserable, cowardly, lying, reptilian snake."

"There is a certain redundancy there," I pointed out. But what did I know. At this point, I had the intellectual prowess of a tomato. "I'm not going back in that house," I said to Ben. Let's have our conference out here."

We brought the Navigator into Cotton's driveway and tethered Henri, Jake and Janna to the doors of the SUV. I clomped up the front steps and yelled to the folks inside the house. Petal/Fleur's face was pale as Peter led her outside.

"I've been having a talk with Petal," he said in a terse voice. "Seems stealing my name to set up a dummy corporation designed to smuggle diamonds wasn't enough for her. She also became quite proficient at forging my signature on checks. You weren't the only one who was duped, Islane."

"Would you like to use the wrench," she asked picking it up from the ground.

"Maybe later. Did you know your boyfriend isn't from Paris?" We settled ourselves on the steps as Ben began to talk. Cotton stood in the open door. "This fellow's real name is Silvio Bruschetta and he's from Jersey. He and Petal met Maletesta in Turin, where they both—and I use this word somewhat dubiously—worked. Petal was fleecing lonely old men of their life savings and Henri robbed houses. He played the role of a rich, eligible bachelor, escorted ladies to lavish parties in private homes and later returned to steal valuables."

"Not bad, Bloom," Ben said. "How'd you get this information?"

"I'm a top notch attorney. Hardened criminals crumple under my questioning."

Linda S. Clayton 237

"You're modest too," I said. "Just stick to the facts."

Peter preened. "She sang like a yellow tweetie bird once I started to grill her. What else do you want to know?"

Jake shot Petal an evil glance. "You shouldn't have blabbed, my dear. You'll be sorry for that. Remember what I said would happen if you talked?"

I rubbed my temples. These people were beginning to give me a headache. Where was the sheriff when you needed him? "Give us everything you've got," I said to Peter.

"Maletesta was part of the gang of jewel thieves involved in the huge robbery in Antwerp. He has wisely not imparted all the details to his minions, but Petal was smart enough to piece together some of the story. She knew the dummy company was a front for smuggling. And she knew diamonds were in the phony necklaces."

"Let me take a shot at the rest of the story," Ben said. "I've done some research, so I have a pretty good idea of what happened. The robbers were older, sophisticated men who used their brains instead of weapons. They used copies of keys and managed to bypass the cameras and alarm system. They even replaced the surveillance tapes so no one would be able to see what was going on in the vaults." He glanced at Ben. "Our friend here is older and I suppose some would say he's sophisticated. He fits the bill."

"*Mon Dieu*," Islane said.

"So," Ben continued, "they stole the diamonds—so many, in fact, they had to leave some behind. The problem was—what to do with close to $100 million worth of gems. For safety's sake, the gang split up. One man, who wasn't even involved in the actual theft, was arrested, but the rest are still at large."

"Not for long," I muttered.

"I'll take it from here." Peter stood up and faced us as if he were addressing a jury. "Maletesta had to have help getting his share out of the country. He met two small time crooks—Petal and Henri—and offered to trade large sums of money for their complete cooperation

238   A String Of Perils

and silence. To ensure their allegiance, he had photos of Henri breaking into a house and Petal holding a pillow over an old man's face. Jake thwarted her attempt at murder, but he had the evidence he needed if either stepped out of line. They took the diamonds to Morocco, put them in the fake necklaces and sent them to the United States."

"And that would be where the Peter S. Bloom, Import/Export company came into the picture," I said. "They used Jake's boat and the occasional traditional freight company to send the diamonds to America. Jake took over in this country. Believe it or not, the *Lazy Lady* sailed right into Harbour Town with the gems onboard."

We fell silent. Incredible. I put my hands behind my head and leaned back. Hot sunshine filtered through the live oaks dripping with Spanish moss that formed a canopy over our heads. I watched a squirrel scamper from branch to branch. A hawk circled high above, its eye on some unseen prey. It was surreal. We had an international jewel thief and his accomplices attached to our car on a dirt road on Hilton Head Island. It was too bizarre.

"I guess that about wraps it up," I said. "Except we still don't know who killed Otis and that's what started this whole mess."

"I have a theory about that." Lucy bit into a candy bar she pulled out of her pocket. "Otis was providing his plane to transport the diamonds to Maletesta's customers. As Jake said, one day poor Otis discovered the diamonds. Therefore, Jake killed him."

I walked over to Jake. I felt almost sorry for him. Without benefit of shade, the searing afternoon sun was almost unbearable. Sweat poured down his face. I could feel the heat bouncing off the Navigator as I approached. "Did you do it, Jake?" I asked. "Did you really kill Otis?"

"My husband doesn't kill people." Janna looked equally cooked. Her blond hair hung in damp strand down her face."

"He certainly didn't show any reluctance about disposing of us," I told her. "Did I forget to mention he tried to drown Peter, Ben and me?"

"I didn't kill Murbaugh," Jake said. "I don't do that type of work." His eyes slid to Petal. "Why don't you ask someone else?"

"I'm not taking a rap for you," Petal/Fleur screeched. "I know plenty, and I'm willing to tell it to the police." She tried to grab my hand. "I was in Otis's house the night you two broke in. I was looking for the diamonds. I thought maybe the fool had hidden them in a drawer or something. But I didn't kill him."

Jake put his finger to his neck and made a slicing motion. "You should have kept your mouth shut."

Petal/Fleur yanked at the rope binding her hands. "You have to get me out of here. He's going to kill me."

"I don't think so, honey. He's not Houdini. He can't get loose." At least I hoped not. "Are you the one who murdered Otis," I asked.

"I hit him over the head with a board," she yelled. "Otis saw me coming off the *Lazy Lady*. He grabbed my arm and tried to make me go back onboard with him. Said he needed more diamonds and he knew I had some. He wouldn't leave me alone," she whined. "There was a fairly thick board on the dock. I picked it up and hit him. He fell down and didn't get up. Since no one saw me do it. I got in my car and drove away. Later, when I came back, he wasn't there. I figured he was okay and had gone home."

Peter looked disgusted. "You actually cracked a board over a man's head? That's terrible."

"Hey, what would you call taking your ex-wife up in a plane with the sole intention of feeding her to hungry sharks? The sure wasn't Sunday School behavior."

"This isn't about you, Maggie." Peter shot Ben a conspiratorial glance. "It always has to be about them, doesn't it?"

"I wouldn't go there if I were you, Bloom. Maggie has done her best to help you. Surprised you don't recognize that," he said blandly. I wanted to kiss him. So I did.

"This still doesn't solve the mystery of who killed Otis or how he got on the bicycle path where I found him," I said. "Or for that matter, where the missing diamonds are." I looked at Cotton, who up until now hadn't said a word. "You said you found the box by the back door of the shop. Is that true?"

Cotton nibbled on her lower lip.

"You'd better tell us the truth. Don't forget your mother is listening." Panic flooded the poor girl's face. Her eyes darted to the sky. "What's that, Wisteria?" I said, cupping my ear. "Oh, I'm sure she'll give us straight answers. No need to send thunder and lightening." Behind Cotton's head, turbulent, black storm clouds were moving off the water directly towards us. I promised myself I would pay for the poor thing's therapy when this was over.

Cotton began to shiver. "I'll tell them the truth, Ma. Don't get mad. I hate it when you get mad at me."

"Go on," I encouraged gently, hating myself.

"Well, me and Otis were seeing each other." She wrapped a copper curl around her finger. "Sometimes I went in his plane with him. Once we went to his house. Sometimes I'd see him in Harbour Town and he would stop and talk and stuff. The morning you came into the shop, Maggie, Otis had come by earlier. He said he had something to do and asked me to take the box." She looked embarrassed. "I thought he meant I could have it, so I took it into the shop and opened it. The beads were pretty. Ma told me Ms Lowerby would like me if I tried to sell some. And you bought one, Maggie. That was good." Tears spilled down her face. "He never came back."

"I think we need some food," Lucy said. "You'll feel better if you eat, Cotton." She pulled a wicker hamper out of the back of the Navigator and removed a checkered tablecloth, napkins, plastic glasses, plates and utensils, a chilled bowl of potato salad, a platter with generous slices of baked ham and cheese and fluffy rolls. "I had Emerald fix this in case we got hungry. I, for one, am famished. Anyone else?" Greedy hands reached for the food. She held bottles of ice cold water to our prisoners' lips. "You don't deserve this," she said to Jake," but unlike you, I don't let living things suffer."

Linda S. Clayton 241

"You're amazing, Lucy. You think of everything." I made a sandwich and handed it to Ben. "Now, where were we? I remember, Cotton, you told me that morning you returned the necklaces to the owner. But that couldn't have happened because Otis never came back."

"I don't want to talk no more," she whispered.

"But you have to. Come on, Cotton. You discovered there were diamonds hidden in the beads, didn't you?"

She bowed her head and nodded. "I accidentally got one wet. The gooey stuff came off."

"Where are the diamonds, dear? Let me give them to the sheriff." And suddenly, I knew. I flew into the house, snatched the box labeled Gems From The Other Side and rejoined the group. "I'll bet they're in here, aren't they, Cotton. What a clever idea—keeping gems in the Gem box."

Cotton dried her eyes and began to smile. "Ma said to do that."

"I'll bet she did." The others clustered around me as I opened the lid. The diamonds, splashed by sunlight, nearly blinded us. "Well, that solves that," I said when I could breathe again. "All the diamonds are accounted for—except the ones I washed down the drain."

"Maggie," Janna called. "Could you come over here a minute?"

I handed the precious box to Ben. "What's the problem?" I asked when I reached her side.

"I have to go to the bathroom," she said in a low voice. "Could you be a dear and take me to one?"

Lucy heard our conversation. "Tell her to squat on the ground."

Janna frowned disdainfully. "Really, Lucy, such a crude thing to say. I thought you had more class. Please take me, Maggie."

What the heck. She was still a human being. I untied her hands and led her into the house. "I'll wait out here," I said with my back against the door. "Tell me when you're done." Five seconds later I realized what an idiot I was. I raced outside to the open bathroom window I'd entered earlier. Janna was just crawling out. Her rear end and legs had already cleared the sill. I poked her in the butt. "Going somewhere?"

"Oh dear. I'm afraid you've caught me."

"What's up with you, Janna," I asked as I retied her hands. "Are you really as clueless as you seem? Don't you realize your husband is a bad guy? He's in serious trouble."

"He is not," she said serenely. "He's a business man. And I help him. That's why I shot Otis."

"Say again? You shot Otis?"

"I certainly did." She wiped her hands fastidiously on her shorts. "He was trying to cheat Jake. I saw him. First he talked to Petal and she hit him. She didn't hit him very hard, though. He wasn't even knocked out for very long, but he was bleeding badly. After Petal left, he went onboard my boat and came out a few minutes later carrying a box." She smiled benignly. "I couldn't allow him to steal something from Jake. I followed him and shot him. Then I put all that stuff on the body. I found it in a drawer in Jake's desk. I decided your husband could take the rap."

I eyed her closely. There was a hard malice beneath that flaky exterior—and I didn't think she was as crazy as she wanted us to believe.

Cotton was so involved in a celestial conversation with her mother that she didn't even react when I told her Janna had killed Otis.

CHAPTER 33

▼

A heavy mist dampened my hair and made the wooden footbridge spanning the marsh slick as ice. We stopped to watch egrets peck for food in the wet sand. Wally chased a small crab in dizzying zigzags. Outsmarted, he gave up on the crustacean and bounded after a squirrel.

"I hope Cotton will be okay," I said. "Candy is going to take her to Memphis for an extended visit. She promised to make sure Cotton received competent psychiatric help dealing with the death of her mother, and I offered to pay for it. It's the least I can do."

"You didn't do anything wrong, Maggie," Ben said as he tossed a stone into the marsh. "Cotton was messed up before you called on her mother for divine intervention. She's young and resilient. She'll be fine."

I nodded in agreement. "It still amazes me how she could assume her mother's voice. I tell you, Ben, it was eerie. I could have sworn Wisteria was in the room."

"The human mind is capable of anything. Cotton firmly believed she was talking to her mother. I don't think she realizes that all that information she credited to Wisteria actually was a result of her own nosiness."

"She was telling the truth about Lucy's table," I said. "Someone saw her lurking around the garage where it was made. And remember that silly riddle from the séance? I think Cotton was referring to the fake necklace. Subconsciously she wanted us to discover the truth about the diamonds. The poor girl was so bewildered, she didn't know what to do."

"It's all so hard to believe. Jake is being extradited to Belgium to stand trial for the diamond theft and Janna is in jail, accused of murder. I think Jake will be spending a long time behind bars. I heard Petal/Fleur and Henri are quite eager to testify against him."

Ben's hand tightened around mine. "I'm very glad nothing happened to you." When I raised my eyebrows, he said, "I mean, no bones broken and all your parts are intact. Once again you managed to land on your feet. But you're using up your nine lives, Maggie," he said seriously. "One of these days things aren't going to turn out so satisfactorily."

"Pish tosh. You worry too much. Noting is going to happen to me. Besides, I'm absolutely done with trying to help people. From now on, I'm minding my own business." And that was the honest truth. This time, I'd managed to scare myself badly. "No more sleuthing. Ever again," I said. "And I positively mean it."

Ben laughed. "That's like saying Wally won't chew anything but his bone. He can't do that and neither can you."

The dogs raced up the driveway and waited on the front porch for me to open the door. "So..." Ben said. "I guess I'll be going." He pulled me to him and kissed the top of my head. "I have an errand to run. See you later."

"You don't have to leave." I ran my finger along his chest. "Why don't you come in for a while? I serve a very good breakfast."

"Maggie, it is three o'clock in the afternoon. A little early to be thinking about bacon and eggs, isn't it?"

Huh? Was he turning down an obvious invitation? What was wrong with the man? Were things still not right between us? "Peter is gone, you know," I said into his shirt. "He flew back to Boston this morning. The police have impounded the *Legal Pad* until they complete their investigation." When Ben didn't speak I said, "I only tried to help him. I hope you realize by now that he is part of my past. He has no place in my life today—and certainly not in my future. I may, though, have been a bit too energetic about defending him."

"What's that? Ben stroked my hair. "Maggie Bloom is admitting she may have done something wrong?"

"Hey," I said, pulling away. "You have some explaining to do, too. What was up with you and Cynthia Loveday? I saw you coming out of her house one morning."

Ben looked amused. "You were spying on me?

"Not really. I was jogging and stopped to tie my shoe. The front door opened and there you were."

"Did you happen to notice I too was dressed for jogging? She left her sunglasses in my car and I was returning them on my way to South Beach for a run along the ocean."

This was quite possibly true. I hadn't paid any attention to his attire. He still hadn't answered the big question. "Is it true you were going away with Cynthia?"

He held me tightly. "What do you think?"

"I think yes. I mean, twenty gossiping women can't be wrong."

"Well, they were. I went out with Cynthia for one reason—maybe two. She was Janna Maletesta's best friend and knew everything that was going on in Sea Pines. Remember the night of Maletestas' party when someone grabbed you around the neck? That convinced me the people stalking you were somehow connected to that crowd. Cynthia loved to talk. I figured all I had to do was listen and sooner or later she'd tell me what I wanted to know." He grimaced. "It turned into an unbearable chore. The woman was as annoying as a mosquito buzzing around my ear."

I smiled broadly. "You don't say. I shouldn't say this, but I could have told you so. She has had so much of her body hoisted, sculpted and padded, she probably lost some brain mass in the process." I felt good. This was working out nicely. "What was the second reason?" I asked.

"I thought you still had a thing for your ex-husband."

"But you don't anymore, do you," I asked anxiously. I took a deep breath. "I think you know you're the only one for me."

"I have to go," Ben said briskly. He turned and walked to his car. "Say," he said as he opened the car door, "do you want to come with me?"

I ran up the steps, let the dogs into the house and zoomed over to Ben. "Where are we going?"

Ben turned the key in the ignition and the Lexus roared to life. "Remember the diamonds I ordered from the jeweler in Beaufort? And the ring I was going to have made? I have to cancel the order. I feel I owe the man a personal explanation."

I felt the glow fade from my face. Unexpected tears sprang to my eyes. What in the world was the matter with me? I didn't care at all what he did with his ring. "Sure," I said as I fastened my seatbelt. "I'll ride with you. You can't keep the diamond you intended to use anyway. It's part of the evidence."

"I was thinking," he said as he headed out the Greenwood gate and onto the Sea Pines circle. "It would be a shame to waste a perfectly good ring. The jeweler went to a lot of trouble finding those perfect stones for the channel setting. I'm sure he would be happy to sell me another diamond for the center. What do you think?"

My heart began to tippy tap in my chest. Was he asking me what I thought he was asking me? This definitely needed clarification. "Are you asking me what I think you're asking me?"

He reached across the seat and took my hand. "What do you think I'm asking you?"

"Stop it, Ben," I said as I wiped tears out of my eyes. "This is serious. I need a serious answer."

Ben's blue eyes sparkled as he looked at me. "Well, will you?"

First I leaned across the seat, grabbed him around the neck and kissed him as hard as I could all over his face. Then, because I'd promised to curtail my inane outbursts, I snuggled next to him and silently said to myself, "Blackjack, bingo and chocolate kisses. Maggie Bloom's gonna be a missus!"

0-595-32460-6